Dear Reader,

We are delighted to be making our third visit to the lovely town of Marble Cove. Returning to this charming burg—and to Diane, Margaret, Beverly and Shelley—is like going home again.

In this story, themes of family, reconciliation and letting go run strong. When Shelley's estranged father wants to re-enter her life, she finds herself reexamining long-held beliefs about the past and relying on her own family and faith to guide her to the best decisions. At the same time, Margaret struggles with her daughter's desire for more independence. She, too, must dig deep to make the best choices for her family. And the four friends rely on one another and their families as they continue to delve into the mystery surrounding Old First Church.

We're a mother-daughter writing team (Barbara is the mother, and Pam is the daughter) and have been working together since Pam was expecting her first child. That "baby" turns twenty-two soon so, for us, collaborating has long been a family affair. It was a pleasure for us to cowrite this story of faith and family, and we hope you enjoy *Family Heirlooms* as much as we did.

All the best!
Pam Hanson & Barbara Andrews

MIRACLES *of*
MARBLE COVE

FAMILY HEIRLOOMS

PAM HANSON &
BARBARA ANDREWS

Guideposts

New York

Published by Guideposts Books & Inspirational Media
110 William Street
New York, NY 10038
Guideposts.org

Acknowledgments

Every attempt has been made to credit the sources of copyrighted material used in this book. If any such acknowledgment has been inadvertently omitted or miscredited, receipt of such information would be appreciated.

"From the Guideposts Archive" originally appeared as "Family Treasure" by Marilyn Fanning in *Guideposts* magazine. Copyright ©1999 by Guideposts. All rights reserved.

Cover and interior design by Müllerhaus
Cover photo by Jeremy Charles Photography and IStock
Typeset by Aptara, Inc.

Printed and bound in the United States of America
10 9 8 7 6 5 4 3

FAMILY HEIRLOOMS

CHAPTER ONE

I can't stop shivering," Shelley said, sinking down on a leather couch covered with pillows in her friend Margaret's house. "It's the middle of summer, and chills are running through me. When I smelled that awful smoke, I was terrified we wouldn't get out of the church alive. My life flashed before me, and all I could think about was leaving my children motherless."

"You're probably suffering from shock," Margaret said. "Here, wrap this throw around you."

"Who wouldn't be in shock?" Beverly asked. "No one would expect a fire at a church like Old First. Those walls were meant to last for centuries."

"The walls, yes," Diane said, "but the flames were coming from the roof. I give our fire department lots of credit. They certainly got there quickly. Maybe the damage won't be as bad as Reverend Locke thinks."

"He thinks the smoke damage alone will be enough to force the church to close indefinitely," Beverly said. "It's a shame, after all the hard work by so many volunteers, that Founders Day will have to be canceled tomorrow."

Of the four friends, she was the only member of Old First, and Shelley's heart went out to her. Any fire in the small town of Marble Cove was a blow to everyone who lived there, but it had to be especially heart-wrenching for a person who attended services at the beautiful old church.

"Here you are, ladies," Margaret's husband Allan said as he carried a tray into their cluttered but homey living room. "Tea to calm you down, and banana bread just because it tastes good."

"He made it this afternoon," Margaret said, attempting a smile as her good-natured husband did his best to take care of her friends.

Still feeling shaky, Shelley took a cup of tea but refused the banana bread. She was far too upset to swallow anything solid, but the tea felt soothing on her dry throat.

"We never should've been in the church at night," she said.

Margaret nodded in agreement, but Beverly shook her head vehemently.

"It was our only chance to investigate the tower. Reverend Locke was adamant about the timing," Beverly said. "He was only willing to let us inside at a time when he could be there with us. And he specifically wanted the church to be empty of other people."

"It was just bad luck. No one can predict a lighting strike," Diane said, clutching her cup with both hands.

"True. My father was stunned to hear about the fire."

"Oh dear." Shelley put her empty cup on the coffee table and stood up, letting the knitted throw fall behind her. "That reminds me. I'd better call Dan. He wasn't keen on having me go. If he's heard about the fire, he'll really be worried. And I didn't bring my cell phone."

"Use the phone in our bedroom," Margaret offered.

Grateful for the privacy, Shelley hurried to the couple's room, turning on the overhead light but not really noticing her surroundings. Somewhat to her surprise, Dan didn't answer right away. He finally picked up on the fourth ring.

"Yeah," he said in a sleepy voice.

"Don't tell me you slept through the sirens," Shelley said, not sure whether to be relieved or annoyed.

"I heard them, but I fell back asleep. Where are you?"

"At Margaret's. The fire was on the roof of Old First."

"No kidding! Are you okay? Were you in the building when it started? I had a feeling you shouldn't poke around there at night. Do you need me to come over?"

"No, but thanks. I'm fine," Shelley said, although this wasn't strictly true. She still felt shaky and disoriented. "I'll be home in a little while. Get some rest. Diane has her car, so she'll drop me off when she goes home."

"Okay, Shell," he said, sounding unconvinced. "I'm just glad you're all right."

After her brief conversation, she rejoined her friends just as Allan was clearing away the others' cups. Everyone knew Margaret's husband was more at home in the kitchen than she was, but Shelley especially appreciated him this evening. He'd refilled her cup on the table, and she gratefully drank more tea. Distress combined with smoke from the fire had parched her throat, but she wasn't going to feel comforted until she was home in Dan's arms.

"Are you feeling a little better?" Beverly asked.

"Yes, I'll be fine." Shelley tried to sound normal, but she couldn't get the image of the fiery roof out of her mind. What if they'd been trapped in the tower and the flames had spread? Or if they'd been overcome by smoke? Her eyes welled just thinking of the danger they had faced.

"At least we came away with something from the tower room," Margaret said. "Maybe this key is the answer to finding the treasure and saving Old First."

Shelley leaned forward to see the small, dusty bronze key Margaret had grabbed on her way out of the tower. Everyone's attention turned to the unexpected find.

"It's so tiny. What could it possibly open?" Shelley asked.

"A small box," Beverly suggested, passing the key to Diane.

"Like a jewelry box." Diane examined both sides, but there was nothing to support either guess.

"I suppose it could even unlock a diary. When I was a girl, I had one with a lock and key," Margaret said, taking her turn to study it.

"Do you think they had locks on diaries back then?" Shelley asked, reaching out to examine it. The key weighed surprisingly little in her palm.

"I imagine they could design locks for almost anything that needed protecting," Beverly said.

"The question is, is this what Jeremiah Thorpe put in the tower room for his sister to find?"

"And if so, how will it help us find the treasure?" Diane added.

"In spite of the fire, we were lucky Reverend Locke let us into the tower tonight. I doubt anyone will be allowed inside the church for quite a while, at least not until the roof is repaired." Margaret took back the key and started to rewrap it in the aged piece of paper.

"Is there any writing on the paper?" Diane asked.

"Or any hint of a secret message?" Beverly reached for the paper and held it up to a table lamp. "No, it appears to be a plain sheet of rag paper, undoubtedly old but only a wrapping for the key."

"So we have another mystery," Shelley said, feeling weary in every bone of her body now that the crisis had passed.

"Or possibly a clue to the whereabouts of Jeremiah Thorpe's treasure," Diane said. "Wouldn't it be wonderful if we could discover it?"

"This would certainly be an opportune time to find it—if it exists. I imagine the church has some insurance," Beverly said, "but the building is going to need more than a new roof. Everything from carpets to furniture could have smoke damage, and there could even be structural problems as a result of the fire." She shook her head. "There wasn't enough money for all the needed repairs to Old First even before this disaster."

"Unless we really do find a treasure," Diane reminded her. "Anything from the time of the early settlers would no doubt be quite valuable. I can't even imagine what a dealer would pay for coins from that period."

"Yes, even if they weren't gold. Age alone would make them valuable," Beverly speculated.

Now that her chills had passed, Shelley felt drained. Old First wasn't her first fire, and it brought back bad memories of the blocked flue that had started a blaze in their own chimney at home. She still had nightmares about their home catching on fire. There had only been minor smoke damage that time, but it horrified her to think of what could have happened. First thing tomorrow she was going to check the smoke alarms to be sure they had fresh batteries. She and Dan had been entirely too casual about fire protection before their own experience with it.

"Do you want me to keep the key?" Margaret asked.

"Yes, that's only fair since you found it," Diane said. "Of course, someday we'll have to give it back to Old First."

"I don't think Reverend Locke wants anything to do with treasure hunting—or with us right now," Beverly said. "He'll probably be totally occupied with all the problems the fire has created."

"Maybe another church will share space so the Old First congregation can continue having worship services," Shelley said. "Not much happens at our church on Sunday afternoon if Reverend Locke is flexible enough to hold services then."

"That would be a good solution, but I'm not sure how Reverend Locke would feel about that," Beverly said.

"Anyway, the local ministers have some kind of alliance where they get together and discuss mutual concerns. I'm sure they will address the problem."

"I can talk to my pastor about it," Diane offered.

"They'll work something out," Margaret said in a pragmatic tone. "I have my hands full now with the Fourth of July coming up in a few days. All the merchants in town have high hopes for the tourist season this year. Already I'm hard-pressed to keep my gallery walls covered with art to sell, but that's a good kind of problem to have."

"It's wonderful how well your gallery is doing this summer," Diane said. "But right now, I'm exhausted. Ready to go home, Shelley?"

"Yes, please. Dan will be waiting up for me."

Any other time she would've walked the short distance, but Marble Cove didn't seem like the cozy, safe place it had only hours ago. If she'd learned one thing from the fire, it was that even a building with thick stone walls and a long history could have bad things happen to it. She felt very small and vulnerable.

Outside the bad weather had passed, but the end of June had brought unseasonably hot weather. Now the air was cloyingly humid, but she took deep breaths, still able to detect the rancid smell of smoke that clung to her clothing and hair.

Diane seemed to take forever putting on her seat belt and starting the car, perhaps a sign that she was more rattled than she let on. Shelley wanted to tell her to hurry, but, of course, she would never be rude to her neighbor and friend.

Instead of parking by her own cottage and letting Shelley walk from there, Diane pulled into the Bauers' drive and waited until Shelley waved good-bye to her from the front door.

"You're finally here," Dan said as soon as she stepped inside. He was barefoot in sweats and a T-shirt, his hair still unruly from the pillow.

"We had tea and talked a little," Shelley said, then she was in his arms, feeling safe for the first time since she'd been in the church with the others.

"I like your friends, but I hope this is the last time you poke around dangerous places with them," he said, releasing her and speaking only half-jokingly. "I don't know how I went back to sleep after I heard the sirens. I should've known the four of you were in some kind of mess." He smiled, but concern shone in his eyes.

"It's not like we planned to get caught in a fire." She was comforted by his concern but also a bit irritated. Didn't he think she could take care of herself?

"I know you care about that old church, but can't you find another way to help them out? I'm not sure this treasure hunting is really worth it. I mean, what could you possibly find? It's not as if Marble Cove was the Port Royal of the north. If any pirates really did come here with gold, they certainly didn't leave pots of it buried here and there for you to find."

"You make it sound like we're doing something silly. We all read the letters written by Jeremiah Thorpe. He mentioned a hidden treasure. If we can find it, we'll give it to Old First. That church will need it more than ever after the fire."

"Shell, I'm sorry. I know you think there's a treasure, but it's been hundreds of years. I just don't want to see you be disappointed spending time looking for something you'll never find."

"You don't know that."

He walked into the living room, flopped down on the couch, and crossed his arms. "At least try to be realistic."

"You think this is some game we made up!"

"No, I don't, really. I just worry when you're out doing who knows what. What if you'd been trapped in the church when the fire started?"

"It was on the roof. We got out."

Shelley realized it was true. They hadn't been in mortal danger, and she'd overreacted. The shock was wearing off, and all she felt now was a deep weariness—and annoyance at Dan's attitude.

He stood and came to her. "Shell, I was scared silly when you called about the fire. What if it had spread while you were inside the church? What would I do without you?"

His tender words touched her heart, and she understood why he didn't want her in dangerous situations.

"We won't be going back inside the church. Reverend Locke won't allow it while there's any danger from fire damage. Anyway, it's my friendship with Diane, Margaret, and Beverly that's important to me, not just the treasure. But you and the kids come first. You always will."

"I know," he whispered, drawing her close and kissing her.

Dan was able to accomplish what a warm wrap, tea, and friendship hadn't. He made her forget her fear and focus on what was really important in her life.

Still, part of her *knew* there was more to discover about Jeremiah Thorpe's treasure, and she very much wanted to help her friends find it.

Chapter Two

After a calm Sunday that included going to church and enjoying a family picnic on the beach, Shelley felt ready to put memories of the fire behind her—at least during the daylight hours. She was afraid it would haunt her dreams for a long time, but with Dan beside her, she could let go of her fear.

"Is my lunch packed?" her husband asked Monday morning, coming into the kitchen where she ran her baking business.

"In the fridge. I didn't give you any cookies because you said you wanted to cut down on sweets. Your thermos of coffee is on the counter."

"Thanks. It's hard on the waistline being married to the best baker in town." He gave her a little peck on the cheek and carried his plate of scrambled eggs and whole-wheat toast to the dining room table.

Since Dan had gotten his job apprenticing as an electrician, this was often her favorite time of the day. He had to get an early start, and most days the kids slept another hour or more. It was a treat to enjoy a quiet breakfast together while Shelley finished up her baking.

"Where are you working today?" she asked conversationally.

"Same as last week. We'll probably be at the new apartment complex in Danaton till the end of July. I like working on new construction even if it is a long drive every day."

"The last time I was there it was such a pretty little village. I hope all the new construction doesn't ruin it," she mused, nibbling at her toast.

"It's on the outskirts of town, so it won't affect the downtown. I'm grateful for the work, never mind whether a pokey little place gets bigger," he said between bites, obviously in a hurry to leave.

"Would you say that if a developer wanted to totally change Marble Cove?" Shelley asked.

"Depends on what they wanted to do. If it meant year-round employment, I'd say it was probably a good thing."

After Dan's long stint of unemployment, Shelley certainly wouldn't argue with him. But she'd still hate to see her charming little beach town ruined by the wrong kind of development.

"You do have the Fourth off, don't you? I thought we could take the kids to the park for the fireworks," she said.

"Yeah. Too bad it comes in the middle of the week. We'll only have the one day off instead of a long weekend." He finished the last bite of toast and stood to leave. "Give the kids a kiss from me when they wake up. We'll probably pull some overtime, so go ahead and feed them without me."

When he had his lunch bucket in hand, they walked arm in arm to his truck. The days seemed long when her husband worked more than his eight-hour shift, but Shelley was grateful for the financial security after a rough patch. She watched him back out of the driveway and pull away, giving her a wave through the open window.

When she was back inside, Aiden was coming down the stairs in the oversized T-shirt he wore to bed in the summer. His bare feet reminded her that he needed new beach flip-flops, but her baking schedule was full. She doubted whether she'd have time to get them today.

"Can I have waffles?" he asked in a sleepy voice.

"Not today, honey. They were a special treat for Sunday brunch. How about some cereal? You can pick what you want."

"Do we have any pink and purple and green and—"

"Aiden, you know I don't buy the sugary kind. I'll make you a scrambled egg."

"Yuck."

"You like them. Now go get dressed. Adelaide will be here to play with you later in the morning."

"Will she push me on the swing?"

"Maybe, if you're nice to her. While you get dressed, I have to check my orders for today." She knew the holiday meant lots of tourists. The Cove, the restaurant she regularly supplied with baked goods, had doubled their order for the week. The ones in the freezer wouldn't begin to be enough.

Nearly an hour later, after Emma had woken up, she had the kids dressed—which necessitated folding laundry and dumping their dirty clothes in the washing machine—

and fed as well. She let them play near her in the kitchen until Adelaide could come by a little later.

She wasn't expecting Adelaide this early, so it was a surprise when the doorbell rang. Beverly was standing outside the door in her running clothes, looking sleek and athletic even though her face was pink from her morning jog.

"Good morning," Shelley said, gesturing for her friend to come in.

"I won't stay," Beverly said. "I just wanted to be sure you're okay. I had nightmares myself after the fire. It took a while for it to hit me, but we really were in some danger."

"Fortunately, no one was hurt," Shelley said. "Are you sure you won't have a cup of tea?"

"Thanks, I'd love to, but I have work to do for several clients." Beverly pushed a strand of dark hair away from her eyes.

"Sounds like your consulting is going well," Shelley said.

"I've made a good start. It's a challenge to live in a beautiful, unspoiled town like Marble Cove and still make a good living. But I wouldn't change it for anything," Beverly said. "I've fallen in love with the town and all the good people here."

"Dan and I feel the same way," Shelley said. "It's been a tough job market, but I can't imagine a more perfect place to live."

"I agree. Let's hope it stays the way it is for a long, long time," Beverly said. She glanced at her watch. "Well, I'd better be going."

After Beverly left, Shelley went through the orders on her board, thankful her own business was running smoothly after a minor catastrophe when packages from Internet sales had arrived in poor shape. This week she had to concentrate on filling Marble Cove orders. She'd decided to limit online sales to cookies only, to see if it was possible to make a living by focusing mainly on local sales. This summer promised to be profitable with tourists flocking to the beach community.

Occasionally she tried out a new recipe for the Cove, but mostly the owner of the local restaurant preferred familiar best sellers. With lots of baking to do, she decided to stick to Sweet Shoppe rockslide brownies, blueberry crumb cake, and snickerdoodles. She also had two orders for sheet cakes, one for a family reunion and the other a birthday cake. And the upscale restaurant that featured her chocolate cheesecake also wanted pecan and fresh peach pies for the holiday crowds.

"Whew!" she said aloud. Success was sweet, but it was also a whole lot of work.

She went to work, assembling the ingredients and preheating the oven for another batch of cookies, but before she could begin measuring, another knock sounded at the front door.

Only one person softly tapped instead of ringing the bell. Her mother-in-law was always considerate about not waking the children, should they be sleeping. But what on earth was she doing here at this early hour?

"Frances, good morning," Shelley said.

"Here, take this." The older woman lifted a large corrugated cardboard box sitting by her feet on the porch and thrust it into Shelley's arms.

"What is it?" Shelley stifled a sneeze as she involuntarily hugged the decrepit old box against her clean tank top. Putting it down a few feet from the door, she brushed at her shirt but it was no use. She'd have to change before she went back to baking, and that might mean borrowing one of Dan's old T-shirts. It was Monday, and she was already way behind on laundry.

"Sorry about the box," Frances said, bending to pull it open. "I've been packing so much stuff to donate, I didn't have a better one. In fact, it's my summer goal to give our old farmhouse the most thorough cleaning it's ever had. You won't believe how many generations have stored things in the attic and cellar. I've hardly begun to dig things out."

"The kids just went out in the backyard," Shelley said, hoping to distract their grandmother so she could change and get to work.

"I'll say hello, but I can't stay long." Frances pulled something that looked like a wooden spindle out of the box. Apparently it was dusty because she quickly returned it and rubbed her hands together. "I've made an important decision."

When Frances got an idea in her head, it never boded well for her son's family. The box and its contents seemed especially ominous, and Shelley hoped it wasn't something she'd have to store—or even worse, display somewhere in her already crowded house. Refusing a gift from Frances would hurt her feelings, the last thing Shelley wanted.

"Ralph and I aren't getting any younger," Frances said. "We've decided it's time to share our heritage with our children, pass along some of the many artifacts our ancestors left behind. I'm sure Dan will want this old spinning wheel. It's something you can pass on to one of your children."

She used the tip of her foot to push aside one soiled flap of the box and give Shelley a better look at the contents. Nothing live jumped out, but the gift obviously included its share of historic grit and dirt.

"I've no idea who owned it originally, but I'm sure someone in our family used it, maybe as long ago as two hundred years," Frances said.

"It's broken." Shelley looked with poorly concealed dismay at a collection of wooden parts.

"All it needs is a little tender, loving care. I'm sure Dan won't have any trouble assembling and repairing it. He does have a gift for working with his hands. Of course, he mustn't do anything to refinish it. Patina—the sign of aging on the surface—means everything on antiques."

"He's pretty busy these days with his new career." Shelley didn't expect Frances to pay any attention, but she had to try. "I don't know when he'll have time to work on it. Maybe you should keep it at your house until he's ready to tackle it."

"Nonsense. I'm sure he'll be excited to own it. There's no hurry about restoring it."

"I have to check on the kids," Shelley said, rushing away to keep her unhappiness at the "gift" from showing. "Come to the kitchen, and I'll put on the teakettle."

Frances followed, going out the back door to give Aiden a push on the swing and dust sand off Emma's clothes. Shelley hurried to change her soiled shirt, glad she found an old but wearable T-shirt of her own.

Her children's high energy levels soon exhausted their grandmother. She took refuge in the kitchen when Aiden began chasing Prize around the yard, pretending to rope her with a short length of rope he used to practice tying knots. Emma trailed after him, falling flat on her face when she tried to keep up. Fortunately she landed on soft grass, and there were no tears to wipe or boo-boos to bandage.

"They are high-spirited," Frances said, pink-faced from her short stint with the children. "Wouldn't it be nice to bottle it and dole it out to old folks like me?"

For someone who said she couldn't stay, Frances was in no hurry to leave. Shelley poured a cup of tea and put out a few cookies on a plate, but she didn't join her. The kids looked content after their wild romp around the yard, and she desperately needed to mix this batch of cookies.

While her mother-in-law chatted, she began measuring ingredients. Fortunately a conversation with Frances didn't require more than an occasional nod or one word of agreement, but Shelley couldn't get the box of wooden parts out of her mind. Where could she store them away from the kids? Dan wouldn't be at all happy to have them crowded into his workshop space in the garage, and the basement floor was probably too damp. If she knew his mother, she'd want to check on her gift sometime in the future, and a box full of moldy parts wouldn't sit well.

"Don't you think so?" Frances asked.

Shelley had totally lost the thread of the conversation, but fortunately the phone saved her from the necessity of responding. Before she could answer, the front doorbell rang again. She hoped it was Adelaide. The kids were in an especially rambunctious mood this morning.

"I'd better get the door," she said.

"Should I answer the phone?" Frances asked.

"No, you can let the machine take a message," Shelley said, hurrying out of the kitchen.

Adelaide stood on the front porch, dressed in denim shorts and a dark T-shirt for a busy morning minding the kids.

"Whew, am I glad to see you," Shelley said. "My little darlings are in the backyard."

"I like to play with them," Adelaide said.

"Yes, and I'm so glad you do. I was trying to think of a quiet, shady place to play, and I have an idea. I talked to your mother about it, and she thought it was a good idea."

Shelley liked to check with Margaret before she gave Adelaide anything to do that took her out of her comfort zone. As it happened, her parents were trying to let her show more independence.

"I wonder if you'd like to take the children to the park. It's only a few blocks, and the play equipment is in a nice shady area. You wouldn't have to stay long—just long enough to let them have a change of scenery. What do you think about that?"

"That sounds great!" Adelaide said, smiling broadly. "I know the way to go."

"Great!" Shelley said, still a little uneasy about this new adventure, but Aiden knew the way himself. Adelaide was wonderful with the children, and she'd be sure to watch them every minute they were gone.

"I left Emma's stroller in the garage, and Aiden knows he has to walk beside it and hang onto the handle. He's been practicing how to cross streets and is doing well. You only have one on the way to the park, but make him look both ways and tell you when it's safe."

It took several minutes to corral the kids and get them ready for a jaunt to the park, but they set off in high spirits.

Frances smiled at the little expedition. "Aiden is growing up so fast," she sighed. "Time flies when you get older."

She'd poured herself another cup of tea and started eating the last cookie on the plate.

"Now I won't need lunch," she said with a self-conscious twitter as Shelley removed the plate from the counter where the older woman was perched on a stool.

"I'd better see who called. It could be another order, although I already have more than I can handle today." Shelley hoped Frances would take the hint and leave. Time was ticking away, and she had too much to do.

She played the message, listening with growing dismay.

"Shelley, this is Dad. I know it's been a while, but I was thinking maybe we could get together some time. Call me back, or I'll try you again."

Her day suddenly got a whole lot worse. How long had it been since she'd heard from her father? Not long enough! What could he possibly want? Why call her now?

"That's nice of your father to call you," Frances said. "What's he doing these days?"

Shelley was in no mood for a fishing expedition from Frances. She rarely mentioned her parents, which probably made Dan's mother more curious about them.

"Still installing drywall, as far as I know." Shelley scrubbed her hands at the sink, hoping Frances wouldn't ask more questions. "Well, I'd better get a batch of cookies in the oven."

"You were still in high school when they divorced, weren't you?"

"Yes." Shelley cracked some eggs on the edge of a bowl, trying not to remember the bad days when her parents' marriage had gone sour.

It had been a turbulent time in her life and her sister Susannah's with both parents trying to score points off the other through their daughters. When Shelley got married, she vowed never to involve kids of her own in any argument with Dan.

"Did you live with your mother or your father after the divorce?" Frances asked, emptying the teapot into her cup, undoubtedly so she'd have an excuse to stay longer and ask more questions.

Certainly she knew the answer to that! Shelley had shared a shabby apartment with two other girls. Soon after she graduated, her mother had married Ron and moved to Augusta. Her mother's husband—Shelley refused to think of him as a stepfather—was a control freak, and her mother might as well live on the moon for all the contact they had. That's the way Shelley wanted it to stay, but she especially didn't want any kind of reunion with her father.

It was true he'd offered to let her live with him after he got a job in the small town where he still worked, but it was too little, too late. Her biggest quarrel with her father began with a lie. He'd promised to try to work things out with her mother, but he'd never made any effort to live up to his word, and instead, moved out of their house soon after making this promise. She'd never gotten over the feeling of being abandoned by him, and the years of separation did nothing to change her mind.

"I got an apartment with two other girls," Shelley said.

"Divorce is so sad. I don't know what I'd do without Ralph. We've been together so long, we're like two halves of a whole. Think of all we share: our dear children and our lovely grandchildren."

"That's nice," Shelley said, a standard response to one of Frances' monologues.

"Does Aiden know his maternal grandparents? Such a shame if he doesn't."

Dear Lord, Shelley silently prayed, *please give me patience. And please let her leave before I say something I'll regret.* It had taken years to establish a cordial relationship with her mother-in-law. She really did value Frances' wisdom, but she also wasn't ready to talk about such a personal matter with her.

The phone rang again, and Shelley's first thought was, *Saved by the bell.* She picked it up, hoping it was a friend or someone wanting to place an order. It wasn't, but for the first time ever, she was happy to listen to the spiel of a telemarketer.

"I can see you're busy," Frances said after Shelley let the unwanted caller go through his whole sales pitch before hanging up. "Be sure to tell Dan the spinning wheel probably came from my side of the family. I'm sure he'll be excited to restore it."

"I'll tell him, thank you."

"Well, I'll just let myself out. Remember, you're invited to our house for a picnic supper on the Fourth of July." Frances walked out of the kitchen, and Shelley took her at her word, not following.

"I don't remember your picnic supper," Shelley fumed aloud to herself when Frances was gone, "because you didn't ask us!"

Tradition was everything in the Bauer family. They'd had the whole family for a picnic last year and the year before on the Fourth, so this year it was practically written in stone. There went her plan for the four of them celebrating with a picnic on the beach and fireworks at the park.

Plopping down on a kitchen stool, she tried to get her mind back on baking. Frances could be annoying, but she wasn't to blame for Shelley's dark mood. She didn't want to think about the days when her parents were splitting up—the quarrels, the accusations, and the painful process of dividing everything they owned.

Shelley thought of calling Susannah, but it wouldn't be a kindness to vent to her older sister. Susannah had troubles of her own. Maybe if she just ignored her father's call, he wouldn't bother her again.

After several minutes of brooding, she threw herself wholeheartedly into her baking. She didn't have time to be depressed over her parents' failures.

★ ★ ★

The children were in bed when Dan got home, exhausted but pleased by his overtime. Shelley had debated all day whether to mention her father's call, but there was no reason to bother Dan with it right now.

The soiled box of wooden parts did catch her husband's attention. She'd moved them to his workbench so the children wouldn't get into them. He couldn't help but notice when he came into the house through the garage.

"What's the junk on my workbench?" he asked after she'd reheated his dinner and sat with him as he ate.

"Your mother brought it. It's a spinning wheel for you to put together. I guess it's a family heirloom."

Dan groaned. "Like I don't have enough to do."

"She means well. She's cleaning out the attic and cellar and giving things away. I'm afraid that won't be the last thing she'll give us."

"Probably not. I guess it will fit in the storage space above the garage. I can stick it up there until I think of something to do with it."

"We have to keep it," Shelley reminded him.

"Yeah, Mom would have a fit if we threw it away."

"Maybe it has some value," Shelley said without much optimism.

"Maybe, but not as a box of ratty parts. I'll take another look at it, but I doubt whether it's worth my time to restore it. Especially since selling it would be a major crime in her book."

Maybe she should have hidden it for a time when Dan wasn't exhausted from a long day's work. At least she wasn't going to trouble him by mentioning her father's call.

Between fire and family, Shelley was done in. The last thing she needed was an emotional encounter with the father who'd deserted her.

CHAPTER THREE

Margaret was just finishing up with a customer when she heard the door. Earlier that morning she'd murmured a heartfelt "Thank you, God" when she saw the ten-day forecast of continued blue skies and balmy temps. Stormy weather last summer had literally brought the roof down and made her despair of ever making a go of the Shearwater Gallery. What a difference a year made! It was the Fourth of July, but she planned to stay open all day to take advantage of the crowds who came to see the parade.

"Hi, Diane," she greeted her friend after she finished wrapping the painting she'd just sold. "Nice to see you."

"I thought I'd take a break from writing and see if you have time for a cup of tea," Diane said, looking around the crowded gallery. "I can see you're really busy, though."

"Business has been booming all morning," Margaret said.

"I can see why," Diane said admiringly. "Your paintings keep getting better and better. I love the view of the lighthouse at sunset."

Blushing at the praise, Margaret was touched by her friend's words. "You're not exactly lacking in the talent department yourself," she said, surprised to see Diane's reaction. She looked crestfallen by the comment. "Is anything wrong?"

"No, everything's fine. How have you been?"

Margaret had the feeling Diane was trying to avoid talking about herself, but she didn't want to press her friend if something was wrong.

Margaret looked around the shop and saw the last potential customers leave. The elderly couple had spent as much as an hour carefully looking at every piece displayed in the gallery, but apparently they weren't people who rushed into decisions. Or perhaps they were just passing time. Not everyone who came through the door had the means to buy art, and she didn't resent those who enjoyed looking. What was the purpose of art if it wasn't to bring a measure of happiness into viewers' lives?

"Things have quieted down a bit," Margaret said. "Why don't we go in back, and I'll make some tea? If anyone comes in, I'll hear, but the lunch hour is usually slow. Allan will be bringing me a sandwich or something any minute now."

As if on cue, the door opened and her husband and daughter came in.

"Mom, Mom!" Adelaide called out excitedly as she headed straight toward Margaret.

"Hi, honey," Margaret said, stepping forward to give her a hug.

Allan trailed behind their daughter, looking a bit worse for wear. He was carrying her lunch in a brown paper bag, but he wasn't delivering it with his usual cheerful face.

"Is everything okay?" she asked, wondering why he looked so somber.

He nodded weakly at her and said hello to Diane while Adelaide impatiently shifted her weight from one foot to the other.

"Ask her, Daddy, please," Adelaide urged.

"If this is about the trip to New York City, I told you we have to wait until Penny Tyler gets back from her vacation next week. I need to talk to her about it before we make a decision," Margaret patiently reminded her.

"It's one of the things she's talked about all morning," Allan said.

Margaret could understand why he looked worn out. When Adelaide got an idea in her head, she could wear down both her parents.

"But this is about something else," he said.

"What is it, Adelaide?" Margaret asked, starting to wonder whether she should be alarmed.

"Ask her, Daddy!"

"We talked about you asking her yourself," Allan said.

Adelaide wasn't the only one losing her patience. "Will one of you please tell me what's going on?" Margaret asked as gently as she could.

"Maybe I should leave now," Diane said.

Before Margaret could urge her to stay, Adelaide burst out with her news. "I want to watch fireworks with Chloe and Cassie. They asked me. Please, can I?" She looked at Margaret pleadingly.

Margaret looked at Allan before answering. The two of them had been talking for some time about promoting more independence for Adelaide, but they still had reservations. The trip to New York sponsored by the community center seemed an awfully big step, but maybe going to the Fourth of July display with friends would be good for their daughter.

Still, Margaret had too much imagination to feel comfortable letting their Down syndrome child have too many new experiences on her own. Tourists far outnumbered the residents of the town, and strangers might not react kindly to Adelaide and her two developmentally challenged friends. The real question was whether the outing would be good or bad for her. Now in her midtwenties, she was eager to try new things, but her mother couldn't help worrying.

"Is anyone else going with you?" she asked Adelaide.

"Just the twins," Allan answered for her, making Margaret wonder if his resolve to let Adelaide ask herself had given way to the habit of speaking for her.

"Well . . . ," Margaret said, wishing she'd had time to talk to Allan alone before making a decision.

"They go every year all by themselves," Adelaide said.

"Maybe if your father drove you to the park and watched from far away," Margaret said, trying to come up with an idea that wouldn't leave her daughter totally unsupervised.

"No, we walk there," Adelaide insisted, her face pink with emotion.

"What about watching the parade with the twins instead?" Margaret suggested, making her daughter a counteroffer.

An activity during the day seemed a safer way to foster more responsibility. There was less chance she would wander off and get confused or lost if it wasn't dark.

"Only babies like parades," Adelaide said with a pout.

"You loved watching the parade last year," Margaret said. "The bands march, and there are sure to be some floats decorated with bright colors. There's even going to be a clown this year," she added, glancing at Diane and hoping for her support.

"Clowns are scary," Adelaide said, crossing her arms.

"I heard the miniature motorcycles will be back this year," Diane said.

Margaret was grateful to her friend for the reminder. Adelaide had been fascinated by the tiny motorized vehicles last year.

"How about I go to the parade with Daddy," she said. "And I'll go to the fireworks with Chloe and Cassie."

Margaret exchanged a meaningful glance with Allan. "All right, I'm sure Daddy would like to take you to the parade. But you must obey some rules if you go to the fireworks without us."

"Thank you, Mom, thank you!"

"Listen to the rules first," Allan said, making Margaret wish again they'd had time to talk out of earshot of their daughter before making the decision. Now she had to figure out what rules Adelaide should follow.

"Daddy can take all three of you to the park," Margaret said.

"They like to walk," Adelaide insisted.

"I think it will be fine for them to walk to the fireworks," Allan said.

"If you think so," Margaret said with a doubtful glance at her husband. "But when you're done, Daddy will come back to pick you up at the stone gate by the entrance," Margaret said. "There might be a lot of cars leaving as soon as it's over, but you must stay exactly where he's going to meet you. And he'll ask the twins to stay there with you until he comes."

"I'll make up a little basket with soda and treats, so there won't be any reason for you to wander off looking for refreshments," Allan said. Although he felt easier than Margaret did about letting their daughter have more independence, he was still protective of her.

"Will you follow these rules?" Margaret asked in a firm voice.

"I will. Promise I will!" Adelaide hugged Margaret tightly.

"Okay, Adelaide, let's go get some lunch. We'll come back later to watch the parade," her father said. "Margaret, do you want to watch it with us?"

"It's been so busy all morning I think I'd better stay and mind the gallery," she said.

"I figured as much, but it never hurts to ask," he said, winking at her. Margaret was happy to see that his mood had lifted. Their jitters about the community center trip weighed heavily on both their minds, but he was more comfortable than she was about letting Adelaide branch out on her own.

After the two of them left, Margaret turned to Diane apologetically.

"Sorry to involve you in a family debate," she said, "but I appreciate your mention of the small motorcycles. I think Allan would've been disappointed if Adelaide didn't want to go to the parade with him. We've been wrestling with hard decisions about giving her more independence. I have to admit her father is easier in his mind about it than I am."

A lone man wandered into the gallery and started glancing casually at the display of her paintings on the east wall.

"I should be going. You seem to have your hands full today," Diane said.

"Nonsense," Margaret said. "I promised you a cup of tea. Let me make one for both of us. Allan always gives me way too much food. I'll share my lunch with you."

"You're making it hard to say no." Diane grinned at her. "Allan's sandwiches are legendary. I'd gladly settle for just a small bite. I am curious to hear about the community center trip you mentioned."

"I'm really worried about it." Margaret sighed and watched as the man finished his quick survey of her paintings and left the store.

In the back room, she spread out her lunch on the desk, happy to see a club sandwich she could easily share with her friend. Allan had included a hefty slice of his plum upside-down cake as a treat for working on the Fourth, and she was glad to divide it, along with the bag of celery and carrot sticks. It actually made a very nice lunch for two, but their leisurely chat was interrupted by another pair of customers.

"Do begin without me," Margaret urged her friend as she hurried to the front of the gallery to wait on them.

Several minutes later she'd rung up another sale before her tea even finished steeping. This might go down as her best day ever for selling her paintings.

As soon as she was free, Margaret hurried back to join Diane, glad to have a good friend to share her concerns about the trip Adelaide was so keen to go on. Even though she and Allan were in a different situation than Diane as parents, maybe Diane could shed some light on letting children go off on their own.

"So tell me about this excursion," Diane prompted her.

"Well," Margaret began, "Penny Tyler has organized a trip to New York City for the members of the group, which is fairly small. I don't know much about the trip yet because the day Adelaide came home bubbling over about it, Penny left on vacation. She'll be back early next week, and I plan to talk to her then."

"Is this something you might be able to chaperone yourself?" Diane asked. "When Justin was in middle school, one of his classes went on a trip to New York City, and I was one of the moms who chaperoned."

"It must have been difficult for you to let your son go at such a young age. You'd need ten pairs of eyes to keep track of him and the other kids."

"It was," Diane said. "I know your situation with Adelaide is different, but letting go is hard, even when you know your child is ready."

Margaret mulled her friend's words. "You know, Allan and I have been promoting more independence for Adelaide. She has friends now and spending money she's earned helping Shelley with her children. This upcoming trip just seems like such a gigantic step, though."

Diane nodded in sympathy and set her mug on the desktop. "Your plan of waiting to talk to Penny is a good one. You'll know more about the trip before you make a decision. Now, I really need to get back to writing. I've taken up enough of your time already."

Gathering up the mugs to wash them, Margaret said, "It was so good to get a chance to bounce this whole trip thing off someone impartial."

She hugged Diane and was pleased to see more customers entering as her friend exited. Feeling greatly blessed to have her dream of owning the gallery realized, she just wished she could find answers about giving Adelaide a more independent lifestyle.

★ ★ ★

After darkness fell that evening, Margaret checked her watch even though she'd looked at it just moments before. Allan had had more than enough time to pick up Adelaide and bring her home from the fireworks.

"What can be taking him so long?" she wondered out loud, waking Oreo as he dozed in his favorite corner of the couch.

"Go back to sleep, kitty," she said, pacing back and forth in her cluttered but cozy living room. She really wished she'd gone with Allan so she'd know what was keeping him!

What if something had happened to both her husband and daughter? How could she and Allan possibly consider letting Adelaide go off to the Big Apple when she was a nervous wreck waiting for her to get home from fireworks in Marble Cove?

What could be taking so long, and why hadn't Allan called to say they'd be delayed? All sorts of horrible possibilities ran through her mind, especially the possibility Adelaide had wandered off and gotten lost in the dark and confusion at the park.

She'd just started thinking about calling the police or the hospital when the front door banged open.

"Mom!" Adelaide cried out, rushing toward Margaret and enveloping her in a tight bear hug. "I had so much fun!"

"You're all right then?" Margaret asked, looking toward her husband. He looked as though he didn't have a care in the world.

"I'm great!" Adelaide said, beaming.

Margaret stared from Adelaide to Allan, shaking her head in confusion. "You should have been home a long time ago," she said, directing her accusation toward her husband.

To Margaret's chagrin, Allan only looked puzzled.

"Why didn't you call if you were going to be late?" she asked.

"Margaret," he said, coming toward her and putting his arm around her shoulder. "I only left a little over half an hour ago. I walked Adelaide's friends to meet Mrs. Kling and talked to a few friends on the way here. I didn't know you'd be worried so soon after the fireworks ended."

Margaret let out a pent-up breath. "It seemed longer than that to me."

"Go on, Adelaide, tell your mother what a good time you had and how responsible you were," Allan urged.

"Chloe and Cassie and I had so much fun," Adelaide said, still bubbling over with glee. "The fireworks were so pretty. There were red ones, blue ones, green ones, and white ones. My favorites were the red ones. The noise was scary at first, but Chloe said 'Don't be a baby.' Afterward Cassie wanted to get ice cream, but I said no. I told her we had to wait for Daddy."

"Oh, Adelaide, good for you," Margaret said proudly, ignoring the look Allan was giving her. She was going to have to eat crow when the two of them were alone together. Why had she overreacted so much?

"I think we have some fudge ripple ice cream in the freezer," Allan said to Adelaide. "Do you want to go check?"

"Yes!" she said, hurrying to the kitchen.

"I guess I owe you an apology," Margaret said, turning toward her husband but not wanting to meet his gaze. "I know that was just plain irrational of me. I don't know what came over me..."

"I do," he said, putting his arms around her and pulling her close. "You're fretting about that trip to New York City. You let it do a number on you. You've always felt Adelaide was safe and secure in Marble Cove, even during tourist season."

Margaret sighed. How well her husband knew her. How could she have let worries about the big trip "trip" her up so badly?

"Yes, I have," she admitted. "I'm sorry I jumped on you the minute you walked in the door. It seemed like so much time had gone by. I was scared Adelaide might have wandered off."

"No need to apologize," he said. "I chatted with Beverly and Mr. Wheeland while we waited for the crowd to thin out a little. She's still upset about the fire—who wouldn't be?—but she's also excited about the little key you found. Any clue yet about what it opens?"

"No, afraid not, but please don't change the subject," Margaret said thoughtfully. "How do you feel now about the community center trip? Do you think Adelaide is showing enough maturity for us to let her go?"

Allan wrinkled his brow before answering her. "I definitely agree you need to get more information from Penny Tyler first, but we've been talking quite a while about fostering more independence for Adelaide. The trip would give her the opportunity to be on her own without us, but in a very controlled, supervised situation."

Visions of the vast throngs crowding Times Square on New Year's Eve popped into Margaret's mind but she shook them away. It was July after all!

"You're so wise," Margaret said, linking her arm in Allan's and heading for the kitchen.

"I married you, didn't I?" he asked, grinning.

"You know what?" Margaret smiled.

"What?"

"Maybe letting Adelaide have a little independence on Independence Day wasn't such a bad idea after all."

"*Mm-hmm*... And whose idea was that?" Allan asked her with a sly smile.

Margaret laughed as they went to dish up some ice cream. "I think it was Adelaide's."

CHAPTER FOUR

"Good boy, Rocky," Diane said as he stood quietly to let her remove his leash.

Fortunately she'd decided to walk her golden retriever/ Lab mix early in the morning. It wasn't even eight o'clock, and she was flushed and hot. By noon Marble Cove would be sweltering, and the beaches would be too crowded to exercise a dog, especially a friendly one who liked to initiate play with children. Most parents didn't appreciate a big frisky dog intimidating their offspring.

Skipping breakfast for an early outing hadn't been a good idea. She felt a little light-headed and knew she needed breakfast right away to deal with her recent health problem: low blood sugar. But first, she topped off Rocky's water dish and checked her phone for messages—not that she really expected anyone to call this early on the morning after the Fourth of July.

"No one wants to talk to me," she told Rocky, who was busy lapping up water.

His instincts were better than hers when it came to eating and drinking. She'd emptied her water bottle before they left the house. Now she was parched, hungry, and faint. After hurriedly downing a big glass of water, she set out a box of cereal with a bowl and spoon. Maybe she deserved a better breakfast after her vigorous outing with Rocky, but cooking for one person seemed like an unnecessary chore.

After she'd eaten and dressed for the day, Diane felt considerably better, but she was dismayed that she'd missed a call while she was in the shower. Her agent had promised to get in touch with her after the Fourth, and apparently she'd kept her word. Unfortunately, Diane's attempt to call her back was futile. All she got was voice mail.

Life seemed much more complicated since her first book was released. Now she had to worry about selling enough copies to offset the cost of the public relations firm Frieda Watley had recommended for hire. Her agent assured her it was the best way to promote her mystery novel, but lately the sales figures had been a bit flat. She was eagerly awaiting Frieda's call, hoping she would have good news.

"Well, Rocky," she said when he followed her into her compact but somewhat cluttered office, "I still think word of mouth sells the most books, but I'm a newcomer at this."

Although she had work to do on her second book, she took time to send e-mails to Justin and Jessica. Neither of her children had been free to visit over the Fourth, but Jessica had already visited this summer, bringing her new boyfriend with her. She hoped Justin could get there while the weather was still nice. As she finished her e-mails, her phone rang again.

It took a moment to remember where she'd left it. Forgetfulness was a bad habit she was working on overcoming.

But the cottage was small, and she managed to find it in the kitchen before it stopped ringing.

The caller ID didn't show her agent's number, but Diane was pleased to see her sister-in-law was calling. They hadn't talked in a while, but it was always wonderful to visit with Eric's sister. She'd known and loved him even longer than Diane had.

"Good morning, Jeanette," she said. "It's good to hear from you."

"Sorry I haven't called sooner. My new job is taking a lot more time than I first thought," her sister-in-law said. "How are you feeling these days?"

"Pretty good, although I have to be sure to monitor my blood sugar every day. Will you be able to come to Marble Cove any time soon?"

"Much as I'd like to, I can't say for sure. There's so much to do before the fall semester begins."

Jeanette Spencer was a single, career-minded woman, passionate about her job as an English professor at Portland College. She'd recently been appointed head of her department and, like her brother, she loved teaching English literature.

"Maybe you can visit me," Jeanette suggested. "Our theatre department is sponsoring a series of theatre-in-the-round dramas. They'll be doing *A Doll's House* next, then *King Lear.* You don't often have an opportunity to see that."

"I probably can't get there this month," Diane said regretfully. "I have a lot to do on my second book, and it isn't going very smoothly."

"That's a shame. I thought your first one showed real promise—and I'm not saying that as your sister-in-law. Eric would be so proud of you."

With a catch in her throat, Diane tried to imagine what her husband would've said about her mystery novel.

"He was always so supportive," she mused.

"That was Eric," his sister said. "He never let ego get in the way of encouraging new writers, especially not the one he loved."

"Writing novels was only a dream for me when he was alive," Diane said. "Sometimes I imagine him sitting beside me, urging me to go one way or another in my story."

Talking with Jeanette brought back many good memories, but it also made Diane feel sad. Most of the time she didn't feel lonely, but every once in a while, a memory would trigger something and she'd miss Eric as much as ever.

After the call ended, Diane felt slightly guilty for not trying harder to arrange a visit with Jeanette. Much as she loved her sister-in-law and valued her friendship, Diane was melancholy the rest of the morning. Jeanette and Eric were so much alike it was sometimes painful to reminisce with her. His sister reminded her of so many things she missed about her husband. He'd died much too young, and her heart still ached at the loss.

In spite of her best intentions, she couldn't concentrate on the chapter waiting expectantly on her computer screen. It needed something, a clever twist or an unexpected revelation, but she drew a blank. Eric had been so good at encouraging her when she'd been a reporter and struggling with a piece.

With Eric's voice resonating in her memory, she decided to reread everything she'd written, beginning with chapter one. It would take a while and wouldn't advance her word count, but she had a new optimism as she began.

Several hours later Rocky nudged her leg, wanting to be let out. She couldn't believe how long she'd been at it, but she'd found lots of places where changes would improve the manuscript. The story line was beginning to gel, but she was stiff from sitting so long. Still, she hated to stop when she was on a roll.

"Okay, boy, time for basic necessities," she said, realizing how hungry she was.

One of the published writers in her online chat group bemoaned the fact that she always had to do four or five drafts of a manuscript before she was satisfied with it. Maybe, Diane realized, she needed to think in terms of rewrites. As a reporter, she often dashed off a story to meet a deadline with little time for revising. She was trying to write her book the same way, and it wasn't working. Maybe if she hurried through the first draft, then began the serious business of revising, she might not be as troubled by writer's block. There would always be something she could polish or improve, even on days when her creative juices weren't flowing.

The phone interrupted her thought process, and this time she did remember where she'd left it. Rocky followed on her heels as she rushed to the kitchen.

"Hello." She was breathless from the excitement of deciding on a new way to write her book.

"You sound like you've been running," a familiar voice said.

"No, just working. How are you, Shelley?"

"I'm fine, but Aiden tried to climb up the supports on the swing and fell. He hurt his wrist. I don't think it's broken, but the doctor said to bring him in for an X-ray. I hate to ask, but could you watch Emma while I take him? It's hard to keep her entertained if we have to wait long."

"Of course, I'll be happy to."

"I can bring her to your house if it's more convenient."

"No, I'll come there," Diane said, thinking of all the things she would need to baby-proof if Emma came there. "Just give me a few minutes to let Rocky out, and I'll be right over."

When she was ready to leave, she realized she hadn't stopped work for lunch. She grabbed one of the power bars she kept for low–blood-sugar emergencies and hurried to her neighbor's house.

Emma was sleeping when Diane got there, making her wish she'd remembered to bring a book to read. But she knew her sweet little neighbor sometimes took pretty short naps now that she was almost two.

"I can't thank you enough," Shelley said preparing to leave with Aiden, his eyes red from crying. "Dan's working out of town, and there's no telling how long we'll have to wait."

"I hope for Aiden's sake that a doctor sees him soon. But I can stay as long as you need me," Diane assured her. "I'm through writing for the day anyway."

This was probably true. Diane's fingers were stiff from the long session at the computer, and her inspiration had ebbed away like the sea at low tide. She nibbled on her nutrient-rich granola bar with nuts and raisins and glanced through a day-old newspaper she found in Shelley's living room.

"Mama!" A half hour later Emma announced that she was ready to get up.

Diane gave the toddler time to look her over before she went all the way into her bedroom.

"Deedee," Emma said with a winning smile as soon as she recognized Diane.

"Maybe you need a snack," Diane suggested after changing the little girl into a pretty sunsuit.

She took her hand and led her to the kitchen, lifting her into her booster seat while she looked for a snack.

"How about a graham cracker and a nice cup of milk?" Diane asked.

"Cookie," Emma said. Diane supposed she shouldn't be surprised since her mother's kitchen was the cookie capital of Marble Cove.

"I don't think Mama likes you to eat cookies between meals," Diane said, "but I see some Teddy Grahams in the cupboard. Yum, I wouldn't mind having one myself."

Emma was easily convinced when Diane made a game of walking a cracker to her mouth. Wouldn't it be fun to have a grandchild of her own? It was a lovely thought, although she would never pressure her children to become parents before they were ready. She only prayed that someday she'd be blessed to see a member of a new generation.

The snack occupied the toddler for several minutes before she began crumbling pieces with her thumb.

"No, no, sweetie," Diane said, flicking crumbs off her shirt before setting her loose.

"Let's go find something to keep you entertained, little one," Diane said, and Emma led the way to Aiden's room, which was always a magnet for the toddler. As soon as they got in the room, Emma started removing her brother's precious cars from a shelf.

"These are Aiden's cars," Diane said. "I don't think you're supposed to play with them."

Flashing another big smile, Emma climbed onto the bed and watched as Diane tried to replace the cars as close to their original positions as possible. She was pretty sure Aiden would spot the differences, but it was the best she could do.

"You need to run off some of that energy," Diane said, taking Emma's hand and leading her to the French doors in the kitchen.

It was hot outside in the backyard, but Diane gamely pushed Emma on the swing until she was ready to melt into the ground.

"I think that's enough for now," she said, worried because she'd forgotten to rub sunscreen on Emma's face and arms. "We'd better go inside and cool down."

To avoid resistance, Diane gave her a big hug and carried her inside. The child seemed to have doubled in weight the last few months, or maybe she was getting weaker. She put her down and wondered how Aiden and Shelley were doing. Even if Shelley got into the doctor right away, it could be another forty-five minutes or more before she got home, longer if Aiden did have a broken wrist. How did her friend manage to run a baking business and still give priority to her children, which Diane knew she did?

Emma had found Prize sleeping on the doggie bed, but the dog didn't seem inclined to play.

"Let's see what we can do," Diane said, taking the little girl's hand and leading her to her own bedroom.

They both rummaged around in the toy box, but Emma had the short attention span typical of a toddler. Beginning to run out of ideas for entertaining her, Diane spotted a pile of books on the toy shelf. One thing Emma loved was a good story.

"Let's go read a story," Diane suggested, grabbing a handful of books and leading her to the living room where they could snuggle side by side on the couch as she read.

After several readings of the same story, Diane's throat felt raspy, and she could hear it crackling as she finished the book for the umpteenth time.

"Wouldn't you like to play with your dolly?" Diane asked.

"Story," Emma said.

"All right, one more story. How about this one?" Diane held up a book at random, but Emma picked up the Joseph story and gave Diane a look she couldn't resist. Who knew? Maybe she was reading to a future author.

Diane was halfway through the story when Shelley and Aiden got home. Emma forgot about finishing the book and scrambled to her mother for attention.

"His wrist's not broken," Shelley announced. "Just badly sprained."

"No more climbing the swing set," her son solemnly announced, striding toward his room.

"Emma played with my cars," he roared in disapproval when he got there.

"I'm sorry about that," Diane said. "She got to them before I could stop her."

"No matter," Shelley assured her. "It happens about three times a day. Time-outs don't faze her. She loves getting into her brother's things. If I didn't have Adelaide to watch her, I'd never be able to get my baking done. Thank you so much for coming over on such short notice. It would've been a nightmare to take Emma to the doctor's."

"You know I'm always happy to help out," Diane said, bending to give Emma a little hug before she left.

Walking the short distance to her cottage, Diane felt ten years older than she had before babysitting with Emma. Had her children been that full of energy when they were that age? Not that she remembered, but she'd had a long time to forget how active little ones could be. Fortunately, she adored both of Shelley's children, and taking care of them once in a while was a pleasant interlude from writing.

The trouble was, she'd let too many things keep her from working on her book.

There was still plenty of time to write, but she was yawning as she drank a bottle of green tea in her own kitchen. Maybe a short nap would be refreshing and make her work go better.

First she checked her phone for messages and groaned aloud. Her agent had called again, and she hadn't thought to take her cell phone with her to Shelley's.

Again she tried returning the call, and this time Frieda picked up.

"Diane, we've certainly been playing phone tag today," her agent said. "I don't have good news, but I don't have bad either."

"What does that mean?"

"Well, the latest print sales figures are pretty flat, but you have had some e-book sales. Mysteries appeal to the right demographic for electronic usage, so we'll keep our fingers crossed on that. How's the new book coming?"

"Slower than I'd like," Diane admitted.

"We don't want the gap between books to be too long," Frieda warned, not for the first time. "Don't give the people who read your first book time to forget your name."

This was what agents were supposed to do, wasn't it? Diane knew she needed a good strong push to complete her manuscript. The big question was whether a whole new draft would be beneficial. And did she have time? It would be awful if her publisher dropped her because she couldn't complete the second book in a timely way.

"I was hoping for good word of mouth," she weakly suggested.

"Never hurts, but you can't take it to the bank. Keep me posted on your progress. Bye now."

The agent abruptly ended the call, and Diane didn't know whether to be encouraged or discouraged. She guessed it was a good sign the woman was still talking to her. Frieda must think she had potential, or she wouldn't invest any more time urging her to finish the second book.

Work or nap? Diane stretched out on her couch to relax for a few minutes. A nap won.

CHAPTER FIVE

Friday was an especially busy day for Shelley. The influx of tourists doubled the number of people in town, bringing in larger orders from her business customers. Add to that the number of special family events scheduled to take advantage of the warm summer weather, and she was swamped.

When she began work for the day, she first tried to design some clever decorations for the sheet cake the Bertchfields had ordered for a family reunion, but Aiden was unusually whiny. His sprained wrist hurt, and he was hanging around her instead of playing where Adelaide could watch him. Granted, her helper had her hands full with Emma these days, but her son usually played near them and kept himself entertained.

"When will Daddy be home? He said he'd take me to buy new flip-flops," he complained, fiddling with the sling the doctor had given him. Wearing it was optional, but it did help remind him not to use his wrist too much until it healed.

"It's still morning. If he has to work overtime, you may have to get them tomorrow." She felt a twinge of guilt for failing to buy them herself.

"I need them," Aiden insisted.

"You can't go to the beach today. I have to work, and anyway, it's too hot."

A frosting beach ball with a sand pail and shovel would be a creative way to decorate the Bertchfield cake, she decided, a nice change from big sugary flowers. It was fun when the client left the decorations up to her. She remembered the fun she'd had making a cake with an army insignia for Diane's son and a realistic-looking cat-shaped cake for Adelaide's birthday.

"Aiden, do you want to play outside?" Adelaide asked, stepping into the kitchen with Emma riding on her hip.

"Naw." He slumped down on the floor by his mother's feet, not his usual response to playing outside.

"You like playing outside," Shelley coaxed. "Go with Adelaide to get sunscreen and your baseball cap."

"I don't want to go," Aiden insisted.

"We can play Mother-may-I," Adelaide suggested. "You like that."

"That's no fun." He wasn't going to be persuaded easily.

"I have a good idea," Shelley said, remembering Margaret and Allan's determination to help their daughter be more independent. "Would you like to take them for a little walk, Adelaide?"

"That would be fun," she said, obviously pleased.

"Emma can ride in her stroller, and Aiden can walk beside it, just like the other day," Shelley said.

"I want to ride my bike," her son said.

"Not with your wrist in a sling," Shelley pointed out. "But you can show Adelaide how you've learned to look both ways before crossing the street. Show her what a big boy you are."

Shelley helped the little procession get going, glad to see Adelaide was wearing a cute sailor hat to shield her head.

"Don't walk too far," Shelley said. "It's only going to get hotter."

"We won't," Adelaide promised as she pushed Emma's stroller out of the garage.

Alone in the kitchen, Shelley went into high gear, heating the oven and rapidly mixing up the cake. As soon as it was in the oven, she could get started on cookies for the Cove. They were selling as fast as she could make them, which was gratifying but a lot of work.

Her first cake, a chocolate-and-white-marbled creation, had to be made in two separate batches. She'd frost them side by side to make one large sheet cake, but experience had taught her that the recipe didn't come out as well if she doubled it.

Her head was full of recipes and work steps when the phone rang. She almost hoped it wasn't a last-minute order, or she'd be baking well into the night.

"Lighthouse Sweet Shoppe," she said, trying to swirl the two separate batters, white and chocolate, with one hand while she picked up the phone with the other.

"Hi, Shelley. It's your father."

For several moments she was too stunned to say anything. He was the last person she'd expect to be on the other end of the line, and she could feel her heart racing. Why hadn't she checked the caller ID? She didn't want to talk to him, and he couldn't possibly say anything that wouldn't distress her.

"Dad," she forced herself to say.

Pushing the mixing bowl farther back on the counter so she wouldn't knock it over, she tried to think of reasons to avoid talking to him. She'd never been able to forgive her father for moving out of their house after he'd promised to try to work things out with her mom. She'd convinced herself she was happier without him in her life.

"It's been awhile since we talked," he said.

His voice sounded lower and huskier than she remembered, but, of course, he was getting older.

"Quite a while," she agreed, wanting to tell him it hadn't been long enough. She couldn't imagine what they had to talk about. "Why are you calling?"

"I just want to know how you're doing." He sounded unsure of himself.

"Fine."

"Dan's working, is he? Jobs have been hard to come by lately. Lots of unemployment around the state."

"Yes, Dan has a job," she said, wondering where this was going. "He's an apprentice electrician."

"That's a good field for a bright young man like Dan. How are the kids?" he asked in a tentative voice.

"They're fine too." She didn't want to go into Aiden's sprained wrist.

"Glad to hear it. I bet Aiden is getting tall. I have his baby picture on my dresser."

If he thought that made him a good grandfather, he was dead wrong.

"Why are you calling, Dad?"

"It's been too long," he said. "I thought maybe we could get together. I'm on vacation this week and next. It'd be awfully nice to see you, Shelley."

"This isn't a good time. I'm sorry, but I'm up to my ears in work. My baking business has really taken off."

"I see." His voice told her he thought it was only an excuse.

"Maybe some other time," she said, hoping to get off the phone.

"Tell you what," he said in the voice he used when he wanted to strike a bargain. "Give it some thought, and I'll get in touch with you in a few days. It's not right that a family doesn't get together from time to time."

She wanted to tell him he should have thought of that when he gave up on his marriage—and his daughters. To his credit, he'd asked Shelley to come live with him, but his tiny apartment in another town seemed more like a prison than a home when she was still in her teens.

"Okay. I have to go. I have a cake in the oven." It was a small fib, but she did have batter to go in.

"Talk to you again, sweetheart. Bye now."

Sinking down on a nearby stool, she stared at the phone in her hand for several minutes after saying good-bye. When she was little, she'd adored her father. He always made her laugh, and she basked in his attention. The divorce had ruined their relationship, and she didn't know how she felt about him now. Had she completely stopped loving him? Did she have any feelings at all for him? Would it be a good or a bad thing to see him again?

Why didn't she give him a definite no? Now she had to agonize over whether to see him again. What would Dan think? Would it be a good thing for her children to see their grandfather?

Silently praying for several moments, she couldn't reconcile her deep Christian faith with her father's request. Was it her duty to let him back in her life? Or would he bring more hurt and discord into her life and her family's?

Time was passing much too swiftly, and she'd hardly begun her day's baking. She forced herself to concentrate on what had to be done, but she couldn't help wishing her father hadn't called.

Her mother would tell her to forget him, but she was living an entirely separate life with her second husband. Shelley rarely heard from her, although she didn't feel any enmity toward her.

What should she do about seeing him again? It was a dilemma she didn't want to deal with. Maybe he wouldn't call again—but that was a futile hope. He would. Her choices were plain: refuse to see him or risk the hurt of letting him back into her life. Seeing him would bring back all the bad memories of her parents' divorce.

She stood with a bowl of batter in her hands, momentarily paralyzed by the decision she'd have to make.

Why had he called now, when things were going so well for her?

★ ★ ★

Inhaling deeply, Beverly enjoyed the aroma of roasting coffee beans as she entered the Cove, one of the many things she loved about her newly adopted town. Even though it was midafternoon, the place was crowded with tourists—no doubt lured there by the tantalizing smell wafting out to the street. She admired the worn pine floors and wood-paneled walls, wisely left unchanged since it was a pub for fishermen many years ago. Families were crowded around the small wooden tables, and it made her smile to see children munching on her good friend Shelley's treats. Business was booming for the young mother, and Beverly couldn't have been happier for her.

"Over here," Dennis Calder called out, waving her over to a small table tucked away in the corner.

Weaving her way through the crowded room, she didn't know whether to be flattered or annoyed when she saw Dennis had already gotten coffee and a cherry Danish for her. It was late in the day for that kind of treat, and she wasn't a big fan of sweets anyway. But he had been very helpful in the fight to save Old First, a cause near and dear to her heart. As long as he knew they were just friends, she did enjoy his company on the occasional casual coffee "date."

He rose and pulled out the chair for her, a somewhat theatrical gesture but one she did appreciate. She didn't see men doing it very often.

"You're looking wonderful, as usual, Beverly," he said, sitting down across from her and taking a sip of his coffee.

"Thank you . . . and thanks for ordering for me," she said, trying to be gracious.

"Everyone's been talking about the fire at Old First," he said. "I guess an old building like that is pretty vulnerable. Good thing it was empty when it happened." Beverly didn't mention being on site with her friends at the time the fire occurred. She didn't see any reason to confide in him. The last thing any of them wanted was to answer questions about why they were there.

"That really was fortunate," she said, taking a sip of her coffee and breaking off a small edge of the pastry to nibble. "It would have been a terrible disaster if people had been hurt."

"Do you know whether the building can be repaired? It might be an opportunity to build a nice new one."

He sounded casual, but Dennis was too much the entrepreneur not to see other potential for the property. Still, she hoped she was misjudging him. He'd been a huge proponent of renovating the historic old church.

Stop being so suspicious, she silently chided herself, breaking off another small bite of the Danish. She didn't want to invent something to worry about. Since selling her house in Augusta and settling into her consulting business, she felt at peace with her decision to make a permanent home in Marble Cove. Leave it to her to look for things to worry about when her life was calm and peaceful.

Still, he'd touched a sensitive issue. She was upset about what the fire would mean for the future of the church. Maybe that was why she was skeptical about the concern Dennis was showing for the fate of Old First.

"I've no idea what will happen." She almost slipped up and said she hadn't talked to Reverend Locke since the night of the fire. "It's a shame the Founder's Day celebration had to be canceled."

Dennis nodded. "I didn't ask you for coffee to talk about Old First, although it is a tragedy," he said. "I have something I want to show you."

He pulled out several large rolls of paper from a portfolio resting out of sight under the table. "Let me just get rid of these coffee cups, unless you'd like more?" He wiped the table with a paper napkin to make sure it was dry.

"No, thank you. I'm good," she said, her curiosity piqued.

The big Danish was still almost whole, and it seemed a waste to let him throw it away. While Dennis got rid of their cups, Beverly wrapped the pastry in a napkin and stuck in her purse. Her father couldn't eat it, but Mrs. Peabody, his part-time cook and housekeeper, would probably enjoy it.

"Let me give you some backstory," Dennis said when he returned to the table. "My development company is going to start a new project on land I own beyond Sunrise Shores. These are plans for a new complex designed to make Marble Cove a real tourist destination."

He carefully unrolled one of the long cylinders and spread it out on the table, keeping it flat by resting his arms on the edges.

"I thought Marble Cove already *was* a real tourist destination," she said, perplexed by his statement. "We get a large influx of visitors and summer residents. Look at how busy the Cove is in the middle of the day." She gestured around the still-packed coffee shop. Through the window she could see people lined up waiting to get in. She was starting to feel guilty for taking up a table.

"This?" he asked, looking around the small space. "This is nothing. I'm talking about something akin to what the Carolinas draw. Look at these plans."

"Why are you sharing this with me?" she asked, genuinely curious about his reason.

Dennis looked up at her, and she wished his eyes weren't Technicolor blue, intense and riveting. He was good-looking and keenly aware of it, but her feelings for him only extended to friendship. She'd made it clear to Dennis on several occasions she was in a relationship with Jeff Mackenzie—albeit a very slowly developing one. She and Jeff had grown closer when he'd been so supportive during the process of selling her house.

"I'm telling you about my plans because you're sophisticated and able to see the big picture," Dennis said in his most persuasive voice. "I think you could be influential in swaying some of the locals who aren't as farsighted as you and I. I'd love to have your father's support too. He's pretty well connected in town."

Beverly frowned, wondering where this line was leading. Just what was he up to?

He carefully smoothed the renderings out. "I'm confident the town council and Mayor Waters will give the whole project a green light. But there are always a few naysayers in every community who object to progress for the sake of objecting."

"What exactly are you proposing?" Beverly asked, craning her neck to get a better look at the plans.

"The complex will feature up-to-date attractions for the whole family, including high-rise vacation condos and an adjacent water park and miniature golf course."

"Why do you need a water park when you have the ocean?" she asked, but he only laughed at her question.

"I'm talking about building a premier vacation destination, Beverly."

She watched him unroll another set of plans before continuing. "The amenities in the units will include extended ceiling heights, private elevators into the penthouse units, concierge service for occupants, hardwood floors, and oversize tubs and showers. I'm also envisioning twenty-four-hour babysitting service and eventually a bowling alley, restaurants, and a retail area." His excitement was contagious—and alarming.

Beverly looked around the Cove again before choosing her words. "But what will your plans do to local businesses?" she asked, trying not to sound as critical as she felt.

"Locals will either prosper or fail," he said matter-of-factly. "What my firm is proposing will change the face of Marble Cove forever."

That's exactly what Beverly feared as she envisioned boarded-up shops all along Main Street. Not just the Cove would be affected. What would happen to the Mercantile and the charming little specialty shops? Even Margaret's gallery might fail if his idea for a retail development took a huge share of business away from the downtown area. She envisioned a financial disaster for the people who depended on the tourists who came for the beach and the spectacular view of the lighthouse.

"Dennis, you do realize this complex has the potential to ruin the charm of Marble Cove, not to mention the livelihoods of many of its residents?"

"You say that like it's a bad thing," he said in a smug voice.

"It *is* a bad thing!" she said loudly, then was embarrassed when patrons looked their way. She was angry though. How could Dennis not care about what his plan would do to the residents of Marble Cove? It was a potential disaster, and he brushed it aside as though it was inconsequential. The town managed to be a bustling tourist attraction in the summer and still retain its quaint charm and historical relevance. What Dennis was proposing could wreak havoc on all that.

"Don't you care anything about the town and the people?" she challenged him.

He rolled up the plans and neatly replaced the rubber bands before answering her.

"This complex will be a revenue booster for Marble Cove," he said. "Can't you see the potential for jobs? Property values will soar."

"So will taxes on property. People won't be able to afford homes that have been in their families for generations. And what kind of jobs can you offer? Do you plan to employ bankrupt businesspeople in minimum-wage jobs?" The more she thought about it, the worse it seemed.

"Beverly," he said with exaggerated patience. "You're overreacting, only looking on the negative side." He was starting to sound angry, but Beverly didn't care. His idea was terrible, and she couldn't believe the mayor and town council would approve it.

"Marble Cove is a wonderful place to visit and to live just as it is," she argued. "Your development will ruin the charm of the area and turn Marble Cove into a generic playground for the well-to-do like so many others along the Eastern Seaboard. You'll be destroying everything that makes the town special."

Dennis just stared at her, and Beverly felt her cheeks reddening. She rarely lost her cool, but she'd just lost it big-time.

"I never thought you of all people would be against progress," he said coolly, carefully putting the rolled plans back into his portfolio.

"I'm not opposed to progress," she said defensively. "I just think things of this magnitude need to be carefully considered by the people most affected instead of being forced on them."

She wasn't naïve. If Dennis got the approval he wanted, he wouldn't be satisfied with family vacationers. His condo plans were geared to a much faster lifestyle. Next he'd want legal gambling and all the problems that came with it. Marble Cove would be spoiled and corrupted.

"Thank you for your input. However, what you think really doesn't have any bearing on the project. The mayor and town council are sure to approve this complex," he said as a parting shot.

Watching him go, she was sure of two things: She'd lost a friend and gained a cause.

CHAPTER SIX

W hy get together on a Monday night?" Dan asked as
Shelley kissed her son good night before leaving.

"I'm not really sure. Beverly has been trying to get
Margaret, Diane, and me to come to her house for some
kind of meeting since last Friday. This is the soonest all of
us could make it."

"Mama, can Prize sleep with me?" Aiden asked as he
settled down for the night.

"You know she isn't allowed on your bed," Shelley said.
"Now be good for Daddy and go to sleep."

"How long will you be?" Dan asked as he followed her to
the front door.

"I wouldn't think very late, but Beverly was pretty
mysterious."

"Well, be safe. I don't want any emergency calls this
time," he teased good-naturedly.

"I think we're just talking," Shelley assured him. "All
Beverly said was we needed to have a meeting. She made it
sound important."

"Well, don't stay too late," her husband said. "I'll watch
TV until you get home."

"Why not go to bed? You know you'll doze off in your chair and I'll have to wake you up."

Her wifely advice was interrupted by a soft knock on the front door.

"That will be Diane," Shelley said, going to answer it.

She slipped out the front door before Dan could say anything else. Fortunately, he never minded staying with the kids in the evening. He knew she was in the house most of the day and needed some time with friends. Also, she tried not to take advantage, knowing he really missed spending time with her after they got the kids settled down.

"What do you think this is about?" Diane asked as they walked.

"No idea," Shelley said. "Beverly was sort of secretive. She said it's urgent we get together, but she didn't want to go into it on the phone."

"Same here," Diane said. "Maybe she has news about Old First. I can't get the fire out of my mind."

"Or she has a new idea about the treasure."

"I guess we'll find out soon," Diane said with a light laugh. "But it's not like Beverly to be so vague."

When they arrived, Margaret was already seated in the living room with a cup of tea. More surprising, Beverly's father and Mrs. Peabody were there too, so the meeting probably had nothing to do with lost treasure. They tried to keep their conversations about treasure amongst themselves as much as possible.

"I don't know what's up," Mrs. Peabody said, "but I made a nice pineapple upside-down cake for the occasion."

"It's delicious," Beverly said, although she wasn't having any herself.

"It's made with that artificial sweetener," her father said, holding his plate close to his chest to avoid dropping crumbs. "I don't care much for it as a rule, but this is good."

"Can I slice you up a piece, ladies?" Mrs. Peabody asked.

"That would be nice," Diane said, and Shelley nodded in agreement.

They found seats on the couch, but Beverly remained standing, fidgeting until Mrs. Peabody served the cake and poured iced tea. Shelley could tell her friend was impatient to tell them why they were there, but, to her credit, she let the older woman play hostess first.

"Let's get on with this," Harold Wheeland said. "It's nearly my bedtime."

He didn't sound cranky, only a bit impatient. Shelley felt the same way. The cake was good, the tea was refreshing, and she enjoyed being with her friends, but it had been a long day. She was eager to hear why Beverly had called them together.

"I had coffee with Dennis Calder," she began.

"I like the Mackenzie boy better," Mrs. Peabody interrupted. "You could do worse than him."

"Please, Mrs. Peabody, this isn't about my personal life. Dennis had ulterior motives for asking me to coffee. He has a nightmare plan for Marble Cove, and we've got to do something to stop him."

The atmosphere in the room changed. She had everyone's full attention.

"Dennis invited me to coffee to show me some plans. He wants to develop land adjacent to Sunrise Shores. Fortunately, it's within town limits, so there's still a chance to stop him."

"What kind of plans?" Diane asked.

"He wants to put up high-rise condos to attract wealthy summer people, but that's not the worst. If he gets his way, he'll build an amusement park complete with miniature golf, water features, rides, you name it."

"Won't that help the town by bringing more visitors?" Shelley asked.

"More likely it will destroy Marble Cove as we know it," Beverly said in a heated voice. "He wants to include a large shopping area with all the amenities of places like Atlantic City."

"Then you can kiss most of the downtown businesses good-bye," her father said, quickly helping to explain her concern.

"That sounds terrible," Margaret said in a stricken voice. "I might as well close my gallery on the day it opens. Tourists will flock to the new complex, and everyone on Main Street will be left high and dry."

"If I know history—and I do," Mr. Wheeland said, "speculators don't build fancy accommodations for the family trade. He must have something else in mind, very likely gambling."

"Does he have the political clout to get licensed for it?" Diane asked with concern.

"Who knows?" Beverly threw up her arms in consternation. "Money talks, and Dennis Calder must have powerful financial backing to attempt a project like this."

"Never had much use for the Calders," her father mumbled.

"I'm sure folks won't stand for something like that," Mrs. Peabody said.

"If I know Dennis," Beverly said in a solemn voice, "he'll begin construction the day after the town council approves his plan. By the time the people in Marble Cove muster opposition, it will be too late."

"Why did he tell you about it ahead of time?" Shelley asked.

"Good question." Beverly paced the length of the small living room, wringing her hands. "He misjudged me. He thought I'd be supportive because it would bring outside money into town. And, of course, my father knows a lot of people. If I could get him on Dennis' side, a lot of people might be deceived into thinking it's a good idea."

"Marble Cove would turn into—what do you call those towns where nobody lives anymore?" Mrs. Peabody asked.

"Ghost towns," Beverly said. "Only it could get even worse. If businesses fail and people have to leave, guess who might buy up property cheap to expand his project? Dennis even asked me what the plans were for Old First. He suggested it was a good time to think of a new building. I think he meant something besides a church."

"I never!" Mrs. Peabody said indignantly.

"Wouldn't his plan create jobs?" Shelley asked, thinking of how hard it had been for Dan to get steady employment.

"Possibly," Beverly admitted. "But there aren't any local contractors that can handle a development this large. Once it gets going, the people in town will be lucky to get minimum-wage jobs. Dennis Calder's plan has nothing to do with helping out Marble Cove, and everything to do with building his personal empire."

"The bottom line is about change," Diane said thoughtfully, "but not the kind of change that will benefit the town. Everything that's historical and charming will be wiped out. It sounds like his project is a clone of developments up and down the Eastern Coastline."

"Sounds like a foolish idea to me," Mrs. Peabody said. "There's no guarantee the thing won't go belly-up after it's built. The country doesn't need another playground for folks with more money than sense."

"But what can we do about it?" Shelley asked.

"That's why I asked you here tonight," Beverly said. "You're the people I trust most in Marble Cove."

"The only way to stop it is to make sure the town council doesn't approve it," Diane said thoughtfully.

"Isn't there an election coming up soon?" Shelley asked. "Maybe they won't dare approve it until they're reelected."

"That could work both ways," Mr. Wheeland said. "They might hurry it through before the election. No telling what's in it for some of the council members."

Shelley didn't want to believe Mr. Wheeland's cynical comment, but she was hard-pressed to deny the possibility he was right. In her heart, she didn't want to live in a community of boarded-up stores and empty homes. It wasn't at all what she and Dan had wanted for their family when they decided to make Marble Cove their permanent home.

"I see where you're going," Diane said. "We have to get the word out and build a viable opposition."

"If you're all agreeable, here's my plan," Beverly said. "We have to persuade enough residents to sign a petition protesting the approval of Dennis Calder's project. It's the only way to stop him."

Shelley added her murmur of agreement to the general assent. She couldn't imagine living in a town dominated by a commercial amusement complex. Like most residents, she appreciated the influx of summer people, but she shared the townies' sense of relief when the season was over and the town belonged to the residents again.

"How do we do that?" Shelley asked, hoping the others didn't think she was naïve.

"The first step is to see an attorney," Beverly said. "We want to be sure we're doing everything in a legal and effective way."

"I'll take care of that," Mr. Wheeland said. "I know just the lawyer. He owes me, so he probably will look into it pro bono."

"Then it will be up to us to get signatures," Beverly said.

"We can enlist others too," Margaret said. "I imagine every business owner in town will be willing to help. I'll make it my responsibility to contact everyone on Main Street."

"That would be immensely helpful," Beverly said. "I'll get a map of Marble Cove and divide up the neighborhoods for door-to-door canvassing. That way two people won't go to the same area."

"I'll take a petition to church. I don't think our minister would object if I ask people to sign in the parking lot after services," Shelley said.

"I'll circulate one at the community center and keep one at my gallery too. I'm sure Allan will want to help too if you give him some streets to cover," Margaret volunteered.

"If all my relatives sign, it should put us over the top," Mrs. Peabody. "My granddaughter can talk to young folks of voting age."

"I don't know a lot of people, but I'm certainly willing to go house to house in whatever area you assign to me," Diane said.

"I can't thank you all enough," Beverly said with a catch in her voice.

"Well, I don't know about the rest of you, but it's my bedtime," her father said. "Sounds to me like we have a plan."

"Oh dear," Mrs. Peabody said. "It's time for me to get home too. I'm glad you invited me to your meeting. I'll have nightmares about that Calder fellow taking over the town."

When the older pair had left, Beverly smiled at her friends. "I knew I could count on you."

"Before we break up, I have one question," Margaret said, taking a small plastic bag from her canvas carryall. "Does anyone have a new idea about the little key I found just before the fire?"

"Wish I did," Diane said thoughtfully. "Maybe it doesn't open anything anymore."

"Still, it must have been special. Why else would it be in a room no one has seen for ages?" Beverly asked.

"I wonder how much Reverend Locke knows about Jeremiah Thorpe," Shelley speculated. "He pastors Thorpe's church. Wouldn't that make him curious about the founder?"

"You'd think so." Margaret took back the key to put it in her bag for safekeeping.

"Can I see the key one more time?" Diane asked.

"Of course." Margaret handed it to her. "What if one of us showed it to Reverend Locke?"

"I'm not sure that's a good idea," Shelley objected. "What if he insists on keeping it? That would be the last of our only good lead."

"Shelley may be right," Beverly agreed. "If he takes it, the treasure may never be found. We know how much he's opposed to the whole idea. I was surprised he let us into the church the night of the fire."

"Still, he may know things we don't," Diane suggested. "He may be more forthcoming now that Old First has been closed down by the fire."

"Maybe you could feel him out, Beverly," Shelley said.

"I guess the worst he could do is throw me out," Beverly said with a forced laugh. "Maybe letting us into the church was a sign he's softening his opposition to our treasure quest."

Would something come of Beverly talking to her minister? Shelley believed there was something to find, maybe not gold or silver but something valuable enough for Jeremiah Thorpe to hide it.

"I'm glad you called us together," Diane said. "I think we're all 100 percent against Calder's plans. Now I'd better get going, if you're ready to leave, Shelley."

"Actually, there's something I'd like to run by all of you," Shelley said with hesitation. "I'm in something of a quandary."

"What's wrong?" Margaret was quick to ask. "Is it something about your children?"

"Only indirectly." Shelley struggled for just the right words to explain her predicament. Would her friends think she was terrible because she didn't want to see her father?

"You can tell us," Diane said in a compassionate voice.

"Well, it's complicated." Shelley took a deep breath. "All of you know my father has pretty much been out of my life since my parents divorced. Anyway, he called me last week. He wants to see me."

"That's good, isn't it?" Beverly asked. "My father and I are a lot closer than we were a few years ago. Maybe your father regrets all the time he's lost."

"It's not just the divorce. It's the way he left us. I don't trust him enough to rebuild our relationship. Does that make me a bad person?"

"Certainly not," Margaret said. "But do your children know him? Sometimes the love between a grandparent and a grandchild is pretty special."

"I adored my grandfather," Diane mused. "Whenever I was sad or worried, he was the one person who could always cheer me up."

"Did your father say why he wants to see you?" Beverly asked.

"No, but if he likes the idea of being a grandparent, he's waited a long time to do anything about it. His call upset me so much I can't think straight."

"Maybe he just misses you," Diane suggested in a kind voice.

"Maybe, but I don't miss him anymore. I've gone on with my life with no help from him. I've prayed about it, but I can't seem to find the love I used to feel for him."

"You might not know how you feel until you actually see him," Margaret suggested in a compassionate voice.

"And talk to him," Diane added. "People change, sometimes for the better. Maybe you can find common ground again."

"I imagine Aiden and Emma would be excited to have another grandfather." Margaret stood and checked to be sure she had the key tucked securely into her carryall.

"If the reunion doesn't work out, you'll at least know you tried." Beverly could always be relied upon for practical advice.

"Well, thanks for your input," Shelley said, trying to sound happier than she felt. "I guess I should get home now. Thanks for having me, Beverly. I'm behind the petition drive 100 percent."

"Thank you all for coming," Beverly said, walking them to the door.

Shelley really didn't want to talk on the way home, and Diane seemed to sense it. Her friends' wholehearted support of meeting with her father had taken her aback, and Dennis Calder's threat to the town only added to her distress.

"I love cool, calm nights like this," Diane said as they approached their houses. "It really would be a shame to turn Marble Cove into one more generic amusement complex."

"Yes," Shelley answered absentmindedly.

Should she feel guilty about depriving her children of the chance to get to know their grandfather? Someday they might become curious about their roots. How would she explain grandparents who were divorced and a grandfather who was estranged from his family?

"Good night," Diane said when they parted company. "I'll be eager to start circulating Beverly's petition."

"Me too," Shelley said without enthusiasm, still vaguely hurt by her friends' advice. They didn't seem to understand how hard it was to let her father back into her life. She couldn't forget how her father had evaded her questions and outright lied to her. When trust was dead, what was left?

After she stepped into her home, she wasn't surprised to find Dan sound asleep in his chair with the TV still on. All the lights were out, and the glow from the television screen made the familiar room seem eerie.

What would her husband think about reconnecting with her father? No doubt he'd leave it up to her.

"Time to go to bed, sweetheart," she said in a soft voice, bending over to kiss his forehead.

"Oh, you're home!" he said, startled awake in spite of her gentle approach. "What was the big meeting about?"

"I'll tell you in the morning," she said, linking her hand in his to pull him to his feet. "Let's go to bed."

"Good idea," he murmured, still more asleep than awake.

He tumbled into bed before she could get her teeth brushed. When she was ready, she stood over him and thanked the Lord for her wonderful husband and the love they shared.

Would her father disturb the tranquility of her family or add another dimension to their happiness? She was afraid to risk seeing him again. Was she protecting her family or being selfish?

Crawling in beside Dan, she lay awake for a long time. For the first time ever, her three friends had failed to see her point of view. They just didn't understand why she was so reluctant to see her father. Much as she regretted asking them, she was honest enough to admit she'd hoped to reinforce her decision not to let him back in her life. Unfortunately they'd left her in an even worse quandary. Was it possible she was wrong in rejecting her father? Was she strong enough to put aside the past and try to begin again?

CHAPTER SEVEN

Margaret put the box of cereal on the kitchen table next to the small stack of brightly colored mismatched bowls she enjoyed using. As she was pouring herself a healthy breakfast, Adelaide rushed into the kitchen.

"It's Tuesday!" she sang out, coming up to Margaret and wrapping her arms around her.

"Careful, honey," Margaret said cheerfully, "or these flakes will end up all over the floor."

"Sorry. I'm just so excited," Adelaide said contritely.

"Excited about what?" Allan asked, coming into the kitchen.

As she poured milk on her cereal, Margaret couldn't help being amused by the exasperated look their daughter gave him.

"Daddy, it's *Tuesday*," Adelaide said emphatically.

Margaret was tempted to laugh out loud at the expression on her husband's face. Poor man, she thought wryly. He obviously didn't remember the significance of the day. She hadn't been thinking of anything else since she'd gotten up. In fact, today had been weighing heavily on her mind for several days.

"Am I missing something?" he asked, genuinely bewildered as he looked from Margaret to their daughter.

Margaret took pity on him. "Tuesday is Penny Tyler's first day back from vacation. I'm going to go talk to her about the life-skills group's trip to New York City."

Allan nodded knowingly. "Oh, *that* Tuesday," he said.

"You can come with me if you like," Margaret offered.

"No, thanks," he said, reaching for a box of his favorite cereal.

The two of them had agreed Margaret would talk to Penny before they decided whether Adelaide could go on the trip. She was still uneasy in her mind about letting her daughter go, although Allan thought it would be a good step toward giving her more independence. No matter how busy she'd been at the gallery the previous day, the trip had never been far from her mind. It was one thing to discuss giving Adelaide more freedom and allowing her to manage some money. It was quite another thing to send her off to the Big Apple without her mother or father.

"When are you going to talk to Miss Penny?" Adelaide asked, carefully adding the milk to her cereal.

"As soon as I finish eating, dear. I'll go before I open the gallery," Margaret promised. "I won't even have a second cup of coffee."

"Thank you!"

Adelaide looked so happy Margaret felt a pang of guilt. What if she and Allan decided *not* to let Adelaide go on the trip after she talked to Penny? But there was no sense fretting about that until she went down to the community center and got the facts. Margaret had a whole list of questions she and Allan had compiled about the trip, and she knew Penny would have the answers. Whether they were the answers she and Allan—and Adelaide—wanted was still uncertain.

After breakfast, Allan started clearing the dishes away while Adelaide continued to chatter at Margaret about the trip.

"I'm going to go in just a few minutes," Margaret reassured her excited daughter. "Remember I'll have to go straight to the gallery after I talk to Penny, so the two of you will have to come see me at lunchtime to find out what I've learned."

Adelaide looked crestfallen. "Please, can you call? Please?"

Turning to Allan for backup, Margaret saw him shrug.

"Afraid I'm with Adelaide on this one," he said. "Can't you at least call and give us a quick rundown before we come down to talk to you at lunchtime?"

Margaret felt sympathy for her husband so she nodded assent. Adelaide was so keyed up she probably wouldn't give her father a moment's peace. He loved spending time with their daughter, but Margaret knew this trip had them all on edge.

"I'll call when I know something," she promised. "But remember, Adelaide, even if Miss Penny gives me good answers, your father and I will still need to discuss things further. Alone."

"I know," Adelaide said so solemnly it saddened Margaret again to think of her daughter's reaction when, or if, she was told no. With a heavy heart, Margaret headed to the community center.

"Come on in," Penny Tyler said, ushering Margaret into her small yet neat office after the short walk across town.

Margaret sat down on the seat Penny indicated. "Thank you so much for talking to me when you've just gotten back from your vacation. Did you have a good time?"

"It was lovely. Thanks for asking. I went to visit friends and stayed at an adorable bed-and-breakfast in Delaware," she said, sitting down across from Margaret. "It was a great break, but I'm happy to be back. I missed the people here, especially my special group."

"If Adelaide is any indication, they missed you too," Margaret said with a broad smile. "I must have heard your name a dozen times a day."

"That's sweet," Penny said with an answering smile. "Now what would you like to know about the trip? I was sorry the information came out right before I left so there was no time to answer questions. But I'm glad you're here now. The deadline to sign up is soon."

"Well, I actually have a list of questions," Margaret said, digging into her carryall for the piece of paper she thought she'd dropped right on top. "Here it is."

Penny picked up a stack of papers on her desk. "I have more information for you to take with you after we talk, but I'll be happy to answer any concerns you may have. I know it's a big step to let Adelaide go without you."

"Wonderful," Margaret said, glancing at her list. She and Allan had put their questions in order of priority, but now, looking at the list, Margaret wondered what she should ask about first: chaperones, transportation, cost, or accommodations? The answers seemed equally important in her eyes. The prospect of actually sending Adelaide alone on this trip had her stomach twisted in knots.

She knew Penny could sense her anxiety and appreciated the warm smile she gave her. "I have so many questions, I'm not sure where to start," Margaret admitted.

"What are your biggest concerns?"

"Everything!" Margaret said, happy to feel the knot of tension lessen a bit. "First of all I guess I should ask you the dates of the trip."

Penny briefly consulted a piece of paper. "The van from the transportation company leaves Friday, the twentieth, and the return date is Monday, July 23. The deadline to sign up is this Friday."

"So soon?" How could they make the decision that quickly? The looming deadline made the decision seem even more difficult.

"The trip is being made available to the members of the life-skills class and others in the community through a special grant from a private donor," Penny said. "The funds earmarked for the class need to be used by the end of July. Normally the deadline would be the start of the new fiscal year, which is July 1, but we got an extension until the first of August."

"I didn't realize the trip would be subsidized," Margaret said. "It's very kind of your donor."

"The cost to the individuals is quite reasonable." Penny handed Margaret one of the sheets of paper lying on her desk.

Margaret quickly scanned it and was taken aback. The trip would cost them next to nothing, thanks to the generosity of the unknown sponsor. Margaret was ashamed of herself because she'd secretly hoped the expense would be prohibitive. She could have used that as an excuse for saying no to Adelaide.

Scanning the information, Margaret noted the activity level ranged from low, which involved very little walking, to medium, which required participants to be fairly mobile. Two or three activities were planned each day with time for rest and refreshments built into the schedule.

"In addition to the van driver, the company provides extremely well qualified, trained chaperones. Of course, I'm going along too as the community center chaperone."

"Has anyone signed up yet?" Margaret asked.

Penny consulted a list by her phone. "Yes, Hank, Lisa, Chloe, and Cassie."

Margaret sighed at the mention of Adelaide's friends. All the ones she liked best had already committed to go. No wonder she was so eager for an answer from her parents.

Looking down at her list, Margaret moved on to her next questions. "What exactly will they be doing on this trip, and where will they be staying?"

"Those are excellent questions. I have the info sheet for you right here," Penny said. "In fact, let me give you all this information so you can refer to it while we talk."

"I should have asked for it," Margaret said. "What's my excuse for being so absentminded?" she was asking rhetorically, but Penny looked at her sympathetically.

"You're a mother about to send her daughter off on her first big adventure—alone. This is a situation that gives any parent pause," Penny said, smiling kindly.

"You're so right," Margaret sighed. "It's not that Allan and I feel you won't take wonderful care of Adelaide. And I'm sure the other chaperones are very good at their jobs. I'm just…apprehensive. I don't suppose you could use another chaperone, could you?" she asked tentatively.

Margaret watched Penny lace her fingers together before answering. "Do you really want to go?"

The way Penny put the emphasis on the word *really* made Margaret feel sheepish. No, she didn't really want to go, nor could she. Business at the gallery was booming and showed no sign of letting up. She'd worked hard for a long time to make it a success. Not even Allan could step in and "business babysit" for her. He was as busy with his handcrafted furniture as she was with her gallery. It would be a real financial hardship to leave both endeavors in the middle of the tourist season. The purpose of their activities was to leave Adelaide with an adequate inheritance when they were gone.

"I can't," she admitted to Penny. "Although I would like to see New York City someday." Taking a trip alone with her husband wasn't an option, not while they had so much responsibility, but it was a pleasant thought.

"Maybe you will someday." Penny looked sympathetic. Although she didn't have a special-needs child of her own, she understood how it limited what a couple could do.

Taking a moment to look over the pile of information sheets Penny gave her, Margaret was impressed with all the attention to detail. "So they'll be staying in a group of rooms close to their chaperones?"

"Yes, and I'll be available at all times if any problems arise. The hotel provides a breakfast every day as part of the room rate, and a couple of lunches and dinners are also part of the package. As a special treat we'll be taking the group to a popular restaurant. They should enjoy all the movie memorabilia on display. At the end of the trip, they'll get a keepsake video so they can remember all the things they did."

"That's a wonderful way to keep memories of the trip alive. The whole plan is very impressive," Margaret said, not sure she wanted it to be such a great opportunity. The better the trip, the harder the decision would be.

"We haven't talked about the highlights of the trip yet," Penny said.

"Oh my goodness, you're right," Margaret said, rifling through the papers to find the tour schedule. "I didn't notice this page because it was blank side up."

"I should've stapled them together in order," Penny said, clearly not pleased with herself for the organizational oversight.

"You did," Margaret said sheepishly. "I pulled the staples out to spread them out better."

Penny looked relieved and reached for the stapler sitting on the right side of her desk. "I'll do it again. You won't want to misplace any of the pages. They show exactly where Adelaide will be at all times on the trip."

Penny's attention to detail was one of the things Margaret admired most about her. It made her more comfortable about the prospect of Adelaide going off under her care. Penny was not a woman who would allow her charges to wander off and get lost. Margaret was sure she would be an excellent chaperone.

"As you can see, the tour offers highlights of the city without overwhelming our travelers. We'll take the ferry to the Statue of Liberty and Ellis Island on separate days. I'm sure everyone will enjoy going to the top of the Empire State Building Observatory. They'll get a 360-degree perspective that includes Manhattan, the other boroughs, and four states. My, I sound like a travel brochure, don't I?"

The two of them laughed, and Margaret was beginning to think she had enough information to make a decision.

"One more thing," she said. "Have you made any provisions for homesickness?"

"Adelaide's or yours?" Penny asked with a big grin.

Her answer made Margaret burst into laughter. "I guess it's more likely Allan and I will miss her than she'll miss us."

"Not necessarily," Penny said. "But, in all honesty, I think Adelaide is more than ready for a trip like this. You know I wouldn't say that if I didn't believe it."

Margaret knew Penny was right on all counts. What's more, she knew deep down in her heart that letting Adelaide go was the right decision. Adelaide was ready. Margaret was the one who wasn't prepared for such a big step, but that didn't mean she was going to say no.

"I know you're right," Margaret said. "Thank you so much for taking time to talk to me."

"Does this mean you're going to allow Adelaide to go on the trip?" Penny asked, looking almost as hopeful as Adelaide had when Margaret left the house to go to the community center.

"I need to talk to Allan, but yes, I think we will let Adelaide go on the trip."

Penny beamed at Margaret and practically clapped her hands together in glee. "Wonderful! The permission slips you need to sign are in the packet I gave you, plus information about the deposit. Please remember everything is due by Friday."

Margaret put the papers securely at the bottom of her carryall. "I promise we'll get everything turned in on time."

"I'm so happy you are going to let her go," Penny said. "It will be a wonderful growth experience for her."

Again, Margaret knew Penny was right. It was going to be difficult to see her daughter off on a trip without her parents, but Adelaide should benefit a great deal. It was a real test of her independence, and a step that needed to be taken.

She thanked Penny again and left the community center. It was past time to get the gallery open, but concern for her daughter took precedence over everything.

She was in such a hurry to get to her business she nearly bumped into her own husband walking up to the center.

"Allan...Adelaide...what are you two doing here?"

Allan had the grace to look sheepish. "Adelaide was afraid you'd forget to call, so she asked if we could come down and walk you to the gallery."

Adelaide looked like she was bursting to talk. "What did you find out? Can I go? Please?" she asked as she fell into step beside her mother.

This wasn't how Margaret wanted to tell Adelaide her decision. First, she really wanted to discuss it with Allan, but she knew the time had come to stop talking and start having a little faith.

Looking from her beloved daughter to her husband and back again, Margaret carefully weighed what she would say. "It all sounds wonderful. Miss Penny answered all my questions. If your father doesn't have any more, I'm inclined to say yes, if that's okay with you, Allan?"

"Oh, thank you!" Adelaide said, enveloping Margaret in a huge bear hug.

Allan smiled at her. "If you're satisfied with what you learned, then I'm satisfied. Yes, you can go Adelaide."

"Thank you, Daddy!"

Margaret was still anxious about the trip, but seeing the joy on Adelaide's face lessened her worries.

"What's the next step?" Allan asked as he and Adelaide joined Margaret on the walk to her gallery.

"I have all the information here," she said, holding up the sheaf of papers she'd gotten from Penny. "The deadline to sign up is Friday, so while I'm at the gallery, maybe you can start filling out the forms."

"I'll get right on it," he said, taking the papers from her.

Margaret linked arms with Allan and Adelaide and basked in the warmth of her husband's and daughter's smiles.

Adelaide was radiating happiness, and Allan looked pleased with their decision. Together, the parents could weather whatever life threw their way, including a trip to the Big Apple for their daughter.

CHAPTER EIGHT

T he decision is entirely up to you," Dan said over breakfast on Wednesday. "If you want to see your father, that's fine with me. If not, that's okay too."

"I'm sorry to keep bringing it up," Shelley said, picking at the scrambled eggs she'd made for their breakfast. "The truth is, it's keeping me awake at night. I feel like a steamroller has run over me."

"You look good for someone who's been squashed," Dan teased. "In fact, you're the prettiest cookie-maker in town."

"Oh, that narrows it down a bit. The only other person I know who's famous for her cookies is eighty-seven."

Before Dan could tease her anymore, Aiden shuffled into the room, wearing his father's bedroom slippers.

"Trying to fill my shoes, are you, scout?" Dan joshed. "Better you wearing them than Prize chewing them."

Even though she was still stewing over whether to see her father, Shelley appreciated her husband's good mood. The longer he apprenticed as an electrician, the more he seemed to like it. He made it a point to do his work well, often bemoaning substandard wiring that could lead to fires. And, of course, a regular paycheck helped with family harmony. There wasn't the stress of wondering whether they could pay their bills every month. She could run her baking business without the burden of keeping them afloat.

"You're up bright and early," she said to her son.

"The sun woke me up. It was shining in my eyes."

"Whoops! Did I forget to close the blinds when you went to bed?" Dan asked, taking blame for Aiden's early rising. "At least I get to see my best bud before I go to work."

He pulled his son onto his lap and grabbed a slipper, pretending to make him smell it.

"It's stinky, Daddy!" Aiden said, wiggling free.

"You two!" Shelley said with mock indignation. "I don't know which of you to put in time-out."

"Choose me!" her husband said. "I'd love a few extra hours of sleep."

"You're going to be late if you don't get a move on," Shelley warned, handing him his lunch of thick cheese and bologna sandwiches, an apple, and carrot sticks.

"Here's the superhero Electric Man, rushing to his winged truck to save the world from flames," Dan shouted, lifting Aiden and swinging him around before he gave him a good-bye hug.

"Your truck doesn't have wings," he said giggling. "You're being silly, Daddy."

"They're invisible. Don't want everyone to know my secret identity. Now be a good boy today. If I get home early enough, we'll throw the ball after dinner."

Dan had to leave for work, but his good mood had been contagious. Aiden teased his mother by balancing a slipper on his head, and she threatened to feed him broccoli for breakfast.

After both children were fed, dressed, and happily playing in the backyard, she couldn't stop thinking about how blessed she was to have such a wonderful husband and two healthy, lively children. She paused to give thanks for all her blessings before she began her day's baking.

Had her own father ever been as playful as Dan? She tried to think back to the times when he took the family to the beach or to visit relatives in a nearby town. On the way home he always bought them cups of frozen custard with strawberry sauce, not minding when some of it dribbled on her clothes.

Sometimes her mother criticized him for being a big kid himself, but Shelley had adored him before the bad times began. Arguments and hostility changed him. He became dour and short-tempered, someone she tried to avoid after he had particularly bitter fights with her mother.

If she saw him again, would he be anything like the father she remembered from her early childhood? Her biggest fear was that adversity had changed him forever. Would they even have anything to talk about? It would be easier if her sister could be there. She could always find something to talk about, but Shelley drew a blank when it came to a conversation with her father.

Emma's shrill cries interrupted her thoughts, and Shelley had to race outside with flour-covered hands to brush off her daughter and make sure she wasn't hurt. It was only a false alarm this time, but it was unfortunate Adelaide couldn't come today. How could she get everything done without her helper? As usual, she had cookies to bake, not to mention a special order for three fresh peach pies.

If she did decide to see her father, when would she find time? Her days were so busy she scarcely had time to do a minimum amount of housekeeping.

Sometimes she could beg or bribe Aiden to play nicely with his sister, but today he was short on sleep and cross with his sibling.

"I have to work, Aiden. Please help me by keeping Emma out of trouble."

Hurrying inside, she wasn't optimistic. All she could do was hurry through her baking, she hoped without making any mistakes as she kept a wary eye on her children through the window.

Her piecrust wasn't rolling as well as usual, and Emma was wandering around the yard looking for mischief. Shelley had just sprinkled a little more flour on the marble surface she used for rolling dough, hoping to get her usual good results, when the phone rang.

"Shelley, this is Frances," the voice on the phone said, as though she wouldn't recognize her mother-in-law's voice.

"How are you today?" Shelley asked to be polite, hoping this wouldn't be a long conversation.

"My arthritis is acting up a bit. No wonder after all the cleaning I've been doing."

She hoped she wasn't going to bring them another "gift" from her attic. Dan had stored the pieces of the spinning wheel in the garage rafters, disguising it in a plastic bin in case his mother happened to look up there someday.

"That's too bad," Shelley said with one eye on the oven timer. She had to take cookies out in three and a half minutes. With luck, Frances wouldn't talk longer than that.

"The reason I'm calling is that I found some old board games at the back of a closet shelf. If Aiden would like to come over, his grandpa would love to teach him how to play a few."

Shelley knew her day would be more complicated if Aiden wasn't home to keep a reluctant eye on his sister, but how could she deprive him of his Grandfather Bauer's company? "I'm sure Aiden would love it."

She thought about her son's special relationship with Dan's father. Was she right in not letting him know her father?

"Good, I'll be right over," Frances said. "Emma can come to our house too. Don't want her to feel left out. I'll give them both lunch and bring them home after her nap."

"That would be wonderful! Adelaide couldn't come today, and I'm swamped with orders." Shelley leaned against the edge of the counter, relieved that both children were invited.

After the pan of golden brown snickerdoodles was done, she hurried to bring the children inside and get them cleaned up. Fortunately she'd just done laundry, although it lay in a big heap on her bed because she hadn't had time to fold it. After a quick washup, she dressed Emma in pretty pink overalls Frances had given her and made Aiden change into a clean blue tank top. By the time they looked reasonably presentable, their grandmother was at the front door.

"Something smells delicious," the older woman said as she walked into the house.

"I just took out a pan of snickerdoodles. Would you like to try one?"

"I'm afraid that would set a bad example for the children. Maybe we can take a few home to share at lunchtime."

"The kids are in Aiden's room. He must be busy with his cars, or he would've run out to answer the doorbell. I'll put some cookies in a bag for you."

Frances followed her into the kitchen, and Shelley couldn't help but notice an opaque plastic bag she was carrying. It had the logo of a store that had closed before she and Dan moved to town, making her a little uneasy about the contents.

"I found a little something for you in the attic." Frances pulled out a motley stuffed bear and sat in on the counter to be admired.

"It looks..." Shelley was appalled by the beady-eyed animal. It had all the charm of roadkill, and she didn't even want to touch it, let alone give it to Emma. "Old."

"Yes, it's over a hundred years old. It's a Teddy Bear, named after President Theodore Roosevelt."

"That's interesting." It was the best Shelley could come up with.

Maybe the bear on her counter had once been cute and cuddly, but now the wooly fur was worn and dingy brown.

Clumps were missing, and one leg had suffered some serious chewing. She imagined a hundred years of grime and dust collecting in the straggly remnants of the toy. Why didn't Frances pitch it in the rubbish? No child should be allowed within a block of the forlorn creature.

"It's a Steiff," her mother-in-law proudly said. "An early example like this could bring thousands of dollars if it were in perfect condition."

"What's a Steiff?" Shelley didn't want to ask, but she felt obligated to do so.

"It's the name of the German toymaker. Look at the little button on its ear. That shows it's genuine."

Shelley looked but didn't touch. She was suspicious of the musty smell that seemed to come from the bear.

"Maybe you can sell it at the antiques shop," she suggested, very much afraid it was another gift she'd have to hide away.

"Oh, I couldn't possibly do that!" Frances exclaimed. "It's a family heirloom. Just think of some little girl getting it as a gift back in the day. Emma will treasure it when she's old enough to appreciate it."

"I'll pack it away with some cedar chips until then," Shelley said, admitting defeat. Frances wasn't a person who took no for an answer.

"There's nothing more important on this earth than family." It was a pronouncement Shelley had heard often from her mother-in-law, but it was one thing they agreed on.

"Speaking of family," Shelley tentatively began, "remember when my father called the other day?" Even though she'd had differences with Frances, she respected her opinion on some things. Maybe she would understand Shelley's dilemma better than her friends had.

"Yes." Frances was tucking the cookies in her handbag. "Did you call him back? Is he well?"

Embarrassing as it was, Shelley didn't know. She hadn't thought to ask about his health. Did he have a terminal disease? Was that the reason he wanted a reunion with her? If that was true, she was an awful daughter to put him off. But wouldn't he have mentioned it?

"I guess he's okay. He wants to come to see us."

"That would be hard for you," Frances sympathized. "The longer an estrangement lasts, the harder it is to put things right. What are you going to do?"

"I don't know. Maybe it's not fair to my children never to know their maternal grandfather. Of course, they're really lucky to have you and Ralph. You spoil them in the best way—with lots of love."

For a moment she thought Frances would get teary. This was the first time Shelley had admitted how important Dan's parents were to her children.

"It's sweet of you to say so," her mother-in-law said. "Are you going to invite your father to visit?"

Shelley shrugged. "It seems so awkward after all this time. I don't begin to know how to go about it."

"Yes, it is tricky. Sharing a meal is always good, but then you have to decide whether to make it a family affair or meet him somewhere on your own."

"Meemaw, can we go now?" Aiden called out from the kitchen door.

"Pretty soon. Your mama and I are having a little chat. Be good for a few more minutes. Then we'll go to my house."

He grumbled a bit, then remembered Emma was in his room and raced off to defend his turf.

"You and Dan are blessed with beautiful children. Maybe the Lord wants you to share a little of their time with your father. No matter how you feel about him, it's a little harsh to deprive him of knowing his grandchildren."

"You're probably right."

Surprisingly, Shelley didn't resent her advice. Frances could be a tad snobby about her ancestors because they were among Marble Cove's founding families, but she thought the world of her grandchildren. She was willing to forgive and forget almost anything for the welfare of her family. The lesson wasn't lost on Shelley.

"He's going to call me back. At least that's what he said. I don't know what to say to him. Should I try to smooth over our relationship on the phone, or wait to see what happens if he comes to Marble Cove?"

"I think you can assume he wants to make amends," Frances said thoughtfully. "It was probably very hard for him to call you. Maybe you'll have to show some willingness to forget the past."

"How can I do that? When I heard his voice, all the bad times came back. I'm sure I sounded cold and unfeeling, but mostly I was floored. It felt like trying to put Humpty Dumpty back together. Emma loves that nursery rhyme, but some things stay broken for good."

"Nonsense. Anything can be repaired with good glue. I think you know that in your heart. All you father wants is a chance. If it doesn't go well, you're no worse off than you were before."

Frances' voice was stern, but Shelley knew her advice was well-meant and sound.

"You're right," Shelley conceded. Her mother-in-law was trying to be helpful, not critical. "Now the problem is, how do I do this? Should I call him or wait for him to contact me again? Should I invite him to dinner, or just suggest he come over some evening and see the children?"

"How do you follow a complicated recipe for the first time?" Frances asked.

"I study it and make sure I have all the ingredients," Shelley said, a bit puzzled by her question. "Then I make a batch and test it out, usually on my family. If there are any problems, say, it has to bake a longer or shorter time, I adjust the recipe and try again. I don't try to sell the finished product until I'm sure it's as good as I can make it."

"Exactly!" Frances said with satisfaction. "You take it one step at a time. You don't expect perfection on the first try."

"Yes, I see what you mean." Shelley stepped over and gave her a little hug, much to the older woman's surprise.

"Meemaw, can we go *now*?" Aiden asked, coming into the kitchen trailed by his sister.

"We certainly can. Give your mama a good-bye kiss, and we'll be on our way. Pappy can hardly wait to play a game with you."

Shelley walked them to the door, making sure Frances had Emma's diaper bag with changes of clothing for both of them.

"Be good at Meemaw's," she admonished her children, although they were too hyper to pay any attention.

Watching until Frances drove away with both kids buckled into the car seats her in-laws kept for their use, she said a prayer of thanksgiving for the gift of family. Once she would've resented advice from her mother-in-law, but now she could see the wisdom in what she'd said.

If the visit with her father went badly, nothing in her life would change. If they managed a successful reconciliation, her whole family would benefit, especially Aiden and Emma. They would gain a grandfather, no small blessing in the lives of children.

Back in the kitchen, she looked more closely at the stuffed bear. It was ratty, no question about that, but it had been well loved. Maybe Emma would treasure it someday as part of her heritage. Meanwhile, Shelley gingerly put it in a heavy-duty plastic food storage bag and securely sealed it.

Somewhere in her little house there had to be a niche to store the bedraggled bear. She scrubbed the counter where it had sat and went back to her baking, her mind full of the possibilities a visit from her father might open up. She was still apprehensive, but she realized he deserved another chance.

CHAPTER NINE

"Well, Rocky, we should beat the crowd today," Diane said early Thursday morning as she attached his leash.

Her recent hospitalization had shaken her into being more diligent about controlling her blood sugar, so it was easier to get up early and tackle the day's routine, beginning with a brisk walk on the beach with Rocky. It was only a little after 6:00 AM, and it was highly unlikely any tourists would be enjoying the ocean that early. She checked her small waist pack for plastic bags and a clean scoop repurposed from her laundry detergent to clean up after Rocky, and added her house key and a bottle of water from the fridge. After rubbing in sunscreen, she put on her favorite baseball cap and sunglasses. The sun would still be low in the sky, but she wanted to be prepared for the bright July sun.

As she got under way with her walk, she thought about how much she hated the idea of turning Marble Cove into a combination circus and money machine for outsiders. Would the majority of townspeople agree with Beverly's crusade to stop unwanted development? Diane was eager to start the campaign against it.

Her goal for the morning was to jog to the lighthouse and back. This morning the beach had a trampled look from the many visitors who flocked to Marble Cove to enjoy sea and sun. Tomorrow the town would bring out their big machine to sift out lost belongings and smooth the sand for the weekend, but today she chose to run close to the ocean where waves had damped the sand and packed it down. Rocky wasn't restrained by uneven terrain. He raced up and down with enthusiasm, having a sniff fest in the process and reminding Diane how much she enjoyed his company.

An elderly couple was walking hand in hand as they returned to town, and she greeted them with a smile and a nod, feeling a pang of sorrow at her single state. She tried not to dwell on what her life would be like now if her beloved Eric had lived, instead counting her blessings. Her two children were happy and successful by any definition that counted, she was started on a new career writing books, and she'd done what the little ditty from her childhood said, one her mother liked to sing to her:

Make new friends,
But keep the old,
Some are silver
And others gold.

She was so preoccupied with her thoughts that she didn't see the lone man sitting on the beach near the lighthouse.

"Diane!" Dr. Leo Spangler stood and called out to her as she approached. "I knew that was you when I saw Rocky."

"Good morning, Leo. Are you out without Limo?" she asked the vet, who was also her friend.

"I had to remove a benign growth from his side. He's doing well, but I didn't think he was up to a run this morning."

"Sorry to hear that. Rocky loves to play with his pal. He really doesn't see many other dogs."

She was genuinely glad to see the slender, gray-haired veterinarian. They'd gone out a few times, and although Diane wasn't as ready as he was for a relationship, she enjoyed his conversation. They shared a love of animals and old movies.

"What have you been up to lately?" Leo asked, sitting down again and patting the sand beside him.

She slumped down, happy to rest a bit before she ran back to town. The rising sun was too brilliant to look at, so they sat facing each other as the breeze rippled his sparse hair. Leo was a kind-faced but unexceptional man until he started talking. Then his wit and intelligence made him an excellent companion.

It was still much too soon to even think of another man replacing Eric, but for now, she valued him as a friend, and their accidental meeting was a pleasure.

"It's been an exciting summer so far—which isn't necessarily a good thing," she said, going on to tell him about her presence at the fire and the pressure to complete her second book. "What have you been up to?"

"I've been tied up supervising the workmen who are expanding my animal hospital to include a sheltered run for patients who are well enough to exercise. I like to return them to their owners in tip-top shape."

"Marble Cove is lucky to have a vet like you," she said sincerely.

"It's a good place to live—and to retire, but I can't imagine life without my practice."

"Speaking of our lovely town, do you know Dennis Calder?"

"By sight. He's pretty conspicuous around town."

"Well, he's trying to develop the land near his apartments." She explained his idea for an amusement complex that included high-priced condos and a shopping area.

"I don't like the sound of it," Leo said, shaking his head. "There has to be more than tourist trade behind an investment like that. The season here is too short to make it pay unless he has other plans, say a gambling casino. I wonder if he has political influence."

"That's what Beverly Wheeland thinks. In fact, she's so upset she's putting together a petition to block approval by the town council and having an organizational meeting on Monday evening. I've agreed to help get signatures."

"She can count me in too." He frowned and pursed his lips thoughtfully. "A development like that could be the end of Marble Cove as we know it."

"I'll tell her," she said as Rocky came bounding up, scattering sand. "Well, I better go home and get to work, but I'm glad we met this morning. Beverly will be delighted to have your help."

"I'll see if I can get my service club behind her efforts. Quite a few businesspeople belong, and they have the most to lose if a new shopping complex goes in."

They walked back to town, discussing ways to thwart Dennis Calder's plan.

"Nice seeing you," Leo said as they parted company with Rocky walking sedately beside her. "Maybe we can get together sometime soon and talk about this some more."

"Good idea," Diane said. If he wanted to add his efforts to stopping Dennis Calder, he would be a valuable member of the opposition. She planned to send Beverly an e-mail about him as soon as she got home.

The sun felt warm on her arms and face, so it was a good thing she'd exercised Rocky early in the morning. She said good-bye to Leo and walked at a slow pace toward her cottage.

Her cell phone was ringing when she stepped into the house. She remembered it was still on her bedside table, another example of how absentminded she could be. She really should take it with her when she went to the beach. Fortunately the caller allowed enough rings for her to get to it.

"Good morning," Shelley's familiar voice said when she answered. "I knew you were up because I saw you walking home with Rocky."

"Yes, we had an early run on the beach. What's up?"

"I made a double batch of blueberry muffins for our breakfast. I wonder if you'd like to pop over and have one. Dan just left for work, and the kids aren't up yet."

"I'd love to," Diane said. "Let me fill Rocky's water bowl, and I'll be right over."

When Diane got there, Shelley was waiting at her front door, looking pert in pink shorts and a flowered tunic.

"I didn't want the doorbell to wake the kids. Come out to the kitchen where we can talk without whispering." She led the way to her combination family kitchen and business hub, where they could sit on stools and visit.

"You only have two muffins left," Diane said when Shelley lifted one out of a pan. "I don't want to deprive your children of a breakfast treat."

"Oddly enough, Aiden doesn't like them. He calls the blueberries 'yucky squishy things,' and Emma is in a phase where she imitates everything he does. Anyway, I put some in the freezer, so both of these are for you. Would you like orange juice or tea—or both?"

"You know what I really like with muffins? Milk! Just a small glass if you have enough on hand."

"No problem. I buy it by the gallon." She quickly poured out a full glass to go with the muffin she put on a small china plate.

"This is delicious," Diane said after her first bite of muffin. "This is a treat for the tongue. I bet these are popular with your fans."

"Thanks, but I wouldn't call my customers fans," Shelley said, her cheeks pink from the praise. "Right now I'm getting a lot of orders for cookies, pies, and cakes, almost more than

I can handle some days. But I'm certainly not complaining. How is your book coming?"

"I'm making slow progress." Diane appreciated her friend's interest, but she was finding it harder and harder to talk about writing problems with the people she knew in Marble Cove. She suspected her friends were more kind than interested when they asked.

"I have to confess something," Shelley said. "I had an ulterior motive in asking you over for a muffin."

"That sounds mysterious," Diane said with a soft laugh. "Don't tell me we have another mystery on our hands. We aren't exactly knocking it out of the ballpark on the one we have."

"No." Shelley joined in her laughter. "If we were private investigators, we'd surely starve before we'd find Thorpe's treasure. My predicament is much less complicated. I'm not quite sure how to communicate with my father. The whole situation is so awkward, but my mother-in-law has convinced me to give it a try."

"You want to begin a dialogue with him?" Diane asked, to clarify her friend's position.

"Exactly! You put it much better than I could. He has a computer, and I've known his e-mail address for a while. My question is, do you think I should contact him online and maybe exchange a few messages? Every time I think of picking up the phone and calling him, I get too nervous. What can I possibly say to him?"

"E-mail is a great way to break the ice," Diane said. "Just begin with a simple message, maybe 'How are you?' If he's really serious about having a relationship with you again, he'll jump at the chance to communicate any way he can."

"That's what I think, but I'm glad you agree. I was worried it might seem too cold or artificial to suddenly start e-mailing. You don't think he'll think it's only a way to get out of talking to him on the phone, do you?"

"Absolutely not! You're opening a door that's been closed for a long while." Diane realized how hard this must be for her friend and tried to be encouraging.

"You're right, of course," Shelley said, sliding off the stool and giving her friend a hug. "I can't tell you how much I appreciate your wisdom!"

It was Diane's turn to blush. "I didn't tell you anything you hadn't already figured out for yourself."

"Maybe not, but you make it sound so right."

As cozy as it was to sit visiting in Shelley's kitchen, Diane knew they both had work to do. She decided to leave before the children woke up and tempted her to stay longer.

"Thanks for the muffin," she said as she was leaving. "Now all I need is a quick shower, and I can get to work."

Slowly walking home, Diane thought about Shelley's plan to use the computer to work on her relationship with her father. Being a freelance writer was sometimes a lonely occupation, especially since she couldn't get together with other authors on a regular basis. But she did belong to an online writers' group, and the members seemed to be congenial and very interested in the craft of writing. Maybe she should pay more attention to them. After all, who better to understand the ups and downs of a writing career?

After hurrying through her morning shower, Diane was excited about the prospect of talking to other authors online. She'd already communicated one-on-one with several in the group. In fact, one woman, Janice Rimes, gave especially helpful and encouraging advice when she spoke to the chat group. Diane suspected she'd published a number of books, although her name never showed up on sales lists.

Settling down at the computer with a cup of tea, she tried to decide what to say. Since she rarely spoke up herself, she had to think of a good way to proceed. She didn't want sympathy for her problems with the second book, but she did want to know if her writer's block was unique or common.

After some hard thinking, she inserted her question online: "Did any of you find the second book harder to write after your first published book?"

It was short and to the point, but would any writers be interested in sharing their experiences?

Since it was silly to sit and wait for an answer, Diane called up her most recent chapter and revised a scene that didn't quite work for her. Before she thought of her question again, nearly two hours had passed. She was stiff from sitting still so long, and Rocky was due to go outside. Still, it couldn't hurt to check her e-mail on the off chance there was a message from an author.

Much to her delight there was a message on her personal e-mail.

"Hi, Diane, I really sympathize with your dilemma. I had the same experience after my first book was published. It didn't seem as if I could write a second successful book. I suspect we have a lot in common. I'm a multipublished author of cozy mysteries, and I rarely get to see other writers in person. I live in a tiny town in northern Michigan. The main interest of folks here is hunting and fishing. Since I'm an only child who never married, I don't have much of a network. Where do you live? What have you published? Regards, Janice."

Diane typed as fast as she could, amazed at the friendliness of her fellow author. After she'd told a little about herself, she asked a big question:

"I've looked for books under your name, but not even Amazon has any," she wrote. "So do you write under a pseudonym?"

"Two, actually," Janice replied. "One for each of my publishers. I prefer no one but my agent know them, but if you'll promise to keep my secret, I'll be glad to tell you."

"Certainly I'll promise! I'd love to be able to read some."

Once she knew the author's pseudonyms, Diane was thrilled to realize she actually had several of Janice's books on her shelf. Without the least bit of exaggeration, she could say she was a favorite author. Not only that, they had the same agent, and both were very happy with her.

"Do you ever have writer's block?" Diane asked.

"I think it's an occupational hazard," her new friend replied. "I try to have more than one piece going at a time. If a book stalls, I turn to an outline I'm working on or some promotional work. I try to have an alternative to whatever chapter I'm working on. Sometimes I write magazine articles on speculation, just to keep my juices flowing."

"That's how I worked as a reporter," Diane wrote. "I might have several long-term investigations in the works while I did routine stories. I've read your book *Misty Murder* twice. Where did you get such a wonderful idea?"

More than an hour passed as Janice recounted the experience that had inspired her book, and Diane worried she'd taken too much of the busy author's time.

"I hope I haven't kept you from your work," she apologized.

"Not at all! I haven't enjoyed a conversation so much in ages. Please do keep in touch! I'm going to order your book as soon as we sign off. I can't wait to read it!" Janice wrote back.

After reluctantly breaking off their exchange, Diane sat for several minutes digesting all she'd learned about Janice Rimes. Who knew a muffin with Shelley could prompt her to start a wonderful online friendship with another author? She hadn't felt so energized in ages!

Without more hesitation, she went to her current chapter, full of ideas to improve it. The one thing that had been missing in her life was contact with another serious author. Even as she worked, she thought of more things she'd like to discuss with her new friend.

CHAPTER TEN

Beverly was tempted to ignore her cell phone Friday morning as she got ready for her meeting with Reverend Locke. She was debating whether to wear a lightweight navy jersey dress or her beige pantsuit. Her unusual indecision had everything to do with bolstering her confidence. She was nervous about talking with him, especially since his attitude toward their treasure quest had been mostly negative so far.

Fortunately, she grabbed her phone before it stopped ringing and was pleasantly surprised by her caller.

"Good morning," Jeff Mackenzie said in his familiar deep voice. "Am I interrupting anything?"

"No, I'm going to see Reverend Locke, but I have plenty of time." This wasn't strictly true, but she was pleased to hear from Jeff. "Where are you?"

"Seattle. I'm almost through with an assignment, but I'm going to stay the weekend with an old college friend. He's rented a motorcycle for me so we can make a run on one of his favorite routes."

"Sounds like fun."

She'd rather he come home to Maine, but travel was Jeff's lifeblood. She could imagine riding behind him through beautiful Northwestern scenery, but she didn't have the freedom he did. When she chose to make Marble Cove her permanent home, she took on obligations, especially to her father.

"I'm booked to fly out early Monday morning. I just wanted you to know I'm planning to be there for the organizational meeting at your house. I'm a hundred percent opposed to Dennis Calder's plan. Even though my legal residence is in Portland, I plan to stay in Marble Cove and help with your petition drive."

"Wonderful!"

Beverly was sincerely grateful for his support. The closer the time came for her big meeting, the more nervous she became. Did she have enough support to block Dennis? Would enough people show up at her house and be willing to help circulate the petitions? How many signatures would it take to influence the town council? Success seemed more possible with Jeff on her side.

He couldn't talk long, but she was pleased by his call. Having him there would give her moral support, and he could be very persuasive when it came to swaying people's opinions.

After the call ended, she decided the meeting with her pastor didn't call for a dressy outfit. She pulled on her second-best jeans and a plain white sleeveless top to wear under a casual blue and white striped "big" shirt.

His house was only a few blocks away, so she opted to walk, pulling her best running shoes out of the closet and lacing them over lightweight white socks.

While she dressed, she went over the questions she wanted to ask the minister, trying to frame them in the most tactful way possible. Diane was better at that than she was, but they'd decided it was better for Beverly to see him alone. She was a member of Old First, albeit a new one, and the reopening of the church was a legitimate concern of all the members of the congregation. Reverend Locke might resent outside interference, but she had a right to worry about the future of the venerable old building.

After walking across town and climbing the wooden steps to Reverend Locke's porch, she paused to gather her thoughts. When she'd called to ask if she might have a few minutes of his time, he'd agreed without even asking her why.

This would be the first time she'd seen him since the fire had caused her friends and her to flee Old First. They'd all been a little surprised when he had finally—though still very reluctantly—agreed to let them explore the bell tower under his watchful eye. He'd continued to dismiss any possibility Jeremiah Thorpe would have hidden treasure. She suspected he only let them into the tower to prove there was nothing to find.

She lightly rapped on the door, expecting a short wait. Instead Reverend Locke opened it so quickly she was startled. Had he seen her approach through a front window?

"Beverly, come in," he said kindly, gesturing for her to step into the front room.

"Thank you," she said, following him but not knowing what kind of reception to expect.

Beverly had been to his house before, but this time she noticed some rather striking ship prints hanging on his off-white walls, the kind Currier and Ives might have produced in the nineteenth century. A wood-cased barometer sitting on a bookcase was obviously old and fine, although the upholstered furniture didn't match the quality of the antique items.

Silas Locke gestured for her to take a seat on a tweed sofa in a rather vile shade of avocado. As she waited for the minister to settle himself on a matching chair, it struck her as incongruous that the chair and sofa looked to be vintage 1970s furniture, but the other big chair in the room was an expensive-looking leather recliner. Reverend Locke's taste in decorating ran the gamut from thrift shop bargains to touches of elegance. There was no sign of a woman's touch, and she wondered whether he was a lifelong bachelor. She didn't really know much at all about the man, and his sermons had been uniformly impersonal. Unlike some preachers, he rarely used stories from his own life as sermon illustrations.

"Would you like some coffee?" he asked.

Beverly had the distinct impression he was trying to be an affable host, and she appreciated the effort. The sooner she got to her reason for coming, the better he probably would like it.

"No, thank you. I'm fine," she said, declining the offer. "I won't take much of your time. I'm sure you're very busy. Do you have any idea when Old First will reopen?"

She didn't expect a definite answer, but the question was a way to begin a conversation.

He looked at her as though he was suddenly aware of her presence for the first time and seemed to be weighing his words carefully before he spoke.

"I am really not sure," he said formally. "There are a lot of factors involved."

Beverly waited for him to elaborate further, but he didn't.

"I assume insurance will cover the cost of repairing the fire damage?" she asked.

Beverly had spent enough time with Diane for some of her friend's reporting skills to rub off on her. She hoped her questions about repairs and insurance would help establish rapport and lead to any thoughts he might have about Jeremiah Thorpe's treasure, but it was soon obvious he wasn't going to be forthcoming about anything. His reserved demeanor wasn't a surprise. He didn't have a warm, fuzzy personality, but today he certainly seem distracted. Was he hiding something?

You're being ludicrous, she told herself. *What could he possibly be holding back?* He had agreed to let them into the tower room, after all.

"I don't know the specifics about repairs yet. For now, we're just very fortunate that Marble Cove Community Church is letting us share their worship space when it's available. Is there something else you want to know? I'm pressured for time today."

She hesitated before answering. He wasn't going to like her bringing up the topic of treasure.

Taking a deep breath, she said, "We—my friends and I—still believe Jeremiah Thorpe possibly left more clues about the location of a hidden treasure. We don't want it for our own benefit. Anything we might possibly find would go to Old First to help revitalize it."

"That's what you want to talk to me about? I can't believe you haven't given up on that preposterous idea." He didn't raise his voice, but the scowl on his face was intimidating.

"Yes, we believe there must be more information somewhere. Maybe an account that indicates the treasure was found years and years ago. Or writings that would give a clue about where Thorpe might have hidden it. The whole town is anxious to save Old First. It's a precious heritage, even to those who aren't members of the congregation." Beverly was impassioned in defending the motive for their quest, but she was afraid her pleas were falling on deaf ears.

Reverend Locke pushed his gold-rimmed glasses up on his thin nose and regarded her with a stern look on his face. "Beverly, you know how I feel about this treasure nonsense."

Beverly felt chastised, but she'd promised her friends—and herself—she'd pursue any possible lead. "Can you think of anything, as inconsequential as it may seem, that could lead us to some answers? I won't trouble you again if you can assure me you don't know of any old documents or letters or journals from that time."

She knew she sounded melodramatic, but she wasn't going to leave until she was absolutely sure Reverend

Locke wasn't hiding anything from them—intentionally or accidentally.

"Beverly, I'm afraid you're wasting your time, and mine."

"I apologize, Reverend Locke, but you know how much Old First means to me and to the community."

He raised his hands in a dismissive gesture, but she wasn't going to give up without some satisfaction. "Perhaps there are some documents somewhere that could shed light on this puzzle?"

She deliberately did not mention the key Margaret had found the night they fled. Beverly knew it was silly to hope Reverend Locke would turn over a diary that fit the key, but it was worth trying.

He sighed and pushed his glasses up again. "I'm certain there's nothing in the church. I've been here long enough to be familiar with the church records and everything in the library. But my predecessor did donate some papers relating to the founding of Marble Cove and Old First to Portland College. I never saw them and have no idea what they contained, so please don't ask me."

Finally, a lead! Beverly was excited, and her friends would be too, even if nothing came of it.

"Reverend Locke, thank you for your time. I'm glad you believe my friends and I are only acting in the church's best interests."

"Yes, yes," he said impatiently.

His phone started to ring just as she rose from the couch.

"I'll let myself out," she said, as eager to leave now as he was to have her go.

He waved her off and went to answer the insistent ring. She heard his terse "hello" before shutting the front door behind her and wondered again what made him so edgy. Beverly knew he was worried about the fire damage, but he seemed tense and preoccupied rather than engaged in finding solutions.

She decided to walk past Old First on the way home, only a detour of a few blocks. The damage was mostly visible on the roof, and she was pretty sure the building's beautiful stained-glass windows had survived intact. They were her favorite feature of the church, and she felt a need to check once more that none had been damaged in any way. Of course, their true beauty could only be seen from inside with the sun illuminating their brilliant colors, but she still wanted to be as sure as possible that none of the panels had cracked or fallen out.

As she walked, it occurred to her that today was Friday the thirteenth. Fortunately, she wasn't superstitious, and in fact, the day had brought her luck. Now that she had good news to tell her friends about Thorpe's papers, her mind turned to ways of stopping Dennis Calder's development. She was eager for the Monday evening meeting and pleased Jeff would get there in time to attend. The petitions were ready to pass out, and she could hardly wait to get started.

Lost in thought, she realized she'd walked all the way to the church without being aware of it. She started to look across the street at the lovely windows that always brought a sense of calm and peace to her, but something else caught her eye. A woman pulled on the front door of the church, tugging mightily until she finally accepted it was locked.

Instead of leaving, the black-clad figure began circling the building, moving out of sight behind the church. Beverly watched from a distance, trying to decide whether to ask the woman if she could help her with something. It wasn't long before she reappeared on the other side and once again tried the door, this time pounding as though she expected someone to answer.

Beverly grew even more puzzled when she again began moving stealthily around the outside of the church. Watching closely, Beverly saw a woman of medium height with short dark hair. Her black pantsuit seemed warm for the middle of July, and her movements seemed odd, to say the least. Beverly's first thought was that the woman was an insurance investigator, but her movements seemed to give lie to that idea. For one thing, there were no parked cars anywhere in sight, and she wasn't carrying a clipboard, a briefcase, or even a purse. Her movements were slow and deliberate, as though she was trying to look casual without succeeding. Several times she looked over her shoulder and checked the street in both directions. This time around, the woman was spending a lot of time looking up toward the roof and shading her eyes from the sun. Large sunglasses covered most of her face, but Beverly was pretty sure she'd never seen her before in Marble Cove.

Why was it, Beverly wondered as she gave up on watching the woman and headed home, that every time she got a clue to answers from one mystery, another appeared on the horizon to taunt her?

CHAPTER ELEVEN

When had she talked to Diane about e-mailing her father? Shelley was pretty sure it'd been Thursday, and she still hadn't sent the first message, the icebreaker, as she thought of it. Why was she procrastinating? It wasn't like her to put things off once she made up her mind.

"Maybe I'll e-mail my father today," she said to Dan as they ate breakfast Monday morning.

"You know you don't have to," he said between bites of French toast, one of his breakfast favorites. "Please pass me the sugar, would you?"

Her husband was the only person she knew who liked his French toast with a light sprinkling of powdered sugar instead of syrup. They were out of bacon, but he didn't mind the turkey sausages she'd found in the freezer. As much as she liked sending him off to work with a good breakfast under his belt, she didn't have any appetite herself this morning.

"Aren't you going to eat that?" he asked, indicating the untouched slice of golden brown toast on her plate.

"No, you can have it." She pushed her plate toward him.

"I hate to see you so down," he said. "If your father is upsetting you this much before you even meet with him, I say forget about it."

"Part of me wants to," she admitted, "but he is still my father. What if he's sick or dying or something? I'd never forgive myself for shutting him out of our lives again."

"You're only guessing at that. Maybe he wants to borrow money or have you cosign a loan. You have no idea what his motive is."

"It's not like you to be so cynical." She was sorry she'd brought up the subject.

"Hon, I'm not being cynical. I have nothing against your father except he's made you awfully unhappy in the past. I don't want to see you hurt again."

"Something good could come of reconnecting. Kids can never have too many people to love them." She watched her husband finish his breakfast and stand up to go to work.

"Well, ours already have grandparents who spoil them. Dad was talking about getting Aiden his own TV for his room so he can play games on it."

"I hope you told him no."

"You know I did. We agreed not to raise our kids to depend on electronics for fun. I want my son to get outside and invent his own games, not sit glued to a screen." Shelley had to smile because Dan himself struggled against becoming a couch potato.

"I don't think my father will corrupt the kids. This is about him and me. He really was a good father until things went sour with my mother."

"Whatever you decide to do, I'll support you," he reassured her.

After Dan left, she halfheartedly checked her order board and made preparations to begin work. She wasn't in the mood to make chocolate chip cookies, but the Cove wanted four dozen. In fact, she didn't feel like baking at all, which was certainly unusual. Most of the time she could hardly wait to start mixing and stirring.

"Mama, I want a Pop-Tart," Aiden said, appearing in the doorway and rubbing the sleep from his eyes.

"Hi, sweetie. We don't have any. How about French toast? That's what Daddy had for breakfast."

He frowned, and she could almost see the wheels turning in his head.

"Okay."

Much as she enjoyed the time spent getting her kids ready for the day, Shelley was preoccupied. Should she forget about sending an e-mail to her father?

By the time Emma finished making a sticky mess of her French toast, Shelley knew she either had to send a message today or forget about it. Indecision was wringing the pleasure out of her life.

Aiden wanted to play in his room instead of going outside, and she didn't blame him. The sun was warm already, and the day promised to be a hot one. Emma was in a clingy mood, dogging her mother's steps as she tried to get a batch of cookies ready for the oven. When Adelaide got there, Shelley couldn't have been more grateful.

"I'm going to New York City," her helper said, so excited she wanted to tell Shelley all about it.

"That sounds like fun, Adelaide. When are you leaving?"

"I have this for you. My mother made a copy." She handed over a paper showing when she was leaving and where she was going. "So you know when I can't come."

"Thank you." Shelley hooked it on the board where she kept her orders.

Adelaide bent down in front of Emma and began talking to her in what sounded like a secret language. The toddler giggled and eagerly followed her sitter out of the kitchen.

"Now there's no excuse," Shelley mumbled to herself.

She was talking about her father, not the baking she had to do. Since she couldn't get him out of her mind, she might as well send him a short message and see what happened. If he didn't answer, that would be the end of it. If he did, she'd deal with it when the time came.

After pulling a stool up to the laptop on her counter, she sat for several minutes trying to find the right words. It was too soon to invite him to her home, but she didn't want to rule out the possibility.

He wanted something from her: to renew their father-daughter relationship. Was there anything she wanted from him?

Her eyes grew moist as she thought of how much she wanted to have a real father again, not a man who deserted his family.

It was premature to suggest this was possible, but she did want something else from him: she wanted to know his reason for contacting her after all this time. Was he ill, possibly terminally ill? Would it be on her conscience for the rest of her life if he died without being with her family again?

Shelley thought of calling her older sister, but it seemed unfair to involve Susannah in the decision.

"Okay, Dad, here goes," she said aloud.

She typed in "Dear Dad," then quickly deleted it. The endearment seemed too cozy and compliant. "Hi, Dad" was better.

Diane had suggested something simple like: "How are you?" Maybe that was a little too impersonal—like something she'd say to the mail carrier or a shopkeeper.

No wonder her friend struggled with her writing. Finding the right words was hard. She tried again:

"Hi, Dad, I hope this finds you well."

Did that work? She caught herself biting her lower lip, something she only did when she was extremely agitated.

After staring at the words on her screen for several moments, she decided it wasn't a bad beginning. But what else should she say? She wasn't ready to ask him to visit her, nor did she want to meet him in person—not yet anyway.

"The children are well. Emma is teething, which makes her a bit cross. You always said I was a terror when I cut a tooth."

Was that too personal? Should she reminisce about her childhood before she decided whether to see him again? She deleted the teething sentences, then put them back in. There was no point in sending a note if it didn't say anything.

"Dan is happy apprenticing to be an electrician. Aiden is car-crazy. He can spend hours playing with his toy ones."

There! She'd covered the whole family—except for herself. Was there anything at all she wanted her father to know?

Hey, Dad, I have a great family, and I'll do anything to keep us all together, she thought without adding it to her note. Instead she typed:

"My baking business is doing well. I volunteer at church and have made a lot of good friends in Marble Cove."

All this was true, but was it enough? After several minutes of thought, she ended abruptly: "Yours truly, Shelley."

Her hand shook as it hovered over the command to send. At last, taking a deep breath, she sent the e-mail to her father.

Did she feel better or worse now that she'd reached out to him in this small way?

If he answered, what then? If he suggested a meeting, should she see him alone or with the whole family? Or maybe just with Dan? Would it be wrong of her if she didn't invite him to her home?

Maybe he only wanted to see his grandchildren. He obviously didn't miss her much since he'd waited so long to contact her. Did she owe him the right to know his grandchildren?

Dear Lord, she fervently prayed. *Please show me what to do about my father. I want to love him, but I can't get the past out of my mind. Help me to forgive him.*

What did Jesus say about forgiveness? She remembered the parable of the prodigal son. He behaved badly, but his father forgave him and welcomed him home with a feast. The message was clear, but did she have enough faith to put the past behind her and reconcile with her father?

She knew it would take time, patience, and prayer to forgive her father in her heart, but she did feel good about the small first step she'd taken.

★ ★ ★

Diane was pleased when she opened her e-mail first thing Monday morning and found a message from her new online friend, but she was also surprised. Janice Rimes wanted her help!

"Hi, Diane, I'm stumped! I'm terrible at titles, but just once I'd like to come up with one my editor won't change.

"My new book is about a girl in a mining town in the UP (Michigan's Upper Peninsula). She's in love with a young man who works underground like his father before him, but he really hates it. He's hoping to get a job on a lake freighter—you know, one of the huge ore boats on the Great Lakes. If he does, he'll be gone from the time the ice breaks up in the spring until late fall when the freeze sets in. I'm not quite sure how I'll work out the romance, but I've spent days trying to come up with just the right title.

"Any ideas?

"Regards, Janice."

Diane thought for several minutes, then framed her answer.

"Hi, Janice: Nice of you to ask me. Romance isn't my genre, but I did write headlines for a small newspaper when I was starting out. How about:

When Love Sails Away

or

The Lonesome Heart

or

Winter Solace (since they can only be together in the winter)

"Don't know if any of those would work. All I know about Great Lakes boats is the time when the Edmund Fitzgerald sank. I remember it mostly because of Gordon Lightfoot's wonderful song 'The Wreck of the *Edmund Fitzgerald.*' I get chills whenever I hear it."

"That's exactly how I feel," Janice wrote back. "I was only a kid when it sank in November 1975, but everyone in the UP mourned the twenty-nine men who were lost. My heroine is going to worry about the man she loves working on a boat much like the *Fitzgerald.* Lake Superior is a treacherous body of water, especially in late fall. I love living near it though. It's a constant reminder of how small we are and how vast God's universe is."

"I know the feeling well," Diane typed after a few moments of solemn thought. "The ocean is only blocks from my little cottage, and it's a constant source of wonder. When I stand alone on the beach, I feel an overpowering reverence for God's creation.

"Well, I don't suppose my suggestions are much help, but I do have to get to work. It was so nice chatting with you!"

"Your ideas are better than mine. Maybe one will work. Thanks so much. Talk to you again soon."

Although she didn't expect her new friend to actually use one of her titles, Diane was pleased by how quickly she'd come up with suggestions. In fact, she'd always had the ability to come up with good ideas for friends and fellow writers. It was her own work that lagged for lack of inspiration.

Maybe if she didn't take writing so seriously, her book would progress more smoothly. She remembered a few instances where words seemed to flow from her fingers to the computer screen. If she could capture that mode of composing sentences and paragraphs every time she sat down to work, her writer's block might be a thing of the past.

Before she could open the current chapter, her doorbell rang.

"Beverly, good to see you," she said, inviting her friend to step inside.

"I hope I'm not interrupting anything," Beverly said. "I had to take my father to a lecture in Augusta over the weekend, and we stayed overnight with a friend. This is the first chance I've had to tell you about my meeting with Reverend Locke."

"That's something I really want to hear," Diane said. "Can I get you anything? Coffee or tea?"

"No, thanks, I can't stay long. I have a couple of errands, then I have to get to work. You know what it's like to run a career out of your home."

"My career isn't 'running,'" Diane said with a laugh, gesturing for Beverly to sit with her in the living room. "More like plodding along. Anyway, how was your meeting with Reverend Locke? Did it go well?"

"I don't have a good handle on his state of mind, to be truthful," Beverly said. "He seemed preoccupied the whole time I was there, and either he has no interest at all in the treasure or he's pretending to believe it doesn't exist."

"Will Old First be open for services anytime soon?" Although Diane attended Marble Cove Community Church, she appreciated the role of the venerable church in the community.

Beverly shrugged. "I could've learned more talking to the stones of the building. Reverend Locke was even vague about insurance covering the damage. One odd thing, though. A woman was skulking around outside Old First when I went past on Friday, and she was there again this morning. What could she possibly want in a church that's boarded up?"

"That is peculiar," Diane agreed. "I'll see if I can use my investigative reporter skills to find out something about her. So your visit with Reverend Locke was a waste of time?"

"No, not at all. In fact, that's what I wanted to tell you. He told me one of his predecessors donated some papers to Portland College. He didn't seem sure about their contents, but he thought they were possibly related to the founding of Marble Cove and Old First."

"My sister-in-law Jeanette is a professor there. In fact, she's recently been appointed department head. Maybe she can get access to those papers for us. They might clear up a lot of our questions—possibly even give us a better idea about the likelihood of treasure."

"What a stroke of luck!" Beverly said, rising from the couch to leave. "Colleges can be pretty protective of documents that old, but this is the best lead we've had in quite a while. It would be wonderful if your sister-in-law could arrange for us to see them."

"I just spoke with her recently," Diane said, walking to the door with her friend. "I'll ask her what we need to do to see them."

"Oh, I didn't come just to tell you about my visit with Reverend Locke," Beverly said, stopping and reaching into her large shoulder bag. "Here's a sample of the petition we'll be circulating."

"It certainly looks official." Diane rapidly scanned it, remembering her promise to help. "Is this the only sheet I need to get signed?"

"Dreamer!" Beverly teased. "I have a big stack of them. I'm hoping every volunteer can fill three or four. You will be at my organizational meeting tonight, won't you? I want to pass out the petitions and say a few words about getting signatures, but I'll try to keep it brief. Several more people have agreed to help, which will make it easier for all of us."

"I'll be there," Diane promised.

"And feel free to invite anyone else you think might be interested."

"I'll see you then," Diane said, "and I do hope I can get in touch with Jeanette before the meeting. I doubt Shelley or Margaret can leave their businesses to visit the college, but I'd be happy to go with you."

"Great! See you this evening," Beverly said as she left.

Diane let Rocky out and waited by the back door until he wanted to come in. As happy as she was to see Beverly, she'd lost her momentum when it came to writing. It was great that a multipublished author had asked her for title suggestions, but her main concern had to be finishing her second book.

Her pooch was particularly slow returning to the house, which wasn't all bad. It gave her time to admire her small but tidy garden and the pretty pink impatiens planted in large urns.

She loved the small town of Marble Cove and the friends she had there. Maybe what she needed most was to put her life in perspective. In the great scheme of things, she wouldn't starve if she didn't sell more books, nor did her personal worth depend on the number of novels she sold.

Every time she visited a bookstore in Boston or a public library anywhere, she realized what a great treasure trove of books was available. The multitude of choices was more valuable than gold or silver moldering in the ground, no matter how much her friends hoped to find the treasure and put it to good use.

As long as she believed in the Lord and had the love of her children and many friends, her life was truly blessed. Good health and the ability to read were the icing on her cake, and she was truly grateful for all her blessings.

CHAPTER TWELVE

As she impatiently waited for people to arrive for the Monday evening meeting, Beverly checked one more time to be sure the petitions were laid out in order. She'd put them in different colored folders, one for each volunteer, and labeled them with names. If everyone managed to fill at least two sheets with signatures, they should have a significant number to present to the town council.

So far she hadn't heard from Jeff, other than a short text message before he boarded a plane in Seattle. She hoped he'd get to Marble Cove in time for the meeting, but she'd be happy to see him whenever he arrived.

Her father was still reading in his study, and Mrs. Peabody had hurried off to the market because she was afraid of running out of the salted nuts and candy mints she'd put in pretty dishes around the living room. Beverly had utterly failed to persuade her that people weren't coming to eat.

When the front doorbell rang, she hoped it was either Jeff or Diane. After she'd told her friend about the mysterious woman circling Old First, Diane had promised to see what she could learn about her. So far, she hadn't sent Beverly any information.

"Hey, good to see you two!" she said when she opened the door and saw Diane standing there with Margaret. "I was just thinking about you."

"I came early because I learned a little about your mystery woman," Diane said, following Beverly and Margaret into the front room set up for a meeting.

"Tell me." Beverly gestured at a chair and waited until Diane sat and dug a notebook out of her oversize leather purse.

"I'm eager to hear too," Margaret said. "I hadn't heard anything about this mystery woman until Diane just filled me in."

"I write everything down these days," Diane said. "Seems like I have so much going on, I'm getting absentminded. First of all, I couldn't find out where she's staying or where she came from. I guess my girl reporter skills are pretty rusty."

"Hardly," Beverly assured her. "It's pretty hard to check on a person if you don't know her name. What did you learn?"

"She's been spending a lot of time with Reverend Locke, so much so that several of his neighbors have noticed. I heard them gossiping in the market—not exactly a reliable source, I'm afraid."

"No, but our mystery woman is attracting attention. That tells us something—I'm just not sure what," Beverly said.

"I suppose it's possible she's an insurance investigator," Margaret said.

"Maybe," Diane said doubtfully. "But she isn't acting in a businesslike way. Beverly said there was something stealthy about her movements at the church. By the way, I heard from someone that she was in the Cove in the middle of the afternoon, talking a blue streak on a cell phone. The place was pretty empty, and she was sitting at the table closest to the kitchen so her words were too muffled to be heard. Anyway, my 'source' didn't hear what she was saying."

"Well, that's more than we knew yesterday" Beverly noted.

"Yes, but it's all only speculation. If she is an insurance investigator, why is she staying in town so long? Is there something suspicious about the church fire?" Diane asked.

"I never considered the possibility." Beverly frowned and didn't like the thought that came to mind. "Although, in retrospect, I thought it was a bit odd that Reverend Locke suddenly changed his mind about letting us into the tower room."

"What if we were his alibi? He could've set a timer with accelerants somewhere near the roof." Diane was noticeably agitated now, but Beverly thought it was a bit far-fetched to think of her minister as an arsonist.

"What would be his motivation?" Margaret asked.

"Insurance?" Diane hesitantly suggested. "If the church is heavily insured, the money might stretch to more than roof repairs."

"Highly improbable," Beverly said. "The church couldn't afford to be heavily insured. If the coverage is enough to repair the roof, we'll be lucky."

"Since all we have are suspicions, maybe we'd better keep this among the four of us," Diane said. "I did mention it to Shelley, but she's not a person to spread gossip. We could be totally wrong, and I don't want to be responsible for spreading false rumors."

"I agree," Beverly said. "Until we know more, we shouldn't cast suspicion on Reverend Locke. He's a pretty private person, but I have a hard time seeing him as a criminal."

She was interrupted by a voice calling through the front screen door.

"Hello, am I on time?" Allan asked, joining them when Beverly called out to him. "I took Adelaide to visit a friend before I came here."

"You're early, actually," Beverly said.

"We've both been so keyed up about Adelaide's trip to New York, I'm totally out of the loop," Margaret said. "Have either of you learned anything about the little key I found?"

"I do have a new lead, but not about the key," Beverly informed her. "Apparently one of Reverend Locke's predecessors sent some documents about the founding of Marble Cove and Old First to Portland some time ago. They're housed in the college library's historical collection."

"That's wonderful!" Margaret said.

"My sister-in-law is a professor there," Diane said. "In fact, she's recently been appointed a department head. I'm sure she can get permission for us to see the Marble Cove documents. I'm going to call to make an appointment."

"So we're making progress," Beverly said. "And I can't help but think the little key you found is very significant, Margaret."

"What's very significant?" Mrs. Peabody had come into the house through the back door just in time to hear Beverly's last statement.

"What we're doing here tonight," Beverly said, feeling a little guilty for fibbing to the elderly woman. But she knew Mrs. Peabody was the town crier when it came to spreading rumors. If anyone mentioned the T word to her, the whole town would be on a treasure hunt by tomorrow afternoon.

"The market was all sold out of those little colored mints. I had to go to the Mercantile, and their stuff isn't always as fresh as it could be. Good thing I got my granddaughter to drive me. I don't move as fast as I used to." She busied herself filling the candy dishes to overflowing with more mints and nuts from a can.

"We'd be happy to have your granddaughter join us," Beverly said, wishing she'd thought to invite her sooner.

"Oh, you know young people," Mrs. Peabody said dismissively. "They're always hurrying off to some place of their own. I hope you ladies brought your umbrellas and slickers. Looks like we're in for some rain. I can smell it in the air. Just hope we don't get another lightning storm like the last one. It scared me."

"I don't blame you," Margaret said sympathetically. "I always want to bury my head under a pillow when a bad one hits."

"Well, I don't go that far," Mrs. Peabody said. "I was looking out my front window when a big crack of lightning nearly split the sky. I've heard a bolt like that is hotter than the sun, if you can imagine that."

"Maybe it was the one that hit the church," Diane suggested.

"No, close but definitely not a hit," Mrs. Peabody said emphatically. "I watched out my front window until the storm died down, and lightning never got close enough to Old First to hit the roof."

"Are you sure?" Beverly asked.

Her father's cook was an octogenarian, but her eyesight was still good. And she knew Marble Cove like the back of her hand.

"I think I would've noticed if a bolt of lightning hit anywhere in that direction. Whatever set that roof on fire, it wasn't the storm."

"Why didn't you tell someone?" Beverly couldn't believe the woman would hold back on information like that.

"I told the mister and maybe a few other folks. Maybe you weren't home when we talked about it."

Before she could question her further, Beverly had to answer the door.

"Jeff, glad you made it!" She forgot about the mysterious woman, Reverend Locke's suspicious behavior, and Mrs. Peabody's account of the storm. It was a genuine pleasure to see the tall, rangy photographer.

He planted a quick kiss on her forehead and walked up to the group gathered in the living room with his hand on her shoulder.

"Diane, Margaret, Allan, Mrs. P., nice to see all of you," he said with a broad smile. "How many others are coming?"

"I guess you can count me in," Beverly's father said, entering the room.

Before she could join in the conversation, the rest of her guests arrived for the meeting. Shelley came in right in front of Leo Spangler. The vet had had the foresight to bring Gerald Kimball, the lone reporter for the *Marble Cove Courier*. Beverly wished she'd thought to invite him herself. A write-up in the local paper couldn't hurt. Even if he was opposed to their petition drive, he could draw his readers' attention to what they were trying to do.

"Gerald, I'm glad you could join us," she said, looking up at him. He was tall and had a spare tire around his waist. Although he was only in his midforties, he'd lost his hair except for a tuft right in front, his signature look.

"Now, I'm not sure I'm with you on this," he said, serious but not unfriendly. "Calder's development could bring a lot of money into this town, but I'm willing to listen."

"We appreciate that," Beverly said, hoping she could sway the reporter to their point of view. "I think we can begin now."

"Just let me pass out the iced tea," Mrs. Peabody said. "It'll only take a jiff. You can help with the chocolate chip and lemon bars, if you'd be so kind," she said with a nod at Beverly. "I made enough for everyone to have their fill."

Although she was keyed up to begin, Beverly complied. Maybe it wasn't all bad to soften up Gerald Kimball with some sweet treats.

When everyone was busy sipping and nibbling, she went over her plan to stop Dennis' development.

"What makes you think the town council will be swayed by your petitions?" the reporter asked.

"We can't be sure, of course, but there's an election coming up soon. If we get enough signatures, they'll pay attention."

"It's better to do something instead of letting a project this big get approval without voter input," Jeff said.

"I know my husband might benefit if Dennis hires local people," Shelley said. "But we've talked about it a lot, and Dan agrees the impact on the town would be negative in the long run."

"Where is Calder getting the financing?" Gerald Kimball asked.

"That's one of the things that makes me uneasy," Beverly's father said. "Whoever backs this development will end up practically owning Marble Cove. I'm a little particular about that myself."

"One of our major worries is that he'll manage to get a gambling permit," Diane said.

"The accommodations are too high-end for your average family tourist," Beverly said. "I've seen the plans. He wants to build the kind of luxury condos and hotels they have in Las Vegas or Atlantic City."

"You're certainly giving me something to think about," Kimball said.

"Maybe it would mean a lot of advertising revenue for the *Courier*," Jeff said. "But more likely, the conglomerate would buy the paper and cease publication. Local businesses would be in jeopardy, especially after the new shopping area opens."

"I have petitions in these folders," Beverly said after a lengthy discussion mostly aimed at persuading the reporter they had a valid reason for opposing the kind of progress Dennis Calder wanted to bring to Marble Cove.

By the time the meeting ended, Beverly was exhausted. Her friends had all left promising to begin collecting signatures right away. Leo Spangler even proposed a telephone campaign to recruit more people to help and offered to take responsibility for doing that himself.

With a little gentle persuasion, Mrs. Peabody agreed to worry about washing the tea glasses and plates in the morning and left for home.

"I'll be here tomorrow to make the mister's breakfast," she said, although Beverly had never doubted it.

"I'm ready for bed," her father said. "That went better than I expected. Too much chitchat, but that reporter fellow asked some good questions. Good night, Jeff, Beverly."

"You're incredible," Jeff said when they were alone in the living room. "You almost have Kimball on your side. I wouldn't be surprised if he gives your campaign some good publicity, although I suppose it will depend on the *Courier*'s management."

"Let's hope whatever he writes won't hurt our petition drive," Beverly said. "I'm glad you could be here."

"So am I. It was fun to see you in action. I bet you could run this whole town if you had the chance."

She laughed. "Right now I have all I can do to run my consulting business and the petition drive."

"How long will you be here?" she asked.

"I don't have an assignment lined up right away. I should go home to Portland and take care of a few things, but I'll definitely be spending more time in Marble Cove. I hope we can see a lot of each other before I have to travel again."

"I'd like that."

The idea of him spending a little extra time in Marble Cove made her smile.

His deep, throaty laugh was balm on her spirit. As important as the petition drive was, she wasn't looking forward to pounding the pavement in search of signatures. She hoped the people in Marble Cove wouldn't take too much persuading to sign. She knew, though, that the petitions were only the first step in blocking undesirable development. The town council could still choose to ignore them.

"Why are you frowning?" Jeff asked.

"Just thinking of all I have to do. I didn't even ask how your motorcycle trip went."

"It was fun to be out on the road with an old friend, but I found myself missing you," he said in a muted voice.

She smiled. "That's nice." His words were welcome, and she couldn't help wondering what the future held for them.

After he left, she cleaned up the living room and washed the iced tea glasses because they'd been a wedding present and were too good to put in the dishwasher. She didn't often dwell on her husband Will's untimely death, but she was in a melancholy mood tonight. What would her life have been like if he'd lived? Would they have been able to patch up their differences and make a go of it? Would Jeff have been an obstacle?

Did she want to be in love again? Was that what she feeling for Jeff? He was handsome and fun to be with. More importantly, he supported her decisions and helped if he could, as he had done when she had to sell her house to make the move to Marble Cove permanent. The fact that he'd hurried here to be part of the petition drive pleased her, and she looked forward to seeing more of him before he had to leave on another assignment.

"Dear Lord," she prayed when she was ready for bed but still too restless to fall asleep, "forgive me for barging through much of my life without faith to bolster me. Thank You for the many blessings in my life, especially the love of my father and the friendships I've found in Marble Cove. And if Jeff is to be part of my future, let our love slowly grow in a way that will be pleasing to You."

When she did crawl into bed, the dull rumble of thunder lulled her to sleep.

CHAPTER THIRTEEN

"Today's the day I'm meeting with my father," Shelley said at the breakfast table with Dan. She was feeling as gloomy as the sky outside.

"Oh, I'd forgotten," Dan said absentmindedly as he studied a paragraph in his textbook, part of his required training for his work with Wayne Stover.

"Dan! How could you forget? I've been agonizing over it for days."

"I'm sorry. Between work and all this reading I have to do, I'm been pretty out of it." He gave her a bleary-eyed smile. "I'm sure you'll be fine. Is there any more toast?"

Shelley felt like pouting, but it wasn't fair to expect Dan to be upset about a meeting with her father. Instead of saying more, she quickly toasted two slices of whole-wheat bread and spread them with butter. After dropping them on his breakfast plate, she went back to the kitchen to finish packing his lunch. It was ready when he came into the kitchen.

"Hey, I know this meeting with your father is a big deal. I just needed to brush up on a few things my boss expects me to know." He looked contrite, but she was too worried to give him much support.

"You will be here to take care of the kids before I leave, won't you? I'm really not ready to introduce them to their grandfather just yet," she said.

"Of course I'll be here, Shelley. What time do you need me?" He gulped the last of the coffee in his cup and set it on the counter.

"I'm meeting him at the Cove at 7:00 PM."

"Okay, I'll be sure to be home on time." He leaned forward and planted a kiss on her forehead. "Don't worry about this all day. You'll go, you'll talk, and that's it. I hate to see you stressed out over the guy. You've gotten along fine without him for a long time."

"Yeah, I know." Shelley didn't know how to explain her anxiety. Dan had such a great relationship with his own family. How could he really know what she felt about her father? "Have a good day."

"Kiss the kids for me and tell them Daddy misses them," Dan said on his way out.

As she watched him pull out of their driveway, Shelley remembered all the things she loved about her husband. He'd handled adversity well when getting a job seemed hopeless. As a father, he was wonderful, adoring Emma and Aiden as much as she did. He was the love of her life and the man she wanted to spend the rest of her life with. As long as they were together, did her father really matter?

With a little time to spare before the kids woke up, she hurried to start a load of laundry. It was nice to get ahead on household chores, but even the chance to get a lot done didn't push her father out of her mind.

"Mama!" Emma's call was loud, and Shelley hurried to get her before she woke Aiden.

She was, of course, too late, and her son stumbled out of his room asking about breakfast.

"Can I have chocolate chip pancakes?" he asked, still rubbing sleep from his eyes.

"I think some nice scrambled eggs would be better," she said as Emma clung to her neck.

"Yuck!" It was Aiden's new word, and one she could do without.

"Chocolate chip pancakes are only for special occasions."

Aiden sighed, but sat and ate his eggs grudgingly.

After the children finished breakfast and went to their rooms to play, Shelley checked the notes scribbled on her calendar to confirm Adelaide was coming. She was going to miss her a lot when she went on the New York trip, but fortunately she'd mostly be gone on the coming weekend.

Her order board was full, and she absolutely had to start the applesauce pumpkin Bundt cake she was making for one of her diabetic clients. It was the best-tasting dessert she could make using artificial sweetener, and she was proud of it. She'd altered the recipe just a bit to make it moister and had created a lovely icing to drizzle on.

Before she could assemble the ingredients, she heard a loud howl from Aiden.

"Emma took my red car," he protested, running into the kitchen.

"I'll get it back," Shelley said, looking through the kitchen window rather desperately for some sign of the sun in the heavy gray cloud cover. Her day went much better when the kids could get outside to play, but big splashy drops were already hitting their play equipment.

"Tell you what," Shelley said to both of them. "If you'll promise to play very nicely, I'll give both of you one of your Christmas-in-July presents."

Dan's parents always gave her kids an obscene number of gifts for Christmas. She tucked a few away to open later because the children appreciated them so much more when they weren't overwhelmed with presents. Fortunately, Frances was okay with it, although last Christmas she'd given them even more toys to compensate.

Hoping the gaily wrapped gifts would keep her kids happy until Adelaide arrived, she closed her bedroom door and went to her "secret stash" on the top closet shelf.

The new toys worked their magic and Aiden and Emma played quietly, at least for the time being. Shelley started work on her pumpkin cake, but her mind wandered to her own childhood. Her father always picked out the best presents, sometimes surprising even her mother when he distributed secret packages on Christmas morning. Her mother often chided him for spending too much and spoiling his daughters, but Shelley cherished the memories. Her favorite baby doll had long ago been consigned to the trash with its head flopping to the side, one arm missing, and the plastic face seriously discolored by a crayon makeover. Still, she remembered well how much she'd loved her father's surprises. She liked to think of him in a toy department, spending time to find the perfect gifts for his girls.

Would she be able to forget the bad years and remember her father as a loving, caring man? She just didn't know.

The doorbell rang, and a stampede of little feet raced to answer it. Fortunately, both children loved Adelaide, and Shelley's days went better when she had a few hours to concentrate on her business.

"Good morning," Adelaide said, stooping to scoop up Emma.

Margaret stood behind her, and Shelley invited her to come in for coffee.

"Only for a few minutes," Margaret said. "I have to get to the gallery. Allan is watching it for me, but he has a doctor's appointment coming up."

With the children happily entertained, Shelley welcomed a brief visit with her friend. She made fresh coffee and put out a small plate of Oreos.

"No homemade, I'm afraid. I'm a little behind on my cookie orders," Shelley said apologetically.

"I'm trying to be more careful about my weight," Margaret said, "so I'll just pass, not that I don't love them."

"Have you started on the petition?" Shelley asked, feeling remiss because her sheets were mostly blank. So far, she, Dan, and his parents were the only ones to sign.

"Yes, although Allan got more than I did. We've filled one page and started another. It hasn't been at all hard to persuade people."

"That's encouraging. I'll be more focused after my meeting with my father." Shelley remembered how her three friends had urged her to reconcile, but her resentment had faded. She knew they'd been right, no matter how it turned out.

"I hope it goes well for you," Margaret said.

Although Shelley thanked her for the thought, she really didn't want to talk about it until it was over. She changed the subject, regaling her friend with praise for the way her daughter played with the children.

"I had a reason to stop in," Margaret said after a few minutes of pleasant visiting. "I wanted to remind you about Adelaide's trip. She's leaving for New York early tomorrow morning and won't be back until Monday."

"Yes, I have the days marked on my calendar."

"Maybe you'd better not plan on her for Tuesday either. I imagine she'll be really tired. She doesn't have experience sleeping in strange places." Margaret looked as distressed as Shelley felt about seeing her father again.

"It must be hard, letting her go off on her own," she sympathized.

"Allan says I have too much imagination. I keep thinking of all the things that could go wrong. What if she's horribly homesick? Or someone is mean to her? I'd never forgive myself for giving her permission to go."

"I read in one of my child-care books that everyone should have some difficulties in life. It's better to learn early how to cope. Of course, Adelaide isn't a child."

"She's my child," Margaret said with a slight smile. "I guess I forget sometimes that she's also a young lady who knows her own mind."

"At least it's only a short trip," Shelley reassured her.

True to her word, Margaret didn't stay long, but her visit had cheered Shelley. She was by no means the only person who sometimes found family relationships difficult. She had to accept the situation with her father and go on from there, however painful her memories were.

★ ★ ★

"I'm home," Dan called out shortly before five.

The kids hurried to greet him as he sat on a chair by the back door to take off his muddy work boots.

"Did you ask to get off early?" Shelley asked, picking up Emma when she tried to get her foot in her father's dirt-caked footwear.

"Didn't need to. The rain turned the land around where we were working into a quagmire. The boss called it a day without any overtime. It looks to me like there may be a water problem, but I'm no engineer. I wonder if Dennis Calder checked out the site for his amusement park as well as he should've. It's on pretty low ground."

"Let's hope the town council will put an end to his project."

"We'll see," Dan said pessimistically as he went to shower before dinner.

Dan's early arrival took away one worry, but Shelley was still on edge. She snapped at Aiden for no good reason, but quickly apologized.

At the dinner table, Dan praised her lasagna, one of his favorites that she'd made up ahead of time, but Shelley could hardly eat. The meeting with her father had the potential for disaster. She just wasn't up to a big emotional reunion, not until some of their differences were resolved.

It didn't take Dan long to pick up on her anxiety.

"Are you sure you don't want me to come with you?" he asked. "It's not too late to get a babysitter."

Shaking her head, Shelley thanked him for the offer but refused.

"I think this is something I have to do myself. I've been praying hard that everything goes well, but I'm not at all sure about what I want to happen."

"Whatever you decide is fine with me," Dan said.

"Decide about what?" Aiden asked, increasingly curious about things his parents discussed.

"Eat your peas," Dan said. "Then you can have one of Mom's fresh-baked cookies. I could smell them half a mile away, they're so good."

"You could not, Daddy!" Aiden was critical of exaggerations.

"No, I guess not, but they certainly were on my mind."

Dan kept up a steady stream of conversation through dinner and even helped Shelley clean up afterward, although he was obviously tired after working all day.

"You're a wonderful husband," she said, hugging him as she prepared to leave.

"Thanks! I have to be to deserve you. Whatever happens with your father, I'm behind you 100 percent."

"That means a lot," she said, kissing him good-bye.

It did, but she still had the ordeal ahead of her.

Her first feeling when she went into the Cove was relief. The gloomy day must have kept people home because only a few were scattered around the room. She didn't trust herself not to cry, and she didn't want to break down in front of nosy spectators.

At first glance, she thought she'd been stood up. After deliberately arriving a few minutes late, she expected her father, Sheldon Becker, to be waiting. Although she knew it was rude to be tardy, she'd hoped to avoid sitting alone in case he didn't come.

Taking a hard look around the coffee shop, she realized he was indeed sitting at a small wooden table at the far end of the room. The light inside was dim, a carryover from the days when it had been a fishermen's pub, and he didn't seem to see her either.

Her instinct was to leave before he noticed her, but she steeled herself to approach him. Running wouldn't solve anything, and she was increasingly curious about his reason for contacting her.

"Hello, Dad," she said, stepping up to the table and making a production of slipping out of her rain jacket and hanging it on the back of the chair across from him.

"Shelley," he said, standing until she was seated. "I was afraid you'd changed your mind."

She didn't comment. As much as she'd rehearsed in her mind what to say, she couldn't summon up a coherent thought.

"I hope it stops raining soon." When in doubt, talk weather, she thought.

"How have you been, Shelley?" He obviously couldn't be sidetracked by irrelevant comments.

"Fine. The kids are doing well. Dan enjoys his new job. He always did like electronics." *There,* she thought, *that sums up what I have to tell. Now why am I here?*

"Can I get you some coffee and one of those lemon poppy-seed muffins you used to love?"

"Just coffee. Decaf, please."

Since customers had to go up to the counter, order, and carry their food and drinks back to their table, it gave her a short breathing space.

Her father moved without the familiar spring in his step, and he seemed to have put on a few pounds. Since he'd always been rail-thin, this was a good thing. As he walked back with coffee and a muffin, ignoring whether she wanted it, she had to admit he was aging well. His hair was mostly gray, but he still had quite a bit. He was clean-shaven, the little mustache she liked to pull as a young child gone.

"They were out of lemon-poppy seed, but this blueberry looked too good to pass up. The girl at the counter said it was made with fresh berries. I brought two plates so we can share it, if you like. It's pretty big."

"I actually made those muffins," Shelley said. "I have my own baking business and do all of the baking for the Cove."

"That's great, Shelley." Sheldon smiled, looking proud. "You always did like to bake when you were little. I'm not surprised."

After he carefully divided the muffin in half and shoved a plate toward her, he cleared his throat. She was on the edge of her chair, expecting him to tell her why he'd come to Marble Cove to see her.

"I talked to your mother a few months ago. She's pretty happy but wishes she could see more of you."

Laying on a guilt trip wasn't a good way to begin a conversation.

"She knows where I live. I know because she usually sends Christmas and birthday cards."

"She isn't what you'd call a good communicator. Maybe that was part of the trouble between us—not that I'm blaming her for our breakup. Probably we never should've married. We rubbed on each other's nerves almost from the beginning. All we had in common was our love for our daughters."

It was a long speech coming from her father, and it had the ring of truth. Her parents had tried not to quarrel when their children were listening, but toward the end, their rows grew louder and more strident. Shelley could remember hiding in her room with a pillow over her head to drown them out.

"How are you feeling, Dad?"

She'd wondered whether his reason for calling her was a terminal disease. Certainly she didn't want him to die. It would be a relief if that wasn't why he wanted to see her.

"I'm fit as a fiddle."

When she was little, he'd taught her all kinds of silly little sayings. They tended to pop up in her mind when she least expected them. To delay answering, she took a tiny sip of the very hot coffee.

"I had my appendix out a few years back. No big deal. And the eye doc says I have cataracts, but it'll be a few years before they're bad enough to remove. I probably won't need my reading glasses after the surgery."

"It sounds like you're doing well." She'd given him an opportunity to tell her bad news, and he didn't. So why was he there if it wasn't to get sympathy for a serious ailment?

"I've missed you, sweetheart. That's the unvarnished truth. There's no substitute for family."

Shelley knew how important her family was to her, but she'd long ago stopped thinking of Sheldon Becker as part of it. She didn't know how to answer.

"Well, I won't get all sentimental on you." He broke off a piece of muffin and put it in his mouth. "I just wanted to know how you are."

"Fine."

"Maybe someday you'll let me see your kids. I don't expect to be a big part of their lives, but it'd be nice to know them at least a little."

If she said no, she'd feel mean and vengeful. If she agreed and invited him to the house, she'd have to go through the agony of seeing him another time.

"They're probably in bed by now." Dan tended to give them "late permissions," but it was the only thing she could think to say.

"I understand. Remember how you used to read comic books with a flashlight under the covers?"

"You knew that?"

"Yeah, I was the one who snuck the books to you girls. Your mother didn't approve of them."

If Shelley had ever known that, she'd forgotten.

"I loved Archie. He made high school look like fun." She was hesitant to reminisce with her father, but he was bringing back some good memories.

"The most fun I ever had was taking you girls to the ocean. Susannah was timid about going into the water. Guess they'd talked about sharks in school. But you plunged in full speed ahead. I had to hustle to keep up."

"Mom never went to the beach with us," Shelley recalled.

"She thought the sun would ruin her skin, but she always packed a mighty nice picnic lunch. Remember that big basket we used to take? Fresh-squeezed lemonade in a thermos, bologna sandwiches for your sister, and peanut butter and jelly for you."

"Yes, she always put some nice treats in the basket," Shelley recalled.

"Sometimes I bought pepperoni rolls at an Italian bakery on our way. They were too spicy for you kids, but I liked them. Of course, the real treat was tomato soup cake."

"Yes, I remember. At first I wouldn't taste it. I really hated the canned soup, and I thought the cake would be terrible."

"Guess I sort of tricked you into trying it." He smiled, reminding her of how good-humored he'd been before the bad times. "I told you it was raisin spice cake, and from then on, it was one of your favorites."

"I remember." But did she want to? It was bittersweet to remember the good times with her father.

"I don't want to rush you, but if you could see your way to letting me see little Aiden and Emma, it would mean a lot to me."

He was somber now, and she felt a little tug on her heart. But one brief meeting couldn't erase the stress and lies of the past.

He took a deep breath. "Look, Shelley. I know I was often selfish and unfair during the divorce. I hope someday you'll find it in your heart to forgive me."

Her parents had behaved badly during the divorce and had fought over dividing everything they owned, ending up in court with expensive lawyers. There was even a big argument over who got to keep the living room couch— her mother won that one. Naturally they both wanted to keep their daughters' love, even though they weren't little children anymore.

"Thank you for telling me that," Shelley said.

She wanted to forgive him, but seeing him again brought back so many mixed feelings, she didn't know what else to say.

"I never stopped loving you and your sister," he said in such a low voice she had to strain to hear.

It was her cue to say she loved him too, but the words wouldn't come. She silently prayed to do the right thing, but the whole conversation had overwhelmed her.

"I know I've thrown a lot at you all at once," he said. "Why don't you go home and think it over for a while? I don't want to pressure you."

"I'll do that," she said, wanting nothing more than to be with Dan and the kids. "Thank you for the coffee and muffin."

"I just may finish yours, since you haven't even touched it." He smiled to show it wasn't a criticism. "It was nice seeing you, Shelley."

"Me too." Despite everything, she actually was glad she had seen him again. Now she had to figure out what exactly that meant from here on out.

At least she'd driven to the Cove because of the intermittent rain. She wouldn't have to walk home bawling all the way.

CHAPTER FOURTEEN

"We're supposed to meet Jeanette in her office," Diane said. "She's working most of the summer since she made department head."

"It was really nice of her to arrange for us to see the early Marble Cove documents," Beverly said, pulling into a parking area just below the hill where Portland College sat.

"We'll have a bit of a climb." Diane exited through the passenger door and pointed at the steep steps that wound their way up the grassy hill. "There's only room for a few administrators and tenured professors to park closer to campus."

"No problem," Beverly said, following her up the stairs.

Diane always enjoyed visiting the small liberal arts college. The buildings were arranged around a central quad with a venerable Greek revival structure dominating one side and a chapel with a tall white spire opposite it. The science center was a sprawling modern building, but several others dated to the early 1900s. She led the way to the classic brick building with white columns on the front, once the only building on campus.

"This makes me want to be a student again," Beverly mused. "The setting is so inviting, almost cozy."

"Yes, I know the feeling," Diane said absentmindedly. Although she was very fond of Eric's sister, seeing her was always a bit sad. She looked so much like her brother it was like turning back the clock to her days with Eric.

Inside the building, they climbed marble steps made uneven by many generations of students and faculty. Diane always marveled that stone could wear down under the soft impact of footsteps, but it was a reminder of how long the college had been serving the young people of Maine. She made sure to hang on to the ornate wrought-iron railing so the wavy surface of the stairs wouldn't trip her up.

The hallway was broad, much wider than in modern buildings. The original trustees of the college had spared no expense in creating an elegant facility. It retained much of its original charm in spite of an urgent need for renovations.

Professor Spencer had her name on a small brass plate just below the smoky glass window in the door. When they opened it, Jeanette immediately came out of her inner office to greet them.

"I'm pleased to meet you," she said after Diane introduced her friend. "I'm still hoping to get to Marble Cove before the fall semester starts, but I'm working my way through a mountain of work."

"We really appreciate what you've done to give us access to the early Marble Cove papers," Diane said.

"It was no problem at all. The archives are available by appointment, but we are careful about admitting strangers. Some years back a book thief stole literally thousands of volumes from a number of different colleges and universities. He was caught eventually and sent to prison, but it took a whole team of librarians working with the FBI in Omaha, Nebraska, to sort them all out."

"I didn't realize libraries were so vulnerable," Beverly said.

"Less vulnerable than they used to be, I hope," Jeanette said, pulling off her glasses and letting them hang down on a chain. As usual, she looked elegant in a stylish fawn pantsuit worn with a brown silk blouse. "But serious researchers are always welcome here. Even students can gain entry if they present a valid reason. Some day the archives will be available online, but Portland College is facing a financial crunch these days, as are many private schools."

"That's a shame," Diane said.

Jeanette smiled in agreement. "Shall we go now? I made an appointment with the curator who oversees our small museum and the archives."

She led the way down the marble steps, cautioning them about the worn surfaces.

"You'll enjoy meeting Dr. Standish," Jeanette said. "He's a walking encyclopedia of Maine history."

A long buff brick building was nestled into the hillside next to the science center. Diane loved libraries, and this one was a masterpiece. Dramatic murals depicting the history of Maine were on every wall in the huge central area, but before she could study them, Jeanette led them to a small elevator.

"If you're claustrophobic, we can use the stairs," she said.

"This is fine," Beverly said, and Diane agreed.

The upper corridor was carpeted with a small museum to the right and a series of closed doors on the left. Jeanette knocked softly on the third one, and the woman who opened it could've been forty—or eighty. Diane suspected she was heavily made up and wearing a wig so her employer wasn't reminded daily she was past retirement age.

"Dr. Standish is expecting you," she said. "You can walk right in."

The little man who stood up from behind his desk wasn't at all what Diane had expected. He probably had to stand on tiptoes to measure five feet, but his stance made up for his lack of stature. His beard was a rich mahogany brown shaped in a way that reminded her of a sable paintbrush. The hair on his head sprouted out in all directions. Apparently Albert Einstein had been his style model. He wore a tweed jacket with elbow patches, even though the temperature outside had to be at least 80 degrees on this sunny afternoon.

"So you ladies are interested in the Jeremiah Thorpe papers," he said after a brief introduction. It was a statement, not a question. "He was quite a character, but you'll see for yourself."

"A character in what way?" Diane asked, the reporter in her wanting as much background as she could glean.

"The theory, based on his documents, is that he wasn't on the up–and-up. Apparently he was accused of stealing funds. There's a newspaper article that basically accuses him of being in cahoots with a notorious pirate, a man called Booth Adair. Hard to believe a preacher would be fraternizing with the likes of a pirate, but one never knows." The little curator giggled, a surprising sound emerging from such a serious face.

Beverly glanced at Diane incredulously. "What else does the newspaper article say?" she asked. "That's exactly the kind of thing we're looking for."

"I don't recall all the details, but I'm sure you'll find it here somewhere among the papers," Dr. Standish said.

"I'm going to leave you in Dr. Standish's capable hands," Jeanette said, "but do stop in my office before you leave. I'd really be interested to know what you learn from that newspaper article."

After giving her sister-in-law a circumspect hug, Diane turned her full attention to the little man.

"Follow me," he said. "The fireproofing in this building leaves a lot to be desired, but we're state-of-the-art on security. Only three people can access the archives, one of them me, of course. I'm not at liberty to mention the other two."

They dutifully followed the curator as he led them to the archives. "When Professor Spencer asked me to schedule an appointment for you, I naturally needed to know your area of interest. You'll find everything we have laid out on that table. All I ask is you wear the white gloves and be very careful. You're dealing with very old, historical papers."

"We'll be ever so careful," Diane said, picking up on Standish's way of speaking.

"I'll have to lock you in, but never fear. All you have to do is press that buzzer, and I'll come in a jiff." He pointed at a button surrounded by old brass on the wall, certainly a relic from earlier days.

"Thank you," Beverly said, looking somewhat askance at the prospect of being locked in. "Is there any way we can make copies of the pertinent documents?"

"You'd have to fill out form 472. I'm the only one allowed to reproduce them. Generally I can get them to you in four to six weeks, although we are rather rushed around here."

"We probably won't need to do that," Diane said, taking a little notebook out of her handbag as he left.

The door closed with a loud click, and they looked at each other and shrugged.

"Let's get at it," Beverly urged.

"Agreed," Diane said. "He was under suspicion in his own time. That fits in with a possible lost treasure. I wonder how he befriended that pirate. What did Dr. Standish say his name was? Adair, Booth Adair?"

"Yes, that adds a whole new twist to the story, doesn't it?" Beverly pointed out. "I wonder if that newspaper article is here."

"Well that would be fascinating, but we really need to know what the little key opens," Diane said. "I'm hoping Thorpe's diary is here, but this pile doesn't look promising."

"Maybe we'll find that old newspaper clipping," Beverly added.

Diane pulled on a pair of white cotton gloves and sat on one of the polished oak chairs in front of the hoard. She began dividing it into piles so they could make quicker work of going through them. She really wasn't keen on being locked in a room in this antiquated building.

Nearly two hours later she took off the gloves and blinked her tired eyes. Between them, they'd puzzled their way through all the papers. She'd taken pains to record every pertinent mention of Thorpe in her notebook, but she didn't have much to show for her efforts.

"What do you think?" Beverly asked. "Do we need to fill out a form and request copies of anything?"

"I learned more from what the curator said than from reading all this stuff," Diane said in a discouraged voice.

"I know what you mean." Beverly took off her gloves and stood to stretch. "There's nothing here remotely resembling the newspaper article mentioning Thorpe and Booth Adair. There's no diary, and the letters and other papers are too vague to pin down any concrete reference to possible treasure."

"Or even to confirm one actually exists," Diane said. "I can't believe we wasted our time."

Once they'd been let out of the room, Diane led the way back to Jeanette's office, but they didn't linger. After giving a quick rundown on what they'd learned, they started back to Marble Cove.

"Well, we have one new thing to consider," Beverly commented.

"Yes—the possibility that Jeremiah Thorpe was working with a pirate. I can't get that idea out of my mind, but we really didn't find any evidence to support the theory. And we still have no clue what the little key unlocks."

"As much as I hate to admit it, I am discouraged," Beverly said. "Where else could we possibly look for leads?"

Diane shrugged, at a loss to make a useful suggestion. "At some point," she continued at last, "we have to face the fact that we night never know the full story of Jeremiah Thorpe. We may never find out what happened to the treasure, if there ever was one."

"What about Thorpe's own reference to a 'fortuitous maritime discovery,' or however he put it in that letter we found?" Beverly pointed out. "Do you think that really could mean meeting up with a pirate? He mentioned that something that came from bad would be used for good, or something like that."

"Anything is possible," Diane conceded. "It's certainly fascinating to think that something like that could have happened. But at this point, I just don't know what to believe."

"Well the only thing we *are* certain of," Beverly continued, "is the sad state of Old First. It would be devastating if the town's oldest church had to close its doors forever, and I'm not saying that because I'm a member."

"I'm not part of the congregation, and I agree," Diane said. "In a way, it's like the lighthouse: too much a part of Marble Cove's heritage to demolish it."

"Well, we'll see what the future brings," Beverly said, sounding philosophical. "For now, I don't see anything else we can do."

CHAPTER FIFTEEN

W"ell, she's on her way," Margaret said, fighting to hold back tears.

She was standing with Allan outside the community center Friday morning where the large van had just left for New York.

"It will be the experience of a lifetime for Adelaide," her husband said, putting his arm around her shoulders. "We agreed she should branch out and experience the world without our supervision."

"My mind agrees, but my heart is aching. I keep imagining all kinds of bad things happening. She really doesn't know anything about what's out there. How will she cope if the van breaks down or someone gets hurt?"

"You make it sound like she'll be wandering by herself in the big bad city. We agreed the trip is well chaperoned. I completely trust Penny Tyler." Allan patted her arm.

"Yes, you're right about that," Margaret agreed. "But she can't control everything that might happen."

"They're not going by stagecoach in the days before telegraphs were invented," he said, sounding a trifle impatient. "Penny will call if there's any problem at all.

She'll keep in touch through the calling network she set up to let us know when they get there. And remember, we gave Adelaide a cell phone of her own in case she gets homesick."

"I'm not sure she knows how to work it." Margaret knew she wasn't being reasonable, but it was such a wrench to send her daughter off on her own to a huge city.

"I set it up so she only has to push one button to get us. But I also told her she didn't need to call unless she had time and felt like it. Now, can we go home?"

"You can. I have to get to the gallery. An artist from Bangor wants to consign a few of her paintings. They look good online, but I'm going to meet with her at eleven. Some painters think their work should bring thousands of dollars. We haven't talked sale prices yet."

"Well, good luck," Allan said. "It's great you're selling so much you need other artists' work to fill the walls."

"I thought I'd painted enough during the winter to last through the summer, but happily I was wrong. We're only three weeks into July, and the walls are looking bare already."

"Maybe when Adelaide gets back, you'll be able to concentrate better on your painting. Buyers love your lighthouse scenes."

"Tourists must buy them as reminders of the lovely times they had in Marble Cove," Margaret mused, beginning to feel a little less stressed about Adelaide's departure.

"I'll walk you to the gallery, then I have to get home and put another coat of varnish on the two side tables I'm making to sell at the gallery."

"Yes, they can't be done too soon," Margaret said, putting her hand on his arm as they walked. "The pieces you made last winter are mostly sold."

"We're truly blessed," Allan said. "We both have things we love to do, and we're accumulating a nice nest egg to take care of Adelaide when we're no longer able to."

Margaret tensed and squeezed her husband's arm. It was going to be a very long weekend, and she didn't even want to think about the nerve-wracking wait for the van to return Monday.

When she got home in late afternoon after closing the gallery for the day, Allan was in his workshop. She found him there sitting on a stool and going over a book of plans. He usually quit work before she got home, and, truth to tell, she was spoiled. Most days he would have something started for supper or at least have a plan. Some mornings he was so enthusiastic about his cooking he gave her the menu at breakfast.

"How was your day?" he asked when she stuck her head into his workshop.

"I decided to take the Bangor artist's paintings on consignment. She specializes in animals. Her cats and dogs are really cute, so I think they'll sell—especially since she was very reasonable about pricing. Do you want me to start dinner while you clean up?"

"No, I have a better idea," her husband said. "Go put on your prettiest outfit. We're going on a mystery trip."

"Really, Allan, what are you up to?"

"Just do what I say, woman," he teased.

Margaret knew what he was doing: trying to take her mind off Adelaide. He partially succeeded, but as she waited for him to finish showering, her thoughts went back to her little girl in New York without her. Allan was right when he insisted Adelaide was a grown woman now, but mothering wasn't something Margaret could turn off like a faucet.

When he came out of the bedroom, Allan managed to surprise her. He was wearing his best suit—in fact, he only owned a couple—but he looked especially dapper in a summer beige purchased several years ago for a wedding. Her husband was short and certainly not movie-star handsome, but to her he was a beautiful man.

"How do I look?" he asked, straightening the paisley tie she'd bought him to go with the suit.

"Good enough to marry, but what are you up to?"

"What part of 'mystery' didn't you understand?" he asked with a chuckle. "I like that turquoise dress on you. You should wear that color more often."

Intrigued in spite of her reservations, Margaret went to the car with him. When they drove through town and out to a country road, her curiosity changed to apprehension.

"Do you think we should leave town while Adelaide is in New York?" she asked.

"Absolutely. We got the word that they'd arrived. Now it's our turn to have some fun." Allan was enjoying himself being mysterious, but Margaret couldn't get her daughter out of her mind.

His destination became obvious when he turned off on a side road and headed toward Blueberry Hill, a tiny town most Mainers didn't know existed. Margaret didn't say anything to spoil his surprise, but her suspicion was confirmed when he pulled into the parking lot of a country roadhouse on the outskirts of the village.

"The Food Place," she said, giggling. "I'd forgotten all about this restaurant."

"All the more reason why you and I should have a dinner date here. Remember when we were courting, and a friend—I think it was Bernie Hofstadter—told us about it?"

"We couldn't believe how good the food was. From the outside it looks like a barn."

"Which it was before a Boston couple converted it." He walked around the front of the car and opened the door for her. "I made reservations. They're pretty busy on Friday nights, considering their location."

"It's been so long since we were here," Margaret mused.

"It's been too long since we went out for a nice meal, just the two of us," Allan said, walking beside her with his hand on the small of her back. "We've been so busy being parents and building your gallery that we've lost sight of ourselves as a couple."

Staring ahead at the unpretentious building, Margaret felt remorse. Allan was right. Somewhere along the way, they'd forgotten how much they enjoyed each other's company.

"I think this really is a good idea," she admitted.

Inside the tables were covered with oilcloth, and the decor mostly consisted of old farm implements and fishing gear hung on the walls, but the hostess who seated them treated them like royalty. When they were settled at a cozy table in a quiet corner, she handed them menus in leather folders.

"It looks like the same menu," Margaret said, reading through the entrées. "Look, here's my favorite: grilled trout with wild rice. And they still have Cobb salad. And breaded zucchini appetizers."

Allan sat back and smiled at her enthusiasm.

"Why have we waited so long to come here again?" Margaret asked. It was a rhetorical question. She knew their lives were so busy that they'd just forgotten to do things as a couple. "We used to have so much fun looking for new places to visit. I don't regret a single moment with our daughter, but I'm remembering so many of the things we used to do."

"You watched me play softball and pretended you liked the game," he said with a grin.

"I wasn't pretending. I liked watching you. The game just wasn't as important as being where you were."

"Remember when you dragged me to your family reunion? We won the sack race. I think the prize was a big summer squash."

"I cooked it and made you eat some. We were newlyweds, and grocery money was tight."

"Funny thing is, being on a tight budget didn't affect our happiness at all. I thought I was the luckiest man on earth."

"You were the sweetest, that's for sure," Margaret said, reaching across the table to take his hand. "We need to do this more often. Adelaide babysits with Shelley's children.

She certainly can be trusted to stay home alone or go to a friend's so we can have alone time."

"I have a feeling she'd understand perfectly if we set aside some time just for us," Allan said. "Now, do you want to begin with appetizers?"

The gnawing anxiety she'd felt for days was forgotten while they enjoyed a delicious dinner, splitting a succulent chicken potpie with an unusual mix of summer vegetables and an order of lobster rolls so they could try both. They lingered over coffee, and Margaret remembered how they used to talk nonstop for hours just for the pleasure of it.

"I love being a parent," Allan said on the drive home. "Sharing our love for Adelaide has made my life with you complete."

This time Margaret couldn't hold back the tears of happiness that trickled down her cheeks.

"I can't thank you enough for our mystery trip," she said, squeezing his arm. "I won't stop worrying about Adelaide, but knowing you're with me makes all the difference in the world."

CHAPTER SIXTEEN

I'll take the kids to the park," Dan said Friday after he got home from work. "It will give you a chance to get ready for your father's visit."

"The house is clean, but I don't think I'll ever be ready myself," Shelley said. "But thanks. I can use the break. Today was really hectic with Adelaide gone."

"Daddy, can I take my frizzie?" Aiden asked, hurrying into the kitchen where his parents were talking.

"Frisbee," Shelley automatically corrected him, looking in his direction. "Why do you have Prize's leash?"

"So she can chase my friz-be."

"You know Prize can't come to the park with us," Dan said.

Aiden's face showed his recognition and he turned to put away the leash.

Shelley was eager for Dan and the kids to get out of the house. She was uneasy about her father's visit and afraid the kids would pick up on it. It was hard to be calm and cheerful when her insides were churning with anxiety.

She waved them off from the front porch and went inside. It was unusual for her to have time on her hands, but she couldn't think of any urgent jobs to distract her since dinner was already planned.

Maybe she should've said no flat out and saved herself these previsit jitters.

"No," she said, talking to the family pet that followed her into the kitchen now that the children were gone. "I made up my mind to let him come here, and the sooner the better. I don't want to be agonizing over my decision all summer."

Prize stared at her with big brown eyes filled with doggy wisdom, then bounded over to the French door to be let outside.

"Good choice," Shelley said, her mood lightening a little as the dog raced outside to chase imaginary rabbits or whatever else compelled her to sniff and race around the fenced yard.

Slumping down on a kitchen stool, Shelley closed her eyes and thought about her reasons for seeing her father again. Faith was at the top of her list. She well knew the commandment about honoring her father and mother. The Bible said nothing about treating parents as they deserved, but then, who was she to judge?

Perhaps if they hadn't divorced, she might never have come to her faith. A friendly neighbor, Darlene Kearns, knew about the discord in her home and had invited Shelley to come to church with her. Shelley resisted at first, but the church gradually became a refuge from the turmoil at home. She found peace there and would always be grateful to Darlene.

God never promised an easy life, she realized. Maybe she was being tested in some way by her father's desire to be part of her life again. The prodigal son was welcomed home with a feast of celebration, even though he was totally undeserving. What was she doing to make her father feel welcome?

The truth was, she'd only thought of ways to make the visit a short one. He was coming after dinner when it would be close to the children's bedtime. Her hope had been he'd leave after they went to sleep.

Alone with her thoughts in the quiet of her kitchen, she admitted she was wrong to deliberately think of ways to withhold hospitality from her father. It was too late to ask him to come for supper, but she could make a conciliatory gesture.

What should it be? She couldn't think of any words to express what she was feeling, nor was it likely her boisterous children would leave her alone with their newly discovered grandfather. Dan was already worried about her, and she suspected he would hover protectively the whole time her father was there.

Still torn between dread and indecision, she closed her eyes and prayed for guidance. Several minutes later, she had an idea.

One thing she still shared with her father was nostalgia for the time when they'd been a happy family. During their brief meeting at the Cove, he'd reminisced about their picnics on the beach and the nice lunches her mother had packed, especially mentioning her tomato soup cake.

As awkward and uncomfortable as she was about the visit, she still felt completely at ease in her own kitchen. She didn't equate food with love, but what better gesture could she make than to bake a cake for him?

A quick check of her supplies showed that she had the requisite can of tomato soup and a plentiful supply of raisins. Now all she had to do was find the recipe her mother had used.

From an early age, Shelley had been a recipe collector. As soon as her mother trusted her to make simple cookies by herself, she'd started writing favorites in a little notebook. Through the turmoil of the divorce, she'd kept it with her, long after she abandoned childhood mementos like stuffed animals and Barbie dolls. The tomato soup recipe was sure to be in it.

"Now, where did I put it?" she asked Prize when she let her in.

Not surprisingly, the dog wasn't any help in jarring her memory. She checked her shelf of prized cookbooks but knew before she looked that it wasn't there. Of course, she could go online and most likely find the recipe she wanted, but would it be the one her mother used?

With only a limited amount of time before her family returned and needed dinner, she broadened her search and finally found the notebook she'd treasured during her early baking experiments. It was in a box of important papers and other things she'd hidden under their bed so the children wouldn't rummage through it.

She hurriedly assembled the ingredients, preheated the oven, and mixed up the unusual cake, wondering as she did so whether it would be as good as she remembered. When it was done and cool enough, she finished it off with her favorite cream-cheese icing. Aiden wasn't going to like the raisins, and Emma was known to smear frosting from her hair to her toes, but this wasn't about a treat for her children.

Doing what she did best, baking for others, she felt calmer and more ready for her father's visit by the time Dan got back with the kids.

"Something smells good," he said, sniffing as he came into the kitchen.

"Tomato soup cake," Shelley said without further comment. "We can eat supper as soon as you and the kids wash up."

While Dan scrubbed hands, she took a pan of fish sticks out of the oven. It wasn't the kind of dinner they usually had, but the kids liked them. More importantly, she didn't have time for anything that didn't come ready-made from her freezer.

"You seem a little calmer," Dan said as he tied a bib on Emma.

"Thanks to you," Shelley said. "I really needed a little time to myself."

"Can we have cake now?" Aiden asked after nibbling on a single fish stick.

"Not until Grandpa Becker gets here," she said.

Her son was still puzzled by the idea of a second grandfather, but she hoped he'd warm up to him. The visit would be tense enough without her son taking refuge in his room. At least she could count on Emma. She was quick to make friends with everyone, even strangers at the market.

Dan offered to help her clean up after they ate, but she declined, preferring to keep busy until the last moment. After changing into clean jeans and one of her better T-shirts, she'd done all she could to get ready.

Prepared as she was, she still dreaded going to answer the doorbell when it rang. Fortunately, Dan got there ahead of her with the kids on his heels. She was able to hang back while he introduced the children to their grandfather.

"My, you're a big boy now," her father said to Aiden. "I bet you're going to be taller than your dad."

He picked up Emma, but she quickly wiggled to be free. She accepted strangers easily but wasn't keen to be restrained.

"Come have a seat, Dad," she said, trying to get through the awkwardness. She didn't have a clue what they would talk about, but Dan saved the moment.

"Still doing drywalling?" he asked.

"Yeah, work's been pretty good this summer, but last winter we were off a lot. How about you? Shelley said you're an electrician now."

The men talked for several minutes about their jobs, then the conversation turned to sports as it so often did with men. Shelley greatly appreciated her husband's efforts to keep her father engaged. Aiden was eyeing him with reservations, and Emma had wandered off to her room. Shelley wanted to connect, but she was still at a bit of a loss for words.

"I hear your baking business has really taken off," her father said. "If those muffins were any indication, you'll be very successful."

"Thanks," Shelley murmured, not sure what else to say.

Dan praised her success, telling her father about the new kitchen he and his dad had built for her.

"It looks out on the backyard so Shelley can keep an eye on the kids while she works. Want to take a look?" Dan asked.

"Love to," her father said.

Shelley felt left out when the two men went to the kitchen and had a long conversation about construction details. Even though Dan was being wonderful about keeping him occupied, she didn't have a clear idea about her father's motives. Was he there to reconnect with her and get to know his grandchildren, or was he only curious about her lifestyle?

When the two of them wandered out to the backyard, trailed by Aiden and Prize, she set out plates and cups for coffee and cake. The sooner they had dessert, the sooner he might leave.

"I made a cake, if you'd like to have a piece," she said when they came inside.

Partly to keep herself occupied, she brought out a carton of vanilla ice cream and scooped some onto each plate while her family gathered around the table.

"Is this what I think it is?" her father asked with a pleased grin, reminding her of what a handsome man he used to be.

In fact, he'd taken care to dress well for his visit. He was wearing a muted plaid shirt in shades of tan and brown with a bolo tie. His khaki slacks had a sharp press, making her wonder if he'd learned to iron since leaving her mother. Of course, he might take them to a commercial dry cleaner instead. Shelley never had, but a friend used to take her best jeans to be professionally pressed.

"Tomato soup cake," he said after he tasted it. "Thank you, Shelley."

Was he remembering their conversation about enjoying the same cake when she was young? She felt a bit weepy when she remembered the father she'd idolized. She knew this meeting would be hard, but she hadn't expected to feel so confused. They couldn't travel back in time and begin all over, but was there anything left worth salvaging from the past?

Her son called her back to the reality of the moment.

"Do you want to see my cars?" Aiden asked after he finished his cake. Shelley noticed he didn't call him Grandpa.

"I'd love to, sport. Lead the way."

Now that she thought about it, her father had yet to call Aiden by name. Was that his way of saying he didn't like what they'd named their son? Or was she overreacting because it was so stressful having him in her home?

Dan looked at her with raised eyebrows as she washed frosting from Emma's face. "You okay?" he asked in a soft voice.

"Fine." She appreciated his concern but still felt impatient with his question and angry with herself for wanting to keep her feelings to herself. After all, Dan had done everything possible to make the visit less strained.

"He seems to be good with the kids." Was Dan looking for ways to help her accept her father's overtures?

"I guess."

Dan freed his daughter from the booster seat and lifted her into his arms. "Want me to get her ready for bed?"

"Wait a few minutes. I'm not ready to be alone with Dad."

There, she'd said it. No matter how well the meeting was going, she wasn't ready for an emotional reunion.

"That's quite a car collection your boy has," her father said as he came out of the bedroom followed by Aiden. "Reminds me of the Hot Wheels I collected when I was a kid. I wonder what happened to them. I can't remember throwing them away. Probably your mother did. Well, that's water over the dam, but it would've been nice to pass them on to my grandson."

"He's pretty well supplied," Shelley said in a neutral voice.

"He's a smart kid. Knows the makes of all the cars he has. Maybe he'll grow up to be an automotive engineer."

"It's a little early to make career choices." Shelley tried for a humorous tone but was afraid her words sounded critical.

"I wish I'd made better choices in life." Her father sounded regretful but quickly changed his tone. "I've got to be running along. I wanted to bring little gifts for the kids, but I didn't have a clue what to get."

He took out his wallet and extracted two bills, handing one to Aiden and one to Emma. They were fifty-dollar bills, and Shelley quickly took her daughter's before she decided to chew on it.

"Dad, that's more than they need, really," she protested, trying to hand it back. She knew he must work hard for his money, and it was way too much to hand over to children.

"Let them buy something and put the rest in the bank for their college," he said dismissively, reaching down to pat Aiden's back. "It doesn't begin to make up for all the birthdays I've missed."

"Thank you, Sheldon," Dan said. "Tell your grandfather thanks, Aiden."

Their son complied quite nicely, although he was a little perplexed about how much the "dollar" was worth.

"Yes, thanks, Dad, but you really didn't need to do it," she said.

"Thank you for having me," he said. "It meant a lot to see you and my grandkids."

"We're glad you came," Shelley said, almost believing it was true. His presence brought back both good and bad memories, but she was also reminded of how she'd adored him as a child.

"Good to see you," Dan said, shaking his hand and walking toward the door with him.

"I promised to meet an old friend at the Cove," he said. "That's my ride home. Take care, all of you."

He chucked Aiden under the chin and took Emma's little hand in his. Shelley didn't know whether a hug was in order, but her father made the decision by leaving.

"That went pretty well," Dan said when her father was out of hearing. "You did all that worrying for nothing. He only wanted to see you and the kids. You can't blame him."

"I'm not blaming him," Shelley said a bit more sharply than she'd intended. "I don't know about you, but I'm really tired. Let's get the kids to bed and make it an early evening."

"I'm in favor of that," Dan said.

Dan was right. The visit had gone well with none of the dramatic scenes she'd been dreading. Her father seemed to enjoy seeing Aiden and Emma, and he still had a knack for engaging children. He and Dan had talked as though they were old friends, and he hadn't made any demands on her. If he wanted forgiveness, he'd been extremely low-key in seeking it.

"Thank You, God," she said when Dan went to put Emma in her bed. She'd prayed for patience and strength, and her prayers had been answered.

Whether she saw her father again in weeks or years, she felt less antagonistic. They hadn't talked about the divorce or the bad times that came with it, but she felt more ready to put the past behind her than she had before seeing him again.

After kissing Aiden good night, she collapsed on the couch beside Dan and snuggled under his arm.

"I am so blessed to have you," she said. "You made all the difference tonight."

"No, you were the one who put aside old hurts and welcomed your dad into our home. I've very proud of you."

She felt warmed by his praise. The evening had been a success because of her husband's love and understanding. But she had a feeling this was only the beginning of a changed relationship with her father.

Chapter Seventeen

Petitions kept coming in all day Saturday. Beverly couldn't have been more pleased. Everyone who signed up to collect signatures had come through with even more than they'd promised to secure.

In midafternoon Dr. Spangler delivered a whole folder full of petitions, more than any two people.

"You've really gotten behind this," Beverly said, praising his efforts. "Maybe you should run for council."

"No, thanks, that's not for me," he said laughing as he stood in her entryway with his dog. "I just don't want to have to move my practice if Marble Cove becomes another cookie-cutter resort area. People practically lined up to register their protests. This is a very good thing you've done, rallying opposition against Dennis Calder's project."

"I hope it has some impact on the council members. They do have to face an election soon," Beverly said, glancing through the many sheets the vet had handed her. "I can't thank you enough for collecting so many."

"I was happy to do it. Now Limo and I had better get on with our walk. This is his first outing since he had surgery."

What a pleasant person he is, Beverly thought as he went down the walk. The petition drive was having one unexpected outcome: she was getting to know a lot of really nice residents of Marble Cove. Without realizing it at first, she was beginning to feel more a part of the community.

Her project for the day was to check petitions for duplicate signatures, a task that promised to be tedious but necessary. She also wanted to get totals and organize them for a potent PowerPoint presentation. She intended to take the petitions to the next council meeting and back up the signatures with a strong argument when she had her turn to speak during the public meeting.

She'd commandeered the dining room table to spread out the petitions, and her first job was to check her list of people who'd taken one or more to get signed. Happily, every volunteer but one had returned them, most sheets full of signatures. The only person who hadn't turned in hers was Mrs. Peabody. Beverly was surprised because the older woman had been so enthusiastic about helping, but it wasn't too late for her to come through. Now that she thought about it, her father's helper had taken the day before off for a funeral.

By midafternoon she'd found only a few duplicate signatures, almost all of them from Mrs. Cora Blodgett Collins, who'd apparently added her name to every petition she could. After puzzling over it for a few moments, Beverly remembered her as an elderly woman who walked her cat on a leash, regularly visiting almost every business on Main

Street to pass out little brochures about animal welfare. Beverly smiled as she crossed out the superfluous signatures. Fortunately the total was amazingly high, in spite of the absence of Mrs. Peabody's petitions.

Just as Beverly stood up to get some water, she heard someone in the kitchen. Mrs. Peabody had come in through the back door and was bustling around the room, putting away the pots and pans in the drainer.

"It's your day off, Mrs. Peabody. You don't need to do that," Beverly said, knowing as soon as the words were out that any protest was pointless.

"I'll just tidy up a bit," she said, banging pans somewhat more than necessary as she put them in the cupboard. "Don't want the mister to think I'm slacking off."

"He would never think that," Beverly said with a secret smile. In fact, her father would've liked less bustling around from his part-time cook. "I'm glad you're here though. Did you bring your petitions?"

"I surely did," the older woman said. "I have them right here." Beverly's jaw dropped as Mrs. Peabody pulled out a stack that dwarfed even the one that Leo had brought in. "People were happy to sign, I can tell you. Once the word was out, folks called me asking to sign."

"Wow. That's great to hear," Beverly said. "I'll just take your petitions and add them to the others. People really seem to be incensed about the development."

"I should think so! Next some fool will want to build a nuclear plant on our beach," Mrs. Peabody said indignantly.

"I never did think much of Dennis Calder. He has dollar signs for a heart, never mind he has a way of making people like him before they know he's only out for himself. If a man is no good, he oughtn't to pretend to be nice."

"Yes, I see what you mean." Beverly's thoughts turned to Dennis. Certainly he was pleasant company, but had he always tried to use her?

Mrs. Peabody leaned in, conspiratorially. "That Locke fellow isn't what he pretends to be either."

"Reverend Locke?" Beverly asked in surprise. It was the first time Mrs. Peabody had mentioned the minister in a negative way.

"You can bet there's more to him than folks see." Mrs. Peabody brushed a stray wisp of white hair out of her eyes and patted down the dark print dress she was wearing.

Beverly knew she shouldn't listen to gossip, but sometimes Mrs. Peabody saw and heard things that would otherwise have escaped her notice.

"I guess that's true of all of us." It was a weak response, but Beverly really didn't want to hear bad things about the minister.

"Take that woman who's been skulking around Old First. Folks have been seeing a lot of her."

"Marble Cove has lots of visitors in the summer," Beverly said. "Maybe she's just visiting someone who lives here."

"Or maybe she has business with Reverend Locke. Funny business."

"Well, it's probably none of *our* business." She smiled at Mrs. Peabody and gestured pointedly toward the tower of petitions that her friends had helped her gather. "I'm really amazed by the number of signatures we've gathered. The council will have to take notice."

Beverly began shuffling through the petitions on the dining room table, but Mrs. Peabody wasn't ready to drop the subject of the mysterious woman.

"My friend Hettie saw her go into Reverend Locke's house after supper last night. Now don't tell me that isn't suspicious." Mrs. Peabody crossed her arms triumphantly. "And he's a preacher."

"He also does counseling. She could be a person in need. Or possibly someone involved in repairing and reopening the church, an insurance agent or something." It was hard for Beverly to sound convincing when she didn't quite believe what she was saying.

"Well, all I can say is, Hettie isn't one to make up stories. She lives right across the street from Reverend Locke, and she's had her eye on the comings and goings at his house for a long time."

"It isn't nice to spy on people," Beverly said. "Now, I don't think there's anything you need to do this evening. My father is going to have dinner and play chess with a friend, and I won't be here either. I'll see you Monday. Thank you for getting so many petitions."

Mrs. Peabody left with a slight sniff, perhaps a bit miffed because Beverly hadn't been interested in her friend's observations. Beverly was glad to have her petitions, even if they came with a heavy dose of gossip. Hettie might be a good observer, but there was nothing to be gained by spreading rumors about Reverend Locke. He was enough of a puzzle without throwing in a mysterious woman making secretive visits to his house.

When she had the petitions organized and the main points of her presentation nailed down, it was time to take a relaxing bath and dress for dinner. Jeff was going to pick her up at seven, and his timing couldn't be better. She was more than ready for an evening of fun with no worries about petitions or Reverend Locke or Mrs. Peabody's penchant for spreading rumors.

Before she could start to get ready for her date, the front doorbell rang. She hoped it wouldn't be someone who would delay her. She was in the mood for a leisurely beauty treatment from the top of her head to her toes.

The last person she wanted to see was standing on the porch when she opened the door.

"Dennis."

"Hello, Beverly. Do you mind if I come in for a minute?"

He looked overheated and grubby in wrinkled white shorts and a stained green T-shirt. In fact, she'd never seen him looking so unkempt. His hair was windblown and his face red, whether from the sun or anger she couldn't tell.

"It's not a good time, Dennis."

"I'll bet it isn't." He stepped inside. "But I think you owe me an explanation."

"I doubt that." She backed up but was unwilling to ask him to come any further into the house.

"I trusted you with my plans, and you turned against me," he angrily accused her.

"How could I not? Your development would ruin the Marble Cove everyone knows and loves."

"It would revive this sleepy little burg. I'm all about bringing jobs and prosperity. The town is stuck in the last century. People eke out a living on tourists and not much else. My development would change all that."

"Exactly," Beverly said, trying to be rational rather than confrontational. "The bottom line is, the residents don't want your kind of progress."

"You mean you don't want your cozy little world exposed to change. Sooner or later, the town has to move into the twenty-first century or die. There's nothing here but a lot of sand and an obsolete lighthouse."

"I never knew you were so cynical."

"You mean practical. Someone has to jump-start the economy around here." He shook his head and stared at her with cold eyes.

"How exactly do you expect to make your investment pay off?" she asked. "You're planning to build the kind of luxury accommodations they have in Atlantic City or Las Vegas, not family tourist facilities. Do you have a gambling license lined up, Dennis?"

"If I did, you'd be the last person I'd tell," he said angrily. "You're not going to stop me, Beverly. I'm just sorry I trusted you."

"You couldn't have kept something this big a secret for long. Now I would appreciate it if you'd leave."

"No problem, but the gloves are off. You don't know what you're getting yourself into. Not everyone in Marble Cove is as short-sighted as you and your friends."

"If you're counting on the council, you may be in for a surprise." She was saying too much, but he obviously knew about the petition drive.

He took a deep breath, and the expression on his face made him almost unrecognizable. Without another word, he turned and left.

Even though his anger hurt, she knew her stance was right. It wasn't pleasant to lose a friend, but the future of Marble Cove depended on defeating his plans.

The confrontation left her shaky and drained, but she couldn't regret her opposition to the development. Left unchecked, he might build a golf course along the beach and turn the business area into a ghost town.

"Not while I can do anything about it, Dennis Calder," she said as she watched him stomp back to his car.

★ ★ ★

Diane rarely felt lonely these days. When she wasn't with her friends in Marble Cove, she had frequent conversations via e-mail with ones she'd known in the past. And, of course, Rocky was the best of companions, albeit his conversation was limited to barks, woofs, and a wagging tail.

Saturday evening was an exception. She was restless and didn't want to be alone. Since visiting Portland College and seeing Jeanette, she couldn't stop thinking about all the things she and Eric used to do together. When there were no other demands on their time, they loved to order a pizza on Saturday evenings and watch classic movies at home. She loved the silent films from the 1920s, especially *The Thief of Baghdad* with Douglas Fairbanks. The sets were magnificent by any standard, and the acrobatic actor amused her immensely. Anyway, there was no need for spoken film dialogue when she and Eric could talk to each other. He never tired of seeing *Metropolis,* and she enjoyed the bizarre German science-fiction film because he did. They thought of it as their secret indulgence, one they didn't share with anyone else, not even their children. Other couples went out for fancy dinners. She and Eric nibbled popcorn on the couch at home.

Trying to bring back some of the contentment she'd shared with her husband, she put a frozen pizza in the oven and located a DVD movie her daughter had given her last Christmas. Unfortunately, the pizza was too dry and spicy, and watching the holiday classic *It's a Wonderful Life* wasn't much fun in July.

"Come on, Rocky," she said. "When all else fails, we can go for a walk."

The dog quivered with enthusiasm as she put on his leash, and she had to quiet him down a bit before they went out.

"Should I take one of Beverly's petitions with me?" she asked, then decided against it. Saturday night wasn't a time for buttonholing people.

The evening was cool and pleasant with a few other people out strolling. She passed an elderly couple and wished them a good evening, but Rocky was too hyper to stop for conversation. They were close to Main Street when she heard footsteps hurrying behind her. In Boston, she would've worried. Here she only glanced over her shoulder.

"I thought that was you," Leo Spangler said. "I'm headed to the pharmacy. Mind if I walk with you and Rocky?"

"Not at all," Diane said, surprised at how welcome his company was. "We're just having a stroll."

The vet stooped to pet Rocky, then fell into step beside her.

"Here's a thought," he said. "How about joining me for an ice cream sundae? I haven't had one in ages."

"You know, that's a brilliant idea," Diane said, walking with him to the pharmacy.

When they got there, she tied Rocky's leash to an old hitching post embedded in the cement just outside the door for the purpose of securing pets while owners visited the store. After his walk, he was content to hunker down and quietly watch passersby.

Unlike most modern drugstores, the Marble Cove pharmacy still had an old-fashioned soda fountain. A couple of teenage boys were perched on stools at one end, and Leo steered her to the other end.

They read the menu posted on the wall, then she decided on a cherry sundae with whipped cream and nuts. Leo chose marshmallow on chocolate ice cream, and they chatted companionably while a young girl with a blonde ponytail made them.

"How's the signature drive going?" Diane asked as she sampled her treat.

"It hasn't been hard. People are incensed at the idea of turning Marble Cove into a playground for the wealthy and are eager to sign."

They talked about his dog's recovery from minor surgery and Rocky's latest antics. Diane enjoyed his company, especially since she'd been so lonely earlier in the evening. He walked her home at such a slow pace that Rocky kept straining on his leash.

"Thanks for the sundae," she said when they got to her cottage. "It was fun."

"Maybe another time?" Leo asked optimistically.

Torn between enjoying his company and not wanting to encourage him too much, Diane smiled and nodded, then said good night.

Alone again, she realized it was still too early to go to sleep. Saturday evening television programming wasn't worth watching, and she still felt too restless to settle down in bed with a book. Instead she went to her computer, intending to check her e-mail.

She quickly deleted some junk mail and answered a note from Jeanette expressing pleasure at their visit, however brief. A second message held her attention longer:

"Hi, Diane,

"It's too early to go to bed and too late to work. I call it my free time, but actually, it's kind of boring. Color me a workaholic, but I do love what I do.

"What are you up to? Is there any nightlife in Marble Cove? Here the teenage boys park their cars along the main drag and hoot at each other. It begins when the snow starts to melt—say April or May. The object is to take their coats and shirts off and see who can stand the cold the longest. And pick up girls, of course. Ah, the good old days. I don't at all mind being out of that social scene.

"I have a little spare time. Say no to this offer if you like— no hard feelings—but if you'd like me to take a look at what you've written so far, I'd be happy to. Not that I'm an expert, but sometimes an extra pair of eyes is helpful. Take care! J.R."

It wasn't necessary to check the address to know the initials stood for Janice Rimes. Excited by her new friend's offer, Diane was quick to reply.

"Thanks so much for the offer. I'd love to show you what I've written so far," she wrote. "You're right about extra eyes. If you want to get biblical, it's not hard to see the mote in someone else's eye but easy to overlook the beam in your own. That's probably a terrible paraphrase, but I'm delighted to show you my manuscript so far."

Janice was quick to respond:

"I'll watch for your manuscript."

After sending the book, Diane felt drowsy and content. She hadn't found out much about Jeremiah Thorpe this week, and her book was still unfinished. But she'd made a new friend online and had an ice cream sundae with a pleasant man who shared her views on lots of things. A person could have a worse week.

★ ★ ★

After a relaxing aromatic bath, Beverly felt calmer but no less determined to fight Dennis' development with all she had. For tonight, though, she wanted to stop thinking about it and enjoy Jeff Mackenzie's pleasant company. To that end, she dressed in her favorite periwinkle blue sleeveless dress and silvery spike heels that made her ankles look great. She embellished her dark shoulder-length hair with a sterling hair clip, and put an unusual amount of effort into making her makeup as flattering as possible.

This time when the doorbell rang, she was eager to open the door.

"Hi." Jeff smiled warmly and met her eyes. "You look terrific. I don't know if there's anyplace in Marble Cove that's worthy of you."

"Don't be silly," she teased, pleased because he'd worn a lightweight beige jacket with dressy brown slacks. He was more a jeans and polo shirt man, so he'd obviously made an effort to look his best.

"I made a reservation at Spinella's, but we can go someplace else if you like."

"No, that's fine. The company is more important than the place." She was flirting, and it felt good, especially after her unpleasant confrontation with Dennis.

When they were seated at a cozy table for two, a candle lantern flickering between them, Beverly was filled with gratitude for Jeff's attention and support, but she had to get something off her mind.

"Dennis Calder came to the house this afternoon. To say he was irate is an understatement. He was livid."

"I hope he didn't upset you too much. I expect he has his future wrapped up in the development plans, but that doesn't give him the right to harass you." Jeff reached across the table and took her hand, turning it over and rubbing his thumb across her palm.

"I was agitated, to say the least, but you're right. If he wants to argue, let him face me down at the council meeting. This isn't personal between us. There's a lot more than that at stake."

Talking with Jeff was more calming than she could've believed, and soon they were laughing about little things.

"I didn't think I was going to get out of Chicago," Jeff said, telling her about his trip home. "First the plane was there but the flight crew wasn't. Then they got there, and something wasn't right with the plane. The flight was canceled, and I had to talk my way onto another one with a group of women volleyball coaches on their way to a conference."

"You're always having adventures," she said, smiling at the trials and tribulations of flying cross-country. "I'm surprised you still enjoy coming to Marble Cove."

"This is my most important destination," he said. "Where else could I find unsullied beaches, quaint streets, and a beautiful woman who can put up with my wandering ways and my company?"

They were interrupted by a server who took their orders for seafood platters. Jeff was always courteous to waiters, busboys, clerks, and custodians. In fact, he treated everyone with kindness and good humor. It was one of the things she especially admired about him. He had a knack for relating to everyone who came into contact with him. Perhaps that was what made him an extraordinarily good photographer. He loved his subjects and brought out the best in both people and scenery.

"You look serious," he said when she was quiet for a few moments.

"I was just thinking what a nice man you are."

"Keep thinking that way," he said. "I don't want you to discover my flaws."

By the time they'd finished their entrées, she confided in him what she and Diane learned in the Portland College archives.

"Jeremiah Thorpe sounds like a complicated character," he said thoughtfully. "Maybe there really is something to your treasure hunt. To be honest, I doubted it, but I don't think you're wasting your time. I wish I had more time to help you."

"I guess there's really nothing more to do about finding clues right now," Beverly said. "But I would like it if you'd come to the council meeting when I make my presentation."

"I wouldn't miss it for anything," he said emphatically. "And if Calder gives you any more grief, I'll talk to him."

"You don't need to do that." Beverly felt protected by his offer, but her differences with Dennis had to be settled by the town council's decision. She could only pray it went well for the many people who would be hurt if he succeeded.

Later, after a wonderful evening with Jeff, she lay awake for hours. Her mind was too filled with conflicts and possibilities to relax. How would her growing regard for the handsome photographer affect her future? Had she been led to Marble Cove to do more than take care of her father? Was she meant to help preserve the charm and grace of the community, and would she have a role in restoring Old First to serve its congregation again?

Life in a small town was far more complicated than she could've imagined before she decided to make it her home.

CHAPTER EIGHTEEN

Sighing deeply after putting the kids to bed, Shelley realized how much she needed a little alone time. Dan was busy studying and she was up to date on all her baking and bookkeeping. There was one thing she'd been wanting to do, and this was her chance. She hadn't spoken to her sister in a long time, and they were past due for a nice long talk.

After making herself comfortable on a kitchen stool, Shelley punched in the number.

"Susannah, hi. It's me," she said when her sister answered.

"Hey, sis. Nice to hear from you. How are Dan and the kids?" her sister asked. "I love the picture you sent me for Valentine's Day. Emma is an absolute doll."

"A mischievous one sometimes," Shelley said.

"As if you weren't a pill when you were her age," her older sister teased.

"And how are things with you?" Shelley asked her sister.

Susannah sighed. "Not so great, actually. Things are pretty tight. I've been trying to find work, but there's not much out there. I'm just doing what I can to keep things going for Hailey."

Shelley was worried by her sister's tone and wondered what Susannah might not be telling her. "I'm sorry. I didn't realize things were so tough. Is there anything I can do?" Shelley offered.

"No, no. We'll be fine," Susannah said dismissively.

"Um, okay," Shelley responded, not quite convinced. "Well, if there's any—"

"We're fine, sis," Susannah interrupted. "So, what's up? Why are you really calling?"

"Dad was here this week. He wanted to see the kids," Shelley said.

"Yeah? How did that go?" Susannah sounded concerned.

"Not bad. We had tomato soup cake, and he visited with Dan and the kids."

"Did he bring his girlfriend with him?"

"His what?" Shelley was stunned.

"You don't know about Maggie Thomas?" Susannah sounded as surprised as Shelley felt.

"He never said a word about a girlfriend," Shelley said, not sure how to process her sister's news. "He did say he was meeting his 'ride' downtown after he left us, but I didn't have a clue."

"Well, you know Dad. Communication isn't his strong suit," her sister said philosophically. "I guess it was inevitable. After his second marriage broke up so quickly, he was sure to find someone else. He's still a good-looking man for his age."

"But why keep it a secret? All he had to do was mention he was seeing someone." Shelley felt the pain sinking in.

He wanted to be back in her life, so why would he hide this from her?

"Maybe he thought you knew already. Or maybe he was waiting until he knew if you'd want him back in your life," Susannah cautioned.

"This changes everything," Shelley said, close to tears.

"But maybe it doesn't have to," Susannah said. "Shelley, I...People make mistakes, sis. Really stupid mistakes. If you shut everyone out of your life who's done something stupid, then...who's left?"

Was her sister referring to their dad? Or to herself? "I guess you're right," Shelley said.

"There's no guess about it," Susannah said. "If you only knew how much I envy you sometimes. You have such a great life. Really, what harm could it really do to let Dad be a part of it?"

After Shelley hung up, she replayed the conversation in her mind. Susannah was right, of course. Still, her father had told her, *promised* her, that he'd work things out with her mom. And then he'd left. Could she dare trust him again if he was withholding such a major part of his life from her?

★ ★ ★

Sunday morning in church, as she sat beside her husband during a pause for silent prayer, Shelley still felt numb. She'd tried hard to pray for her father in her private devotions the previous evening, but the words wouldn't come. Was she being too self-centered and judgmental?

"Are you okay?" Dan whispered, taking her hand in his.
"I will be."

Shelley forced herself to turn off thoughts of her father and gave silent thanks for all the things that were good in her life, especially her church, her family, and her friends. After the service, she felt more at peace, but the confusion over her father's return to her life still gnawed away in a corner of her mind.

They collected Aiden after Sunday school and picked up Emma in the church nursery where one of the caregivers gave them a guarded report on her activities.

"Your daughter is cute as a button," the grandmotherly woman who was in charge said.

It was yet another reminder of how fortunate Shelley was, and she still couldn't get her sister's words out of her mind.

They only stopped at home long enough to pick up the peach pie and tossed salad she'd made for dinner at her in-laws. Frances made a ritual of Bauer family gatherings, but they weren't always fun for Shelley.

Today, though, she was glad to be with Dan's parents. They were a distraction from thoughts about her father, and she had to laugh when Frances proudly presented Shelley's husband with a pair of tiny shoes he'd worn as a baby.

"What am I going to do with these?" he asked, dangling them from his finger.

"Why, keep them, of course," Frances said matter-of-factly. "Think how much fun it will be to show them to your grandchildren someday."

"Mom, you know I'm not much of a saver. Why don't you keep them here for now?"

"Don't be silly, dear. They're part of your family heritage. Don't you agree, Shelley?"

"I'll tuck them away somewhere," she said. Although Shelley didn't have room for all the objects Frances was unloading on them, she had to admit Dan's baby shoes were cute. Maybe someday she could have them bronzed—or maybe not. She still had Aiden's and Emma's little booties tucked away somewhere. There were some things a mother just couldn't part with, although her mother-in-law was putting sentiment aside in favor of cleaning out a house packed with mementos of the past.

Frances smiled with satisfaction when Shelley rewrapped them in the aged tissue paper and put them in her purse.

Emma began to melt down at naptime, and Shelley took it as a signal to leave. She'd helped clean up after a huge noontime meal, Sunday dinner as Frances called it, and Dan wasn't especially interested in watching a baseball game with his father.

On the ride home, Aiden was cross because he'd hoped to play catch with his granddad, and Emma was fussing instead of dropping off to sleep in her car seat. Dan was still irritated by his mother's housecleaning.

"How can she expect us to take all the junk she'd saved over the years? She knows our house is too small."

"She has good intentions," Shelley said. "The things she gives us mean a lot to her."

"I suppose," Dan said, pulling into their driveway.

Shelley slid off the seat on the passenger side and glanced at the house. Her father was sitting on the front porch step.

"Why are you here?" she asked, racing toward him and leaving Dan to unload the kids.

"Susannah called me," he said in a somber voice. "I never meant to keep Maggie a secret. The subject just never came up."

Shelley didn't know whether to be angrier with her sister for calling him or her father for showing up uninvited.

"Can I come in?" he asked in a humble voice. "Please?"

Shelley was about to ask him to leave. But it was too late.

"Grandpa Becker!" Aiden had spotted her father and came running into his arms for a big hug.

"Hey, sport!"

She wanted him to go, but Aiden was trying to entice him into playing catch.

"Maybe for a little while," her father agreed, looking at her for approval.

She couldn't give it. Instead she went around him into the house and took refuge in her bedroom. Dan could deal with him as he pleased.

Sitting on her bed with her knees pulled up and her chin resting on them, she could hear Dan putting Emma down for a nap and Aiden playing in the backyard with her father. Why had he come back into her life? Why hide his new relationship from her when Susannah already knew? She wasn't proud of the way she was acting, but he'd brought back all the pain and sorrow of the divorce. How could she cope with a revival of all the bad feelings she thought she'd put behind her?

Lying down, she buried her face in a pillow and quietly sobbed until, at last, she fell asleep.

Dan woke her an hour later, according to the bedside clock.

"Are you okay?" he asked.

"I suppose. I'm sorry I stuck you with the kids and my father."

"It wasn't the most mature thing you've ever done," he said in a light tone that didn't sound like criticism.

She started to argue, then realized he was right. Why had she let her father throw her for a loop? She'd gotten along fine without him for quite a few years. She didn't need him in her life now.

"I guess."

"Look, Shell, I know you two don't have a good relationship, but the guy is trying. If you really can't handle it, I'll tell him not to come here anymore. But I'm not sure that's the best thing for you."

Too downhearted to protest or cry, she nodded. "I can't make any decisions right now."

"Okay, I won't pressure you, but it's hard on the kids and me, you know. We can't be happy when you're miserable."

She reached out and took his hand, forcing herself to smile.

"I don't want to be the cause of your unhappiness." She took his hand and gently kissed the top of his fingers.

"You're not. The day I married you was the best in my life. We've gotten through a lot, and we'll get through this."

The kids were subdued during supper, and both went to bed with a minimum of fuss. Shelley kissed Aiden good night, marveling at how sensitive her little boy was to her moods. She'd tried hard to be upbeat and cheerful, but he seemed to sense that all wasn't right with his mom.

"Mama?" he asked as she was leaving his room. "Don't you like Grandpa Becker?"

"Of course I do," she assured him, although she wasn't sure it was the truth. "Why do you ask that?"

He pulled the sheet up under his chin. "I don't know."

"Well, don't worry," she assured him. "The important thing is that Daddy and I love you very much. We always will."

Unsure whether her answer satisfied him, she quietly closed his door and hoped he wouldn't lie awake fretting.

Dan had flopped down in his favorite chair in front of the TV, but the screen was blank.

"Nothing on TV?" she asked.

"I have to get up early tomorrow," Dan said, stretching and yawning. "It sounds silly, but I'm ready for bed already. You kept me hopping this weekend. The lawn is mowed, the recyclables hauled to the collection box, and Prize won't get through the fence again."

"You're a dear," she said, bending to kiss his forehead. "And thank you for handling my father."

"No problem. I'm turning in. How about you?"

"Not this early," she said. "I have to go through tomorrow's orders and make sure I have all the ingredients. Adelaide won't be back until Tuesday or Wednesday, so I hope I don't have to take both kids to the market."

"You're a wonder," he said, standing and giving her a big hug and heading off to bed.

After finishing what needed to be done for the next day's baking, Shelley didn't feel the least bit sleepy. The sweet smell of summer lingered in the kitchen after she shut the window and locked the back door for the night. After a hot, humid day, it felt good to have a cool breeze. She wandered out to the front porch and sat on the top step to enjoy the brilliant night sky and the tranquility of the evening. She was tempted to walk along the beach with her shoes off and let the foamy ocean waves wash over her feet, but if Dan woke up and missed her, he'd be alarmed.

On a night like this when the moon was nearly full and stars twinkled in a midnight-blue sky, it was easy to believe the Lord was watching over her loved ones. Her cares and concerns vanished as she let the wonder of the universe seep into her soul. Lingering beyond the time when she ordinarily went to bed, she cherished this time for reflection and silent prayer. She still didn't know whether it was wrong to put her father out of her life, but for now she put aside her anger.

A car slowly passed her house and turned around at the end of the block. Shelley didn't know whether she should be alarmed when it returned and stopped in the street in front of her. She stood, poised to hurry into the house and lock the door if the occupant got out.

"Are you Shelley?" a woman's voice called out through an open car window.

"Yes," she acknowledged hesitantly.

The stranger shut off the engine and got out of the car. She walked half the distance to the porch and stopped. "I know it's late. But I had to take your father home and drive all the way back to Marble Cove. I'm Maggie Thomas. Do you mind if we talk a bit?"

"Did my father send you?"

"Oh my, no! He's not going to like it one bit if he finds out I came here."

"My husband and children are asleep." Shelley meant it as a reason not to invite the woman into the house, but it seemed she wasn't easily discouraged.

"Do you mind if we visit here on the porch?" the stranger asked.

Now that she was close, Shelley could see she was a tall, willowy woman with long, light-colored hair framing a thin face. She wore a long flowered skirt and a tank top almost covered by multiple strands of beads.

"Okay," Shelley reluctantly agreed, moving over to make room for the other woman to sit.

"You're going to think this is none of my business," Maggie Thomas said, "but I just hate to see your daddy so unhappy."

Shelley was speechless. She didn't know this person, but here she was, intending to plead his case.

"I know the man pretty well," the woman said in a soft voice. "We've been together a fair amount of time. Truth to tell, he wants us to get married, but I told him I want him to get right with his family first. It's not good for people who love each other to hang on to bad things from the past."

Should she be offended? Shelley wasn't sure. A woman she'd never seen before was trying to patch things up between her and her father.

"I didn't even know you existed until my sister told me," Shelley said. "Why wouldn't he tell me about you?"

"I guess he was afraid you'd disapprove. It's like the two of you are standing on opposite sides of a great big canyon. Neither of you can fly, so you both need to take some big steps to get together again."

The woman's folksy tone was appealing, but how could she know what Shelley was feeling?

"My father can do whatever he likes," she said. "It doesn't matter to me whether he gets married again."

"That's just the trouble. He very much wants you to care. I know you think he didn't do right by you in the past, and he certainly made a mishmash of coming to see you again. But he isn't a bad man. He just doesn't know how to talk to you anymore."

"I never sided against him in the divorce, but I was so hurt when he moved out on my mom and my sister and me. All these years I thought he didn't love us."

"It does seem like he could have been up-front with you years ago, but doesn't everyone deserve forgiveness? The last thing he wanted was to hurt you again."

"I'm sure you mean to help my father, but you drove here for nothing. I don't know what to say to you."

"I'm too old to expect miracles, but I pray you'll give some thought to how your father feels. He loves you, and that's the truth. I don't think either of you can be truly happy until you resolve your differences. That's all I'll say." She stood. "I hope we meet again sometime, Shelley."

She left so quickly Shelley didn't have time to say good-bye.

A cloud moved over the moon, and the night suddenly seemed dark and lonely. She couldn't get into the house quickly enough.

Chapter Nineteen

Monday morning Diane woke up with a feeling of euphoria. Things were finally coming together in her career, and this was the day she was sending her completed manuscript to her agent and her publisher.

"We did it, Rocky," she said, padding barefoot through the cottage to let him out.

Not only had she finally finished the book, she'd made a new friend in the process. Janice Rimes had carefully read her manuscript and made some brilliant suggestions, including a way to mask the identity of the antagonist until the very end. More importantly, she'd buoyed up Diane's confidence with words like "sparkling," "insightful," and "imaginative." In fact, her comments were so helpful and encouraging, Diane had printed them out and tacked them up on the wall behind her computer.

Janice's critique also made her realize that mysteries often didn't have quick and easy solutions, something she should've learned from their quest for treasure in Marble Cove. In fact, she and her friends had reached a dead end, with more speculation than facts. They weren't even sure whether Jeremiah Thorpe was a good guy or a deceiver.

After a quick cup of coffee and a piece of peanut butter toast, Diane was eager to get the manuscript off. She showered as quickly as possible and threw on the first pair of shorts and T-shirt she grabbed. All she had to do was format her work and send it through the computer, a timesaver she greatly appreciated.

Now that her second book was done, she had time to wonder why she'd had such a bad case of writer's block. Was it because she expected her work to be perfect the first time she put words on the screen? She'd felt so good since her low blood sugar was getting under control that she suspected it might have contributed to her sluggish productivity.

After dispatching the manuscript, she had a great sense of accomplishment, but she also wondered what to do for an encore. Should she take time off until the revisions came, or was it time to think of book three?

"I need to celebrate," she told Rocky, who responded with a halfhearted tail wag. "But obviously not with you, although if you're a good boy, we'll have a nice walk after lunch."

Sometimes impromptu parties were the most fun, and she knew just the people to help her celebrate the completion of her book.

"Beverly," she said, having dialed her partner in investigations first because she was curious to know how the petition drive had gone. "I finally sent off book two. I thought I'd have a little get-together at my house this evening to celebrate. Can you come at, say, eight o'clock?"

"I'd love to," Beverly said. "It will give me a chance to tell everyone how many signatures we have to present to the council."

Margaret was equally enthusiastic about getting together that evening, provided, of course, Adelaide got home safely and on schedule.

"I suspect she'll be so exhausted she won't even notice I'm gone," Margaret said. "But I won't relax until she's sound asleep in her own bed."

"Well, I'll hope to see you," Diane said, hanging up and calling Shelley next.

Her young friend didn't sound quite herself, and Diane wondered if she wanted to come.

"If you're too busy...," she said, giving her an out.

"Oh no, I'd like to come as long as Dan is home to watch the kids. What time do you want me?"

"Eight or any time after that when you're free," Diane said, a little concerned by her friend's somber tone.

With her little party arranged, Diane took the afternoon off from writing to clean her cottage, a chore she enjoyed when she had time to do it thoroughly. To make the evening more special, she made a lemon chiffon pie with graham cracker crust from a recipe she'd often used when she and Eric entertained.

Today she felt comforted rather than saddened by her thoughts of Eric. She knew how proud he'd be if he were here to celebrate the completion of her second book. Sometimes she imagined him sitting by her side as she wrote, offering little suggestions and encouraging her not to give up.

In the afternoon she decided to give herself a beauty treatment to get ready for her little party. She was lucky to get a hair appointment at short notice and left for the beauty salon in high spirits.

★ ★ ★

Margaret tried not to watch the clock, but it was impossible. Too restless to stay home, she went to the gallery. She even sold a consignment painting showing a pair of kittens chasing a ball of yarn. It was too conventional for her taste, so she was glad to see it go.

In spite of the good sale, she just went through the motions at the gallery, doing a bit of dusting and a little bookkeeping to keep her mind occupied. When Allan brought a sack lunch for her noon break, it meant Adelaide should be home in less than two hours.

"Do you want me to meet her alone?" he asked after she mentioned the sale of the painting.

"Absolutely not! I can't sit here not knowing whether the van gets back on schedule. I'm coming with you."

"I had a feeling you'd say that," he said with a broad smile. "It will be good to get our girl back, but we had fun on our 'date,' didn't we?"

"Yes, we certainly did." She stepped close and kissed his cheek. "I'm not going to forget about our plan for a monthly outing for the two of us."

"I certainly hope not. Going out together brought back a lot of good memories. I'll come back for you a few minutes before Adelaide is due."

"Don't you think we should go to the community center at least half an hour early? What if she gets back and we're not there to meet her?"

Allan smiled indulgently. "Half hour it is, although the van could be late. Then we would have a long wait. I can see you pacing up and down outside the building, checking your watch every ten seconds."

"You know me too well," Margaret said laughing. "Let's compromise and get there about fifteen minutes before the van is supposed to be back."

"A good compromise," he agreed. "I'll come here for you then."

After eating the sandwich Allan had made for her, Margaret wished she'd closed the gallery and gone home with him. Except for a couple of tourists who hardly looked at the paintings on the walls, the gallery was quiet. Time dragged, and she imagined all kinds of disasters that could befall the van.

A slender silver-haired woman stepped into the gallery, and Margaret greeted her warmly.

"Do you have any prints by Wendell Mohr?" she asked, looking over Margaret's paintings without any sign of interest.

"No, I'm afraid I've never heard of him," Margaret admitted.

"Really? I was sure his fame as a watercolorist had spread beyond Iowa, especially since his death a few years ago."

"I imagine you'd find his work in Iowa, not Maine," Margaret speculated, making a mental note to look him up on the Internet.

"Yes, of course, but it was worth asking. I have my own gallery in Iowa, and I can't buy enough to satisfy my clients." She left abruptly without giving a second glance to Margaret's offerings.

Would people be looking for her paintings after she was gone? Margaret had never given it much thought, but she did hope her friends would keep them to remember her.

At least the Iowa dealer had distracted her for a few minutes, but she was the last customer to come into the gallery before Allan came to pick her up.

"The gal at the community center sent out an e-mail. The van is on time. They've done a good job keeping us informed. I'd let Adelaide go on another trip if she asked again."

"We'll see," Margaret said. "First let's find out if Adelaide really enjoyed the experience."

When they got to the community center, several other parents were pacing the walkway, anticipating the arrival of their special children. Allan chatted with a couple they knew, but Margaret couldn't concentrate on the conversation. What would Adelaide say about her trip to the big city? Had it been scary for her? Had she worried about losing track of her group and getting lost?

Her heart was in her throat when the oversize van finally pulled up in front of the community center. She watched as the driver got out to help his passengers down the rather steep step. The chaperones and their charges slowly emerged, most of them loaded with backpacks, packages, plastic bottles, and the remnants of fast food lunches in paper bags. Adelaide wasn't among them.

Margaret nearly hit panic mode when Allan stepped up and looked into the interior of the van. A few moments later he was helping their daughter with the odds and ends she was struggling to carry. Her fine honey-colored hair looked windblown, but she was wearing clean blue denim shorts with an overall top. One strap was unbuttoned, but otherwise she was neatly dressed and beautiful in her mother's eyes.

"Mommy!" She flew into her mother's arms, and everything was right in Margaret's world again.

"Did you have a good time?" she asked when Adelaide released her from a big hug.

"I had the best time ever," her daughter gushed. Then she grew serious. "But I missed you and Daddy."

"You can tell us all about it in the car," Allan said, stepping up to pick her suitcase out of the pile the driver was unloading.

He wasn't fooling Margaret. She detected the tears of relief in his eyes as he set about loading the case in their car.

Adelaide hardly stopped talking to take a breath on the way home.

"What did you like best?" Allan asked when she finally paused for a moment.

"The boat ride. One girl threw up, but I didn't. She was seasick."

"I'm glad you didn't," Margaret said, a bit overwhelmed by all the things her daughter remembered from the trip. "Did you go up high on the Empire State Building?"

"Yes. The yellow cars looked like little bugs."

"New York has a lot of taxis," Allan said. "I bet they do look like bugs from the top of the Empire State Building."

"We couldn't fall off," Adelaide assured them.

"No, of course not," Margaret said, beginning to feel good about her daughter's adventure.

"Tom spilled red juice on the table. The person didn't get mad, but it got on my dress."

"I'm sure I can get it out," Margaret assured her.

"I got you a present. Daddy too," Adelaide said as they unloaded her possessions at home.

First she showed them a stuffed dinosaur she'd bought for herself at the American Museum of Natural History.

"It's cute," her dad said.

"They just had the bones," Adelaide gravely informed them.

"Yes, dinosaurs lived a long, long time ago," Allan said, looking at his daughter's prize purchase.

"This is your present," she said, reaching into a smaller bag inside the large one and handing Allan a refrigerator magnet in the shape of a New York taxicab.

"I love it!" he said, obviously touched because she'd thought of him. "It can hold important papers on the fridge."

"This is for you, Mommy."

Adelaide handed her a pin in the shape of a big red apple.

"I know you like apples," Adelaide said, beaming with pleasure as her mother exclaimed over the gift.

"It was so sweet of you to buy gifts for us," Margaret said.

"I used my own money."

"That reminds me," her mother said. "Shelley said she really misses your help. Aiden and Emma missed you too, but Daddy and I missed you most of all."

"I missed you too," Adelaide assured them.

"I'm glad you had a good time," Allan said. "Did you like sleeping in a motel?"

"I like my bed better. The pillows were funny."

"Well, I put clean sheets on your bed and flowers on the dresser so the room smells nice. We're so glad you're home, sweetheart. You did have a good time, didn't you?"

"I had a great time," Adelaide solemnly confirmed. "I missed you. Can I go again?"

"If Penny plans another trip, maybe you can. We'll have to see, but Daddy and I are so glad you enjoyed yourself."

Margaret felt light-headed with relief now that Adelaide was back with them, but it had been a good experience for her daughter—and for them. She and Allan had realized how vital their relationship was. They needed time to be a couple as much as their daughter needed independent experiences. Her trip to New York had been a plus for their family, well worth the anxiety of having her away.

"Here's Oreo!" Adelaide said with pleasure when her favorite cat came into the room and rubbed against her ankles. "Were you a good kitty?"

She scooped up the black-and-white cat and nuzzled his back. "I missed Oreo."

Margaret smiled a bit wearily. Oreo had been in mischief since the time Adelaide left, scratching at their door at night, hiding in the garden, and ruining one of her favorite couch pillows with his claws. Apparently her parents weren't alone in missing Adelaide.

★ ★ ★

Shelley thought of backing out of Diane's get-together, but her neighbor was such a good friend she forced herself to go. After all, finishing book two was a big milestone for a writer, and Shelley didn't want to let her down because she was depressed about her father.

"Come on in," Diane said when she knocked softly on the front door. "You're the last to arrive."

Also the most underdressed, Shelley realized when she saw Diane in a long silver skirt that shimmered when she moved. Beverly looked as sleek as a fashion model in designer jeans and a form-fitting green jersey tunic. Even Margaret had dressed for the occasion in a pretty flowered dress.

"I didn't think to dress up," she said apologetically.

"You're pretty no matter what you wear," Diane assured her.

Shelley appreciated her kindness but still felt out of place in the shorts she'd worn all day to bake and her only clean tank top with a stain on the front.

"I made punch to celebrate," Diane said, leading her to a large glass bowl with green sherbet floating on top of the beverage. "I made too much. Guess I got carried away, but it's not every day I finish a book. And I don't get to use my grandmother's cut-glass punch bowl and cups every day, either."

Nodding a greeting at the other two women, Shelley accepted a cup of punch and turned her attention to Margaret.

"Did Adelaide have a good time on her trip?" she asked.

"She loved it!" Margaret said. "She talked nonstop about all the great things she did, but she was one tired young lady after her big adventure. She went to bed right after supper, so I don't feel bad leaving her on her first night home."

"Your punch is delicious," Shelley told Diane.

"Before you got here, Shelley, we were telling Margaret about what we saw, or didn't see, at Portland College," Beverly said.

"I can't believe there's a newspaper article floating around out there somewhere that we can't get our hands on," Margaret said. "It would be fascinating to see what that article might reveal."

"Yes," Diane said. "We're hoping Dr. Standish will unearth it and contact us if and when he does."

"I'm more concerned about Silas Locke," Beverly said, frowning and putting aside her empty punch cup. "It's a really bad feeling, not knowing whether a minister is on the up-and-up. I don't usually pay much attention to Mrs. Peabody's gossip, but she has a friend who lives across the street from him. Our mystery woman—if that's what she is—does pay him visits at night. She doesn't act at all like an insurance investigator, which is what I first thought she must be."

"What do you think, Shelley?" Diane asked. "Do you have any clue what Reverend Locke is up to?"

Stalling for a moment, Shelley was reluctant to admit she hadn't given him a thought lately. "Not really. He wasn't very friendly when we were checking the graveyard with metal detectors, but then, I guess we can't blame him. He made up for it by letting us into the church the night of the fire."

"That's odd too," Beverly said. "It's almost as if he wanted us as witnesses in case he was suspected of starting the fire. But it's hard to believe that."

"It was probably just coincidence, but I guess our treasure hunt is over, unless we come up with an answer about the little key I have," Margaret said. "It has to open something, but we may never know what."

"I'm not quite ready to give up," Diane said. "Now that I've finally finished my second book, I'm inclined to believe anything is possible."

"I'm more interested in hearing about the petition drive," Margaret said. "I'm afraid I didn't really do my share, but fortunately Allan more than made up for it. Do you think you have enough signatures, Beverly?"

"More than enough, but it will depend on how the council reacts to them. I don't see how they can ignore the will of so many signers, especially with an election coming up."

"I know Allan plans to attend the council meeting tomorrow night," Margaret said. "I don't know whether I'll go. After Adelaide's big trip, I sort of feel I should stay home with her. It was such a positive experience, I want to hear every detail when she's rested."

"I'm sure Allan can speak for both of you, if the need arises," Diane said. "I plan to attend the council meeting too. Are you going to talk about the objections to the project, Beverly?"

"Yes, I have a PowerPoint presentation if they let me give it. And I'd love to have you there for support if you can come. But you've already come through with flying colors."

Shelley found her mind wandering even though she did care about defeating the proposal. Her thoughts had been in turmoil since her father's girlfriend had talked to her. Was she being too harsh? Or would it be better for her family not to see her dad again?

Diane served her luscious pie, and Shelley forced herself to eat almost half of her piece.

"It's delicious," she told Diane. "I'm afraid I ate too much for supper to finish it."

"I'll put some on a plate for all of you to take home," Diane offered.

"Thanks, that would be nice," Shelley said.

Although she didn't intend to be the last to leave, she stayed behind after Margaret and Beverly went home. Diane asked her to stay a few minutes, and she knew she hadn't been a very good guest so far this evening.

"Is there something you'd like to talk about?" Diane asked in a concerned voice. "I couldn't help but notice your mind was far away this evening."

"I'm sorry. I didn't mean to put a damper on your celebration. It's wonderful your second book is done." Shelley felt like a bad friend not to have shared more fully in Diane's happiness.

"No problem," Diane said dismissively. "I'm just concerned to see you unhappy."

Resisting the urge to cry, Shelley shook her head. "My father coming back into my life has been sort of confusing."

"Why is that? If you want to tell me..."

"Well, he just seems to want to rebuild a relationship with me and get to know his grandchildren, but I still can't forgive him for leaving my mom and my sister and me all those years ago. He promised me he'd try to work things out with my mom, and then the next thing I knew he moved out." Shelley sighed from exhaustion.

"Then I found out he has a girlfriend, but I had to learn that from my sister." Shelley felt awkward discussing her father, but Diane was a sympathetic listener.

"Are you upset because your father found someone else?" Diane sat down across from Shelley on the couch and leaned toward her.

"No. I guess he needs someone in his life. She came to see me. She seems nice."

"Well, have you asked him why he moved out after promising to work on the marriage? Maybe there's more to the story than you know."

"No, I hadn't thought to ask him, really. I mean, what could he say that would make it right?"

"I don't know, exactly," Diane said, reaching out to take her hand. "Shelley, you were pretty young when all this happened. But now you're an adult, and you can talk with your father in a way you couldn't back then. I think you should at least give him a chance to tell you what happened. Things might not ever be the same as they were, but that doesn't mean they can't be good between you."

"I was hopeful about that for a little while," Shelley admitted.

"When Eric and I had a big decision to make, we used to take one of those long legal pads and divide the page with a line down the middle from the top to the bottom. Then we'd list all the positive arguments on one side and the negative on the other. Often we could make up our minds by balancing the good against the bad."

"It would be good for my children to know their grandfather," Shelley admitted. "I guess I'd have to put my lack of faith in him on the bad side."

"Only you can make your list," Diane said as Shelley stood to leave. "You have to think about why he contacted you and why you agreed to see him."

"Thank you for being such a good friend." Shelley hugged her and hurried toward the door before she broke down in tears. "And thank you for asking me to your celebration. I'm sorry I wasn't a good party guest."

"Your pie," Diane said, hurrying behind her. "Although maybe I shouldn't send my amateur effort home with the best baker in town."

Shelley took the covered plate and said her thanks again. Her life was blessed in many ways, not the least of which was having a friend like Diane. Maybe her idea of listing the pros and cons of letting her father back into her life would help her come to a decision.

CHAPTER TWENTY

Looking around the room, Beverly was pleased to see how many people were there for the council meeting. Diane, of course, had come early enough to get a seat, and Dr. Spangler had joined her. Beverly's father was beside her on one of the folding chairs set up to accommodate the unusually large crowd, and Allan was standing at the rear of the room talking to Dan Bauer. She'd expected her friends to come, but it seemed half the town was there.

"Nothing like a hot-button issue to bring folks out," her father commented, looking up from the book he'd brought to occupy himself until the meeting started.

The mayor, Evelyn Waters, was standing at the table behind the stack of petitions Beverly had delivered to her. She kept checking her watch and watching the overflow of spectators who were still trying to find a spot to sit or stand. If she looked more frazzled than usual, it wasn't surprising. This may have been the biggest crowd to attend a council meeting since she'd been elected.

"It's time to call the meeting to order," Evelyn said, clearing her throat several times before people quieted down.

Beverly looked around, spotting more familiar faces, including Charlotte Vincent, chairperson of the chamber of commerce. Now that the meeting had started, she had some last-minute jitters. Would the mayor allow her enough time to deliver her whole PowerPoint presentation? She'd already asked to be on the agenda, but she hadn't gotten a definite answer.

One thing was sure: the people of Marble Cove were upset about Dennis Calder's plans. She looked behind her and wasn't surprised to see him standing alone, leaning nonchalantly against the wall. When he caught her eye, he gave her a challenging smile, as though he expected things to go his way regardless of what she was doing to oppose his plan.

Quickly looking away, she focused on the council members and the routine items on the agenda. Every little item seemed to take forever, but at last, the mayor nodded at her to come forward.

After practicing aloud with her father and Mrs. Peabody as an audience, Beverly could go through the presentation without looking at her notes. She managed to finish without a single glitch, but she hadn't prepared for the question-and-answer period that followed.

Several people spoke up against Dennis' plan, including Leo Spangler, who turned out to be an effective speaker. He'd obviously done his homework and was able to cite several incidences where small New England villages had been ruined by unwanted progress. Beverly wished she'd included them in her arguments but was very glad he had.

"Now I guess it's my turn," Dennis said, making his way to the front of the room without getting an okay from the mayor. "We've heard a lot of whining from people who want Marble Cove to stay the way it was a hundred years ago, never mind that seasonal unemployment is a constant problem, and young people leave in droves for jobs in more progressive communities."

The crowd grew very quiet, and he took full advantage of their attention.

"What's so bad about a project that will give jobs to hundreds and put money in everyone's pocket?" he pressed.

The man could be charming and persuasive. Beverly had to give him that, but her supporters didn't let her down.

"Who's gonna live in all those fancy condos? Who will be stayin' in your fancy hotel?" an elderly man asked in a pronounced Maine accent. "Sure as rain, it won't be anyone here. I don't want my grandkids cleaning up after a bunch of rich people."

Several voices chimed in agreement, but Dennis wasn't rattled.

"There will be a lot more than jobs for just maids and custodians," he countered. "In fact..."

"What about gambling?" a stern-faced man asked. "I don't hold with it."

"At this point in time, I don't have a license," Dennis said. "But I'll be straight with you. It would be a great boon to Marble Cove to bring in all that outside money."

"Wouldn't go to me," his opponent said. "And it would be tainted money. I want no part of it."

A murmur from the crowd agreed with him.

Dennis started to counter his argument, but the mayor rapped her gavel until the room was silent.

"We've given this some thought," she said, speaking for the council. "It's a big decision, and we're unanimous in thinking we need to do more research. We're tabling your request for now, Mr. Calder. The council members don't think a decision should be made until after the election."

Beverly didn't miss the flash of anger that distorted Dennis' face, but he quickly masked it.

"I have to point out," he said, "that I've already invested a great deal in this proposal. I have crews standing by to begin work as soon as the permits are approved. It could be ruinous to delay too long."

"We understand that, Mr. Calder," one of the council members said, pointing at the tall stack of folders Beverly had brought to the meeting. "But this is a decision that will affect each and every person in Marble Cove. We can't just ignore the groundswell of opposition represented in these petitions."

"I understand," Dennis said.

He didn't do humble well, and moments later he left the town meeting room without saying anything else. Unless she was mistaken, Beverly expected him to continue his campaign by trying to bribe or bully individual council members. She hadn't won a victory, but she had managed to postpone the decision. She hoped the council members would respond to public pressure when they did make a final decision.

"One more thing before we adjourn," Mayor Waters said. "As some of you know, my husband is taking early retirement. We plan to stay in Marble Cove, of course, but first we'd like to do some traveling. For that reason, it wouldn't be fair to run for reelection when we expect to be gone a good part of the year."

"I think I can speak for everyone when I thank the mayor for her years of dedicated service," a council member said.

The room applauded in her honor, but Beverly didn't know whether this was good or bad for Dennis' plans.

After the meeting ended, people milled around talking over the mayor's surprise decision not to run again and what it meant for the Calder project.

Dr. Spangler was the first to congratulate Beverly on her efforts.

"Calder's not defeated," he said with a wry grin, "but you surely slowed him down. You can count on me to keep opposing him."

Beverly warmly thanked the vet and several other people who crowded around her. When the people began drifting toward the exit, she noticed Charlotte Vincent hanging back, waiting to speak to her. Although she didn't know the chairperson of the chamber of commerce very well, she did respect her for what she did for the town.

"Congratulations, Ms. Wheeland," she said. "You did a wonderful job bringing the project to public attention. Maybe you should run for mayor. I certainly would vote for you."

When she collected her thoughts after the stunning suggestion, Beverly demurred. "I've never thought of myself as a politician."

"All the more reason to throw your hat in the ring. Marble Cove needs concerned citizens, not professional politicians. You qualify on all counts."

"I really haven't lived here very long," Beverly said. "I'd feel like a carpetbagger."

"Nonsense. Everyone knows you now after your petition drive. Thanks to you, the council didn't dare approve a bad plan for the town's development."

"There's no guarantee they won't," Beverly reminded her.

"No, but the odds have tipped against it," Charlotte Vincent said. "This is a beautiful town with an unspoiled beach and a historic lighthouse. Almost everyone I know wants it to stay that way. But don't kid yourself. The fight isn't over. Even if Dennis Calder is sent packing, there will be others who want to exploit this area for their own gain. That's why we need leaders like you."

"I'm terribly flattered." In fact, Beverly was dumbfounded by the proposal.

"That wasn't my intention," the chamber chairperson said. "I don't know anyone else with your energy and good intentions who could do the job. Don't make up your mind now. Just give it some serious thought."

"I guess I can do that, Mrs. Vincent." Beverly felt as if she'd been thrown into a whirlpool, her head spinning from the possibility of such a major life change.

"If you decide to run, count on me to help in any way I can. And do call me Charlotte. I have a feeling we're going to be working together in the future."

"Thank you for your vote of confidence. I'll give your idea serious consideration."

Beverly made her way to the exit along with her father, who'd certainly heard the suggestion she run for major. She didn't mention it until they were away from other people on the way home. He'd insisted on walking, and she was glad to wind down on the leisurely trek.

"Mrs. Vincent's suggestion certainly took me by surprise," she said. "I can't imagine being the mayor."

"Maybe you should take it seriously," he said. "You're just as well qualified as anyone on the council. I've supported Evelyn for years, but it's time for new blood."

"But think of what it takes to be elected. I'd have to campaign and get contributions for advertising. A person can't run for public office without good backing."

"You'd get supporters. No doubt about that after all you've done so far to thwart Calder." Her father stopped walking and faced her under a streetlight. "It takes courage to put your ideas out there for the public to stomp on, but you've proven you're a force to be reckoned with."

Beverly was torn between not wanting a public life and needing a platform to defeat Dennis Calder once and for all.

"If I run, I'd be a one-issue candidate. I really don't know much about town government," she argued.

"We've got a garbage collector, a goat farmer, and a retired school-bus driver on the council. What do they know that you can't learn in a big hurry?"

"Maybe you're the one who should run for mayor," she teased her father. "You know more about Marble Cove than I'll ever learn."

"I know history, but I'm too old to make it. Doesn't mean I wouldn't stump for you though. These old bones would take to the street campaigning if it would help you become the head honcho."

"The what?" The idea was so preposterous she wanted to laugh, but her father was actually taking it seriously.

"I tell you, Beverly, you have a lot of potential you haven't begun to tap. You're not likely to if you close your mind to possibilities."

"I won't close my mind, Father. If running for mayor means I can scuttle Dennis' ruinous plan for good, I may just give it a try."

"That's the way to think!" He squeezed her arm and sounded prouder of her than he ever had before.

When they got home, he hurried off to bed, but Beverly was so wide-awake she doubted whether she'd sleep at all that night. She was happy about the results of the petition drive and her presentation, but one important person had missed the meeting. Jeff had been given a last-minute assignment from an editor who'd done a lot to boost his career. He'd had to drive to Boston with less than an hour's notice to get ready.

The first thing she did was check her e-mail. Jeff hadn't disappointed her. He let her know he'd arrived safely and wished her good luck at the council meeting. He was a night owl, so she quickly responded:

"Hi, Glad you got there okay. The council tabled Dennis' plan until after the election. Isn't that typical of politicians! You won't believe this, but Charlotte Vincent suggested I run for mayor because the current one is retiring."

His answer came so quickly that he must have been waiting to hear from her.

"Dear Beverly, That's an inspired idea. There's no one in Marble Cove who cares more about the town than you. You're a natural for the job of mayor. Thinking of you, Jeff."

His answer wasn't at all what she'd expected. Didn't anyone think it was a terrible idea, sure to fail?

"Jeff, I'm not at all political. I can't imagine being mayor."

"You know more than you think you do. You did work at the State House in Augusta. They're knee-deep in politicians. No doubt more rubbed off on you than you think. You certainly were quick to oppose Calder's development plan with your petition drive."

"Be serious! It's one thing to get people to sign a paper. Quite another to run a town. When are you coming here again?"

"I'll see you again as soon as possible. I'm hoping this assignment won't take too long. But don't try to change the subject. YOU WOULD MAKE A FANTASTIC MAYOR! In fact, I'm sure you could succeed at almost anything if you put your mind to it. Love, Jeff."

Long after they signed off for the night, Beverly lay awake thinking about the evening and the off-the-wall idea that she could be the next mayor. She felt energized and empowered by the suggestion, even though she still had doubts. Did she really want that kind of responsibility? Eventually she dozed off with thoughts of Jeff in her mind.

Apparently her active evening had taken its toll. When she woke up, she realized she'd slept an extra hour. By the time she showered and dressed, her father and Mrs. Peabody were having a heated conversation over the breakfast table.

"Oatmeal is for winter," her father insisted.

"It's good for you anytime," his cook insisted.

"I don't see you eating it."

"You know I have breakfast before I come here." Mrs. Peabody stood with her hands on her hips, hovering over him as though she could make him eat. "Oh, here's our next mayor!"

"Oh dear, please don't spread a rumor about that," Beverly emphatically insisted. "It was only a suggestion. Most likely nothing will come of it."

She gave her father a stern look, but he suddenly became much more interested in his oatmeal.

"I usually don't hold with politicking," the older woman said. "The council's just a bunch of know-nothings sitting around trying to make life more difficult for the rest of us. But I have to say, I'm taken with the idea of you running for mayor. If you need more petitions signed, I'm ready to go."

"I appreciate that," Beverly said, "but so far it's only a suggestion. If I decide to run, you'll be one of the first people to know."

Her father didn't comment, but he did polish off the oatmeal and make his escape from the kitchen.

"I'm going out for a run," she called after his retreating back.

"My nephew's cousin is good at lettering. I bet he'd give you a real good price on some campaign signs," Mrs. Peabody said, not deterred by the fact that Beverly was halfway out the door.

"I'll remember that," Beverly said, an easy promise since she wasn't a candidate for anything at the moment.

After sleeping so late, she found her run impeded by tourists who'd gotten to the beach before her. Judging by the crowd, Marble Cove was still a very popular vacation destination. She enjoyed seeing families having fun together, the kids scampering in the foamy waves at the edge of the sand and building sand castles destined for early destruction. These were the kinds of visitors who enriched the town without spoiling the old-world ambiance. Once again she was sure Dennis' plans could only be harmful.

After carefully running around the many groups spread out on colorful towels, she finished up by jogging to Diane's house. After celebrating the completion of her second book, it was unlikely her friend was too involved in another one so soon. Beverly softly knocked on her door, gratified when Diane answered immediately with Rocky at her heels.

"Am I interrupting anything?" she asked after Diane invited her to come in.

"Not at all. I feel like the weight of the world has been lifted off my shoulders. It's too soon to get reactions from my agent or editor, so I'm enjoying my freedom from work. Do you have time for tea?"

"Love some. I hurried away from the house. Mrs. Peabody was busy making plans for my mayoral campaign."

"Your what?" Diane asked in surprise.

After Beverly gave her a recap of Mrs. Vincent's proposal and her father and Jeff's reaction, she expected her practical friend to shoot down the idea. She was wrong.

"You know, that's really a good idea," Diane said. "You have management skills, good relations with people, and experience with politicians in Augusta. Now that I think of it, you'd make a great mayor. And wouldn't that put you in a good position to scuttle Dennis' project once and for all?"

"You're kidding! I did consider it for a brief time last night, but, Diane, how could I be the mayor? I'm not a politician."

"You're a concerned citizen. That's even better." Diane put tea bags in two mugs and warmed two store-bought cinnamon buns in the microwave.

Beverly shook her head in wonder. If even her close friend thought she'd make a good mayor, maybe she should consider it. Fortunately it wasn't a decision she'd have to make right away.

"The buns smell good," she said to change the subject. "I went running without breakfast."

"I never know what will happen next in Marble Cove," Diane said thoughtfully. "Who knows? We might find treasure, save Old First, and send Dennis Calder packing. If anyone can accomplish all those things, it's you."

"Wow," Beverly joked, "all that before breakfast! But you're sweet to say so."

"No, my reporter's instinct tells me you'll accomplish great things when you realize you can." Diane smiled encouragement and poured the tea.

CHAPTER TWENTY-ONE

"When is Grandpa coming again?" Aiden asked when he got up Friday morning.

"You just saw him yesterday. Remember, he took you to the hardware store," Shelley reminded him.

"Not Pappy. My other grandpa." He shuffled all the way into the kitchen to watch her rolling out a piecrust.

"Get dressed, and I'll have your breakfast on the table as soon as I finish with this crust."

"Maybe I can go visit him," Aiden hopefully suggested.

"We'll see." Shelley knew it was the least satisfactory answer she could give, but she didn't have a better one.

Was she wrong in depriving her children of the opportunity to know her father? He was constantly in her thoughts, and she'd given prayerful consideration to what their future should be. Jesus preached forgiveness, but even the Lord had taken issue with the money changers who defiled the temple at Jerusalem.

Dan and Diane both thought she should get over it—although they hadn't actually said it that way. She thought of going to her minister for counseling, but she didn't want one more person to weigh in on her father's side.

Was she wrong in not seeing his side? Could she forgive him in her heart and invite him back into her life? It was the hardest decision she'd ever had to make, and no easy answer came to her.

"Mama, I can't find my red shirt," Aiden bellowed from the hallway with predictable results: he woke his sister.

By the time Shelley got Emma up and rummaged in the clean laundry to find a shirt that satisfied Aiden, she'd almost forgotten about the pies she was making for a client. The peaches had to be peeled and sliced up, but not before the kids had their breakfast.

Dan was sure he'd have to work overtime, and Adelaide was at the community center. It was going to be a very long day!

"I want a friend over," Aiden declared.

"Not today," Shelley said as she poured out cereal for both children. "I have so much baking to do that you're going to have to help me by watching Emma."

"I can go to Jeremy's house," Aiden said, deliberately spilling cereal over the edge of his bowl.

"Not unless you're invited." Shelley knew there was little chance of that. Jeremy was in day care every weekday.

By noon she'd had to put her son in time-out twice, once for picking on his sister and once for refusing to do as she asked. Shelley took a break from her baking and shepherded both children to the park, hoping some outdoor fun would calm them down. Instead Emma fell and skinned her elbow. Aiden protested vehemently all the way home because they had to leave so soon.

"I have to clean Emma's elbow and put something on it so she doesn't get an infection," she explained, trying to be patient.

"Why?" Aiden insisted.

"I told you. So she doesn't get an infection."

Emma was still sobbing in her stroller, but she was getting too heavy to carry all the way home. Aiden deliberately bumped into the side of her stroller, the last straw as far as his behavior was concerned.

"That was just plain mean," Shelley rebuked him. "You're going to have a time-out in your room when we get home, and you're going to bed early tonight."

By the time she got home and took care of Emma's scratches, Shelley was ready for a nap herself. She managed to comfort her daughter and get her ready for naptime, but she still had more baking than she had time to do it.

Had she ever misbehaved the way Aiden was today? Her sister liked to tell horror stories about her childhood. According to her, Shelley was hyperactive and constantly in trouble when she was Aiden's age. Of course, Susannah was an older sister who liked to tease, but was Shelley really such a trial to her own parents?

Emma took a long nap, which helped immensely. Shelley was able to finish most of what she had to do, although the fridge was full of cookie dough to be baked after her children were in bed for the night.

As expected, Dan didn't make it home for supper. The kids had to be satisfied with boxed macaroni and cheese, and Shelley elected to wait for her husband rather than eat with the children.

Aiden made a huge fuss about not being allowed to wait up for his father. Maybe it'd been a mistake to put him to bed early, but she didn't know how to be a perfect parent. His behavior had been terrible all day, and she couldn't let him get away with it.

Shelley believed in the teeter-totter effect. When one child was really down, as naughty as Aiden had been all day, the other seemed to make up for it by being supergood. Emma went to bed and fell asleep almost as soon as her mother left the room.

"Mama!" Aiden called out at the top of his voice, and Shelley hurried to his room to keep him from waking his sister.

"You've got to settle down," she said in a calm voice. "It's time to go to sleep now."

"You don't love me," he said, looking so pathetic she was tempted to let him stay up longer.

"Of course I love you!" She sat down beside him on the bed and pulled him into her arms.

"Even when I'm bad?" He sniffled and rubbed his eyes with his fists.

"I'll love you no matter what. You don't have to doubt that," she reassured him. "Daddy loves you too. He always will."

"Meemaw too?" he questioned.

"Of course, Meemaw and Pappy and Emma love you too. We'll always love you."

After gently rocking Aiden in her arms for a few more minutes, he finally seemed convinced that his bad behavior that day wouldn't make her stop loving him.

When Shelley left his room, he had his sheet bunched in his fist, a sure sign he was ready to give in to sleep.

His doubts had shaken her. She took loving her children for granted. How could any parent not love a son like Aiden or a daughter like Emma? But reassuring her offspring didn't give her peace of mind. Did she really question her father's love for her? Just because he'd stopped loving her mother, it didn't mean he no longer loved her. Maybe he had deceived Shelley because he loved her, not the opposite.

She stood looking out the front window, wishing Dan would get home so she could talk to him. Gradually, though, she realized her husband couldn't solve her dilemma. He still took his parents' love for granted, even though they'd had conflicts in the past, and couldn't fully understand her issues with her dad.

One thing became very clear: she was an adult, and it was time for her to accept responsibility for their estrangement. Her father had made the first overture. If she didn't give him another chance, then her behavior wasn't any better than Aiden's had been today. Maybe she and her father would never regain the loving relationship they'd had when she was a child, but if she didn't try, she might always regret it.

The sun was low in the summer sky when Dan finally got home.

"Hey, I picked up a pizza so you won't have to fix anything. Have you eaten?"

"No, I waited for you."

She sat across the table as he hungrily wolfed down a large portion of the delicious cheese, sausage, green pepper, and mushroom pizza.

"Don't you want this last piece?" he asked. "I've made a pig of myself, but we really worked today. Didn't even take a break all afternoon."

"I'm not very hungry. I still have cookies to bake, but maybe I'll get up early tomorrow. There's something I want to ask you."

"That sounds serious." He leaned across the table and took her hand, a gesture she loved even though his fingers were greasy from the pizza.

After telling him about her day with Aiden and his questions about being loved, she made a suggestion.

"I think I should give my father another chance, maybe invite him and his girlfriend for Sunday dinner."

"That's a great idea, Shell. I've been worried you might regret not having him a part of your life after you'd had time to think about it. One thing though, my parents are already coming for Sunday dinner. Do you want me to put them off?"

"No, it would be nice for the children to have three grandparents at one time. And, worst case, if my father and I don't have much to talk about, your mother will certainly keep the conversation going through any awkward moments."

"No one ever accused my mother of being too quiet," he said with a grin.

★ ★ ★

Sunday after church Shelley hurried to change into her best white walking shorts and a pretty tunic with pink and orange flowers. She wanted to look the part of a congenial hostess even if her insides were churning from stress. Entertaining Frances was enough to make her nervous, but adding her father and his girlfriend to the party put her over the top.

Fortunately, Dan couldn't have been more helpful. The day before he'd helped clean the house and kept the kids from trashing it. He'd also volunteered to roast chicken breasts and sweet corn on the outside grill. With the main course in his hands, Shelley had baked two pies, a peach and a mixed berry, and made a pan of macaroni and cheese so the children had something they liked for dinner. She also made her special baked beans with bacon bits and a huge tossed salad. All she had to do before the guests arrived was put things in the oven, including her homemade yeast rolls.

"When will they get here?" Aiden asked for the seventh or eighth time.

"Any time now," Shelley said, giving him the job of putting napkins at every place on the borrowed tables they'd set up outside. It had been Dan's idea to make it a picnic, since the dining area would be pretty crowded otherwise.

"Tuck them under the plates so they don't blow away," she told her son, although the day was sunny and pleasant with almost no wind.

"Hello! We're here." Frances let herself in through the front door, followed by her husband.

Aiden had radar when it came to grandparents. He came running in from the backyard and launched himself at his grandfather, who put down a picnic basket to catch him.

"You didn't need to bring anything," Shelley said.

In fact, she always said that, and Frances always came loaded with extras for dinner.

"I made my special pickled beets and eggs," she said. "You know how Dan loves them."

Shelley knew how Frances thought he loved them, but she didn't say so.

"And, of course, it wouldn't be Sunday dinner without my homemade cinnamon rolls," her mother-in-law said, bending to lift Emma, who'd joined the greeting committee. "You just love them, don't you, sweetheart?" she said, cooing to her granddaughter.

"That's nice of you. Thank you," Shelley said.

Even though Frances tried to make every meal her own, Shelley was grateful for her presence. Her in-laws would help her get past the awkward moments when her father and Maggie arrived.

"Oh, before I forget, I found something else in the attic that might interest you and your friends." Frances put Emma down and pulled a brown grocery bag out of her large carryall.

Dan wasn't going to be thrilled to have more stuff from his parents' attic thrust upon them, but Shelley knew there was no refusing.

After pulling out a weathered box that had once held men's calfskin river shoes, apparently what would be called boots today, Frances handed it to Shelley.

"It's all paper stuff," her mother-in-law explained. "I know you and your friends are interested in Marble Cove history. I thought there might be something worth looking at."

"Thank you. That's thoughtful of you," Shelley said, gingerly carrying the dilapidated box into the bedroom and shoving it under the bed where the children weren't likely to find it.

Before she got back to the front entryway, their other guests had arrived, and her father was introducing Maggie Thomas to the Bauers.

"We haven't seen you since Dan and Shelley's wedding," Frances said as Shelley joined the group.

"Dan is in the backyard getting the grill started," she said. "We're going to have a picnic since the weather is so nice."

As the two couples exchanged views on the universal subject of weather, Shelley hurried to the kitchen to put her rolls in the oven. Emma followed her, perhaps a bit overwhelmed by so much company at once, and Shelley gladly picked her up to use as a shield, although against what she didn't know.

The adults wandered through the kitchen, and Aiden went with his three grandparents into the backyard.

"Your kitchen is lovely," Maggie said, hanging behind the others. Her many bracelets jangled as she moved, and beaded necklaces covered the front of her long white muslin dress.

"Thank you, it's been a blessing when I have so much baking to do for my business."

"I brought you some of my bread-and-butter pickles," her father's friend said. "I do quite a bit of canning, and these are your father's favorite."

"That's kind of you," Shelley said, taking the large Mason jar and locating a dish for them.

"Is there anything I can do to help?"

"Things are pretty much ready, but you could take this pitcher of iced tea out to the table. The glasses are already on the table."

"Gladly, but first I want to thank you for asking your father and me to your home. You don't know how much it means to him."

Although she was still uncomfortable with the situation, Shelley did like her father's friend. She had a warm personality and a ready smile.

"I guess it was time," Shelley said, rather at a loss how to respond.

"I don't have children of my own," Maggie said. "It broke my heart that Sheldon has a daughter he never sees. I knew he'd never be completely happy unless the two of you could reconcile your differences. I hope you don't think I'm interfering."

"No." Shelley still felt tongue-tied, although she easily sensed the goodwill behind Maggie's words.

"He was like a kid going to the circus when he got ready to come here," Maggie mused. "Even bought a new shirt. I think he looks good in blue, don't you?"

"I'm afraid I didn't notice what he was wearing," Shelley admitted.

"Well, I'll take the tea out now. You've made both of us very happy, Shelley. I hope this means we can be friends."

"Yes, I'd like that." Emma was getting heavy, so she set her loose to go outside.

Although she'd never met anyone quite like Maggie, Shelley was drawn to her concern for her father. He'd always been a people person. Now he had a special person in his life, and it was good.

Watching her family through the door, Shelley thanked the Lord for each and every one of them. She had a wonderful husband, lovely children, and in-laws who cared for them.

The rolls were golden brown when Shelley took them out of the oven, and she quickly brushed butter on the tops with a pastry brush. Everyone was milling around outside, and she knew it was time to join them. Before she could put the rolls in a bread basket, the door slid open, and her father came into the room.

"Shelley..."

Whatever he'd meant to say, words must have seemed inadequate. He stepped close and took her in his arms.

"There's something I need to say," he said, backing away. "I should have talked to you a long time ago."

"You don't need to...," she began.

"Yes, I made a bad decision. It's time to own up to it."

She wasn't sure she wanted to hear what he had to say, but she couldn't find the words to object.

"Your mother and I argued a lot during that time and I know we weren't always sensitive to how it was affecting you and your sister," her father slowly began. "I know now we could have handled things better."

"But, Dad," Shelley blurted, "why did you leave after you promised that you and mom would try to work things out?"

"Your mother asked me to. I really didn't want to go, but she had already sort of moved on, you know, and she just didn't want me around."

Shelley was stunned. Her *mother* had kicked him out? She was silent for a moment, letting the shock of the revelation sink in. Her mother had always acted as if her dad left them and never looked back, and she never corrected her or her sister when they complained that Sheldon had moved out without really trying to patch things up.

"But...but Mom always made us think it was *you* who wanted to leave and that you weren't willing to work on the marriage."

"Oh, Shelley," her dad sighed. "I wanted the marriage to work out more than you know, but your mother had already met someone by that point. They were just friends at the time, but I knew that it meant that she didn't consider me her best friend anymore. When I look back now, I know I was emotionally distant. I don't blame her for looking for attention elsewhere, but I wouldn't have moved out unless she insisted."

Again, Shelley sat there, shaken. All these years she had believed the worst of her father without question.

"Look, I'm not blaming the divorce on her alone," Sheldon continued. "I know I wasn't the most attentive husband, and eventually she found someone who paid more attention to her—listened to her." He shook his head. "I didn't want to sour your relationship with your mom, so I never said anything."

"I wish I'd known," Shelley said.

"In retrospect, I wish I would have told you. You were young, and I didn't want to burden you. I've made mistakes in my life, and not being up-front with you was a bad one. But even now, I still don't want you to put all the blame for the divorce on your mother."

Shelley was quiet for several long moments, only vaguely conscious of the happy voices in the backyard.

"I guess that's all I have to say." Her father shrugged his shoulders and started to go outside and join the others.

"Dad..." Suddenly Shelley knew it was time to put the past behind her and not blame either of her parents for their shortcomings. In a way, she'd always known her mother was keeping something from her, and that's why she'd drifted away from her mom as well. But this was her beloved father, and she'd never stopped loving him. The things that had kept them apart dwindled to insignificance. Her eyes opened to another truth: love wasn't something to be discarded when the loved one didn't live up to hopes and expectations. She loved Aiden when he was naughty and Dan when he was in a bad mood. She still loved her father, and nothing in the past really changed that.

"I'm sorry," she said in a hoarse voice. "I've been childish not to believe there was more to the story than I knew."

"I love you, Shelley. The last thing I ever wanted to do was hurt you." He opened his arms.

"I believe you," she whispered. "I love you, Dad."

A big wet tear slid down her cheek, but it was a sign of joy, not sorrow.

"Hey, no waterworks," he teased, but she looked up and saw his eyes glistening.

"Daddy says it's time to eat," Aiden said, bursting into the kitchen and claiming his grandfather's attention.

"We'll be right there," Shelley said. "Would you like to say the blessing, Dad?"

"It would be an honor and a privilege," he said with a happy smile.

Moments later, her family stood and joined hands while her father said words that wouldn't have been possible before today.

"Thank You, Lord, for the bounties we enjoy, but especially for the love in this family. Thank You for letting me be part of it. Amen."

"Nicely said." Frances sat down and started passing dishes with a look of satisfaction on her face.

Shelley exchanged a glance with Dan and silently said her own prayer of thanks.

"Hey! I've got two grandpas," Aiden announced loudly.

"You're one lucky kid," his father said.

Shelley couldn't have agreed more.

CHAPTER TWENTY-TWO

"I t went well, didn't it?" Dan asked that evening when they were alone.

"Yes, it really did," Shelley agreed. "You helped so much. I don't know how to thank you."

"No need," he said grinning as they sat side by side on the couch, enjoying each other's company after the children were in bed. "I just want you to be happy."

"I am." Shelley sighed with contentment. "I just wish that I'd been a little slower to think the worst of my dad all this time. He deserves better than that."

"I like Maggie. She seems good for him."

"She's a dear. I could tell she loved being around Aiden and Emma. They warmed up to her right away."

"Sometimes kids have good instincts about people," Dan said.

"Yes. Speaking of instincts, did you notice what your mother gave me today?"

Dan groaned. "Don't tell me she brought more family artifacts for us to keep. How can I convince her we don't have room to store her hoard?"

"You probably can't," Shelley said giggling. "I really don't know what she gave us this time. It was in a battered old boot box. I stuck it under our bed so the kids wouldn't get into it."

"From my parents' attic to our bedroom. I think I'd rather not sleep with trash in our room. Pests might have gotten into it," Dan said.

"I didn't think of that. Maybe we'd better check it out and find a better place to keep it before we go to bed," Shelley suggested.

"Maybe the garbage bin," her husband suggested hopefully.

"Dan Bauer, you know we can't throw it away. Your mother thinks everything she gives us will be heirlooms for the kids."

"You're right. It would be like her to check whether we still have everything months or even years from now. Let's see what we're saddled with this time."

"It could be something nice," Shelley suggested without much hope, getting up and leading the way to their room.

Dan got down on his hands and knees beside their bed and groped for the ragged old boot box.

"Got it," he said. "One thing for sure. This old cardboard box has got to go."

Shelley watched as he stood and gingerly carried the box to their bedside table, moving the clock to make room for it.

"Well, here goes," he said. "If something bites me, stomp on it."

"That's not funny, Dan," Shelley said, although she did have to laugh at his reluctance to explore his mother's gift.

Just in case, she did stand back a bit while he opened it. She wasn't exactly afraid of spiders, but she didn't want to get bit if a family of bugs had taken refuge there.

"Don't worry. I think Mom dusted this off before she brought it. She may be a bit of a hoarder, but she's a fanatic about cleaning," Dan said. "This doesn't look very promising."

"It's mostly really old papers, books, and magazines," Dan said as he ruffled through the contents of the box. "Wait, there's a wooden box on the bottom. This might actually be something of value."

"Let me see," Shelley said, a bit awestruck when he handed her an ancient-looking box slightly smaller than the book they'd just pulled out.

She attempted to open it without success, then saw a small keyhole.

"I can't even imagine how old this is," she said. "It won't open without a key."

"I suppose I could force it," Dan said, "although I'm reluctant to damage it."

"Maybe all the other stuff was put in the boot box to cushion and hide this," Shelley speculated. "Look, there are iron bands on the top like a miniature treasure chest."

"Exactly like a pirate's chest," Dan said in a teasing voice. "You and your friends have been enjoying the possibility of hidden treasure too long. This is probably only an old document box or jewelry box."

"There's definitely something in it," he said, giving it a gentle shake. "Tomorrow I'll see if I can pick the lock. It probably isn't a complicated one."

"No!" Shelley blurted out.

"You don't want to know what's in it?" He sounded puzzled.

"Of course, I do, but I have a better idea. Margaret found a little key before the church roof caught fire. It's just about the right size to open a box like this."

"Shell, it's not likely her key will open this. Who knows how long it was hidden away in my parents' attic?"

"You said the lock probably isn't very complicated. Maybe Margaret's key will work in it."

"More likely it won't, but you're welcome to try. I really don't want to ruin the box if there's another way to see what's inside," her husband said.

"I'm going to call Margaret right now," Shelley said. "And Diane—she'll want to know. And, of course, Beverly."

"Can't this wait until tomorrow?" Dan asked.

"The box could wait, but I can't," Shelley said excitedly.

"I'm afraid you're going to be disappointed. Some ancestor of mine probably used the old box to keep baptism certificates, property documents, stuff like that. Let's sleep on it, and you can tell your friends all about it in the morning."

"I can't possibly sleep until I know whether Margaret's key will open it," Shelley insisted.

"Well, do as you like. I'm going to turn in as soon as I put this stuff out on my workbench temporarily. There's still no way to know whether something will hatch in it."

Picking up the mystery box, Shelley kissed him good night and hurried to make her calls. Not surprisingly, all her friends agreed to meet at Diane's as soon as they could get there.

★ ★ ★

Margaret couldn't have been more excited when she received the call to meet at Diane's and bring her key.

"You're going there now?" Allan asked from his easy chair where he was reading a book. "It's almost bedtime."

"Frances Bauer gave Shelley and Dan a box from her attic. There's at least a slim possibility the key I found at Old First will open it."

"What are the odds of that?" her husband asked skeptically. "There must be thousands of old keys in this town. Why think yours will open an old box Shelley has?"

"The Bauer family can trace its roots back to the founding families," Margaret said. "Who knows how long it was in Frances's attic?"

"It still seems like you could wait until tomorrow," Allan said.

"Not if I want to get any sleep tonight," Margaret said firmly. "I'm going to get the key and dash over to Diane's."

"If you insist," her husband said with resignation. "I'm going to bed. I'll leave the porch light on."

Margaret hurried to her jewelry box where she remembered putting the key. She sorted through earrings, bracelets, and necklaces, then lifted out the tray that concealed the items at the bottom. There were mementos from her mother and grandmother and a tiny beaded bracelet spelling out the family name. Adelaide had worn it as a newborn in the hospital to identify her. Ordinarily, Margaret would reminisce a bit over this reminder of her darling baby, but tonight she couldn't get to Diane's fast enough.

After sorting through every item in the box, she had a moment of panic. The key wasn't there.

"I was sure I put the key in my jewelry box," she said rushing out to Allan. "But it's not there."

"You probably just forgot where you put it," he said, not looking up from his book.

"No, I'm sure I would remember. I knew how important it could be."

"Do you want me to help you look?" he reluctantly asked.

"Please! I can't tell my friends I lost it, not when they're waiting to try it on Shelley's box."

"Sit down," Allan said.

"What? I have to look for it."

"No, you have to think calmly about the last time you had it in your hands."

As reluctant as she was to stop searching, Margaret realized this was a good idea. She'd put the key in the jewelry box on the night of the fire, but she'd had it out since them. Maybe her memories were mixed up.

"On the kitchen counter!" she almost shouted. "I came home and put it on the kitchen counter, then got distracted. I don't remember returning it to my jewelry box."

"That's a good lead," Allan said, walking to the kitchen. "I could be the guilty party. I tend to sweep everything I see lying around into our kitchen junk drawer."

"It had paper around it," Margaret said, hurrying after him.

He took the drawer out and emptied it on the counter, sorting through it with his fingers.

"Let me," she said. "I remember exactly how it looked."

She sorted through an embarrassing accumulation of junk and a few useful things like batteries and a screwdriver. Just when she was about to give up, her fingers uncovered the ancient slip of paper.

There was nothing wrapped in it.

"It was inside this," she wailed. "But it's not here now."

"It has to be," Allan said. "Keys don't have legs."

"Thank you for that keen observation," she said wryly.

"Let's give this a little more thought. Where do we usually keep keys?"

"On the key board by the back door," Margaret said, trying not to sound as exasperated as she was.

Allan walked over to the special rack he'd made to keep track of household and vehicle keys. A triumphant smile creased his face when he picked up the tiny key and handed it to Margaret.

"I never put it there!" she insisted.

"No, but Adelaide knows where we keep all our keys. She must have seen it in the drawer and put it where she thought it belonged."

Margaret thanked him by throwing her arms around his neck and giving him a big kiss.

"I really didn't want to tell my friends I'd lost the key," she said with relief.

"Well, run along to Diane's but don't stay too late," Allan said with an indulgent smile.

★ ★ ★

As soon as she got there, Shelley set the aged box on Diane's kitchen table. Beverly arrived soon after she did, but Margaret kept them waiting.

"Are you sure she's coming?" Beverly asked after waiting what seemed like a long time.

"She said so," Shelley said. "In fact, she couldn't have been more excited. Should I call her again?"

Before the others could respond, there was a determined knock on the front door. Diane hurried to let her in, and Margaret came into the kitchen red-faced and flustered.

"I couldn't find the key," she explained, flushed with embarrassment. "I put it in my jewelry box, safest possible place, but it wasn't there. As it turned out, Allan found it on the kitchen counter and put it in a drawer. Adelaide must have found it and put it on the rack where we keep all our keys."

Shelley breathed a sigh of relief as Diane and Beverly smiled indulgently. Much as they all loved Margaret, she wasn't a whiz at housekeeping. It wasn't surprising she'd lost sight of the key.

"What do you have here?" Margaret asked when she settled down at the table.

After explaining the circumstances, Shelley urged Margaret to try her key in the keyhole.

"I'm afraid of damaging it," Margaret admitted. "What if the key doesn't fit and the old wood splinters?"

"Dan wanted to pick the lock himself," Shelley said. "I imagine that would have ruined the box."

"Go for it," Beverly urged.

"It's your box, Shelley. Maybe you should try first," Margaret said.

"Let Diane. She has a gentle touch," Shelley said, too nervous to try it herself.

"Whatever gave you that idea?" Diane asked. "I'm famous for breaking handles off teacups."

"I'll do it," Beverly said. "Either it will work or it won't."

Margaret handed over the key after the group's silent consensus. Shelley held her breath as Beverly very carefully inserted the key into the lock.

At first nothing happened.

"It seems to fit, but it's stuck. Do you mind if I try harder, Shelley?" Beverly asked, leaning over the mysterious box.

"No, go for it."

Beverly played with the tiny key until there was audible movement under her hand. Shelley felt vindicated for calling them together when her friend slowly opened the age-darkened wooden box.

"Wow!" Diane said, expressing what Shelley was feeling. "It opened."

"This was in your mother-in-law's attic?" Margaret asked with wonder.

"Yes, I can't believe it, but she just gave it to us today. I had a feeling it was much older than the stuff on top of it," Shelley said.

"Much, much older," Diane said. "How did she happen to give it to you?"

"Frances is a saver, but she'd made a project of passing on family heirlooms this summer. I'm afraid Dan and I weren't very appreciative this afternoon when she gave us a box of old papers and this box," Shelley said.

All of them gathered around to stare at an object covered in what looked like rotting burlap.

"Shall I unwrap it?" Beverly asked, sounding a little awestruck.

"Please do," Shelley urged her.

Beverly gingerly removed the wrapping and held up an intricately filigreed iron key.

"Another key!" Shelley didn't know whether to be elated or dismayed. They'd solved the mystery of what one key opened, only to be confronted with a second larger one.

"Is that all that's in there?" Diane asked. "The outside of the box seems deeper than the inside."

"People were all about secret compartments hundreds of years ago," Margaret pointed out. "Maybe this one has a false bottom."

Beverly carefully searched the inner sides but couldn't find any trigger to get under the bottom.

"Maybe we could pry it up with a table knife," Shelley suggested.

"That's up to you," Beverly said. "I'd feel terrible if I damaged your family heirloom."

"We'll never know unless we try," Shelley said, a bit breathless from excitement.

Diane brought out a stainless steel knife from her tableware drawer.

Shelley was conscious of all eyes watching her. It would be a shame to ruin the box, but none of them would rest easy until they knew whether it contained anything else.

At first the knife tip hit a seemingly solid meld between the sides and the bottom of the box, then, unexpectedly, the wood gave way.

"There *is* a secret compartment," Shelley cried out. "And there's something in it."

Her hand was unsteady as she reached to retrieve it. This time she didn't need to see a date to know she was touching something very old.

"What is it?" Margaret asked.

"A folded sheet of paper. It feels so fragile, I'm afraid to open it up."

"Let me get my white gloves," Diane said. "And a big piece of paper to put under it in case any part of it falls off."

When she returned with the gloves and spread a large sheet of freezer paper on the table, she looked at the women gathered around the table. "Anyone want to volunteer?"

"It's yours, Shelley," Beverly said. "Do you want to give it a try?"

"I guess." She took the white gloves, although they made her fingers feel clumsy. "Maybe you have something I can use to gently unfold it."

"I have a few plastic knives left from a picnic last summer. Would one of them help?" Diane asked.

Nodding assent, Shelley took the knife Diane handed her and ever so gently opened the first fold. When the paper proved a little sturdier than she'd feared, she very carefully unfolded it until a sizeable sheet was spread out in front of them.

"It's a map!" Margaret exclaimed.

"But the lines are so faded, some are almost invisible," Shelley said, excited but also a bit disappointed. A map was only useful if it could be read.

"The writing isn't much worse than on Thorpe's letters," Diane said, leaning close. "I'm no handwriting expert, but the writing seems to be the same."

"If Thorpe actually drew this map, it might lead to his treasure," Margaret said.

"It's the best indication we've had so far," Beverly said. "I think we'll have to scan it and transfer the image to a computer. That's the only safe way I know to enhance the writing."

"My head feels like it's spinning," Diane said. "Every time we solve one step of the puzzle, another presents itself. It's like being lost in a maze."

"And we haven't even figured out what Reverend Locke is up to," Margaret reminded them.

"Yes, not even Mrs. Peabody with all her connections in town has been able to figure out who the mysterious woman is," Beverly said.

"I'm glad the little key proved to be so useful," Margaret said. "Who would believe Shelley's mother-in-law would give them a box this important? Do you think you should return it to her?"

"I wouldn't dare!" Shelley said. "She's cleaning out her attic hoard for the first time ever. It would hurt her feelings if I returned anything. She wants her grandchildren to have heirlooms."

"Well, this is certainly a special heirloom for your children, but I think we should take the map seriously," Beverly said. "There's a lot at stake if we can find a treasure that will save Old First."

"Frances would be the first to agree," Shelley said. "Her family has attended there since forever."

"If I put a clue like this in one of my books," Diane said, "my editor would probably say the coincidence was too fantastic to be believed."

"The little key I found before the fire has unlocked a door to more mysteries," Margaret said. "Who knew such an insignificant bit of metal would turn out to unlock a secret map hidden among the Bauers' possessions for hundreds of years?"

"I can't believe that Dan's family would give us another clue to possible treasure," Shelley said. "I'm learning to appreciate what Frances is doing in passing on these family heirlooms. But what do we do now?" She was still reeling from the amazing discovery.

"We copy the map and put our minds together to solve this mystery once and for all," Beverly said.

Shelley couldn't agree more. This was the second miracle in her day, but reconciling with her father was still the most important. She couldn't help but blurt out her good news.

"I just want you all to know that my father and I have resolved our differences, partly thanks to the good advice all of you gave me," she said.

"That's even better than finding a hidden heirloom," Diane said with a wistful smile.

"I've learned that the best heirloom I can pass on to my children is the sure knowledge that they're loved by their grandparents on both sides of the family."

Her friends all hugged her in turn, sharing in her newfound joy in the importance of heirlooms and family love. "You know," Shelley said, pointing to the map, "we're closer than ever to solving the mystery of Jeremiah Thorpe's treasure. But whatever riches it yields, they can't possibly be greater than a loving family and dear, dear friends."

About the Authors

Pam Hanson and Barbara Andrews are a daughter-mother writing team. They have had nearly thirty books published together, including several for Guideposts in the series Tales from Grace Chapel Inn. Pam's background is in journalism, and she previously taught at the university level for fifteen years. She and her college professor husband have two sons. Reading is her favorite pastime, and she enjoys being a volunteer youth leader at her church. Pam writes about faith and family at http://pamshanson.blogspot.com. Previous to their partnership, Barbara had twenty-one novels published under her own name. She began her career by writing Sunday school stories and contributing to antiques publications. Currently, she writes a column and articles about collectible postcards. She is the mother of four and the grandmother of eight. Barbara makes her home with Pam and her family in Nebraska.

A Conversation with
Pam Hanson &
Barbara Andrews

This installment in Miracles of Marble Cove revolves around the concept of family heirlooms, both actual and symbolic. We asked the mother-daughter author duo to talk about heirlooms that were handed down in their family and what makes them meaningful.

Pam's Grandpa Rock loved antiques, but her Grandma Rock wanted her house to be totally modern and favored white leather furniture and bold carpet colors. When her husband came home one day with a chintz-covered old love seat with carved grapes hanging from the armrests, she tolerated it for a while. Eventually, however, it was hauled to the basement to serve as a bed for the cantankerous family dachshund.

Barbara Rock Andrews inherited her father's love of antiques and, eventually, the 'white elephant' love seat, dubbed so because it was an awkward piece of furniture to fit into a room. As time passed the faded flowery pattern was replaced with a soft burned orange velvet. Today the early 1800s love seat, reupholstered in a charming burgundy striped material, fits perfectly into a corner of Pam's living room. More than a piece of furniture, it's a testament to reinventing oneself while at the same time staying true to one's roots. Grandpa Rock was truly one of a kind, just like the hand-me-down love seat.

Barbara's favorite heirloom is a rolltop desk from the early 1900s. It was in the back room of her father's drugstore when he bought it in the 1930s. As with the love seat, it has been redone several times (going from white to pumpkin orange and restored to its original wood patina) and survived many moves. It sits as a poignant reminder of the loving, creative parent who died too soon at the age of sixty.

Grandpa Rock nurtured Barbara to be anything she wanted to be, encouragement she passed on to Pam.

Heirlooms aren't about possessions. They're reminders of the loved ones who've come before us. Barbara and Pam feel blessed with good memories that mean much more than the antiques they now enjoy.

Baking with Shelley

Tomato Soup Cake

2 cups flour

3 teaspoons baking powder

½ teaspoon baking soda

½ teaspoon cloves

½ teaspoon cinnamon

½ teaspoon nutmeg

½ cup shortening

1 cup sugar

2 eggs, well beaten

1 10¾-ounce can condensed tomato soup

Optional: 1 cup raisins

Sift together dry ingredients, except sugar, and set aside. In a separate bowl, cream together shortening, sugar and eggs. Slowly add can of soup (do *not* add water) to the shortening mixture, alternating with the flour mixture. Then fold in raisins if using them. Bake in two eight-inch greased and floured pans at 375 degrees for about thirty-five minutes.

Cool, turn out of pans and frost with cream-cheese icing. Please note that the cake will be somewhat denser than most cakes–more like a carrot or spice cake.

Cream-Cheese Icing

8 ounces cold cream cheese

5 tablespoons softened butter

2 teaspoons vanilla

2 cups powdered sugar, sifted after measuring

Beat cream cheese, butter and vanilla until combined. Then slowly add the powdered sugar until you reach the consistency and sweetness preferred.

From the
Guideposts Archives

This story by Marilyn Fanning of
Lynchburg, Virginia, originally appeared in
the May 1999 issue of *Guideposts*.

My eighty-five-year-old parents had just sold their home in upstate New York to relocate to a condo in Virginia so they could be closer to me and my husband. But first they had to move out of the roomy old house they'd lived in for years. "We have a lot of stuff to go through," Mom said over the phone. Even when they were young, Mom and Dad couldn't throw anything out. With some trepidation, I volunteered to fly up and help them.

"Good luck," my husband said. "Try to be patient with them, okay? You know how you get sometimes." I nodded, but my insides were churning. *I hope they realize they don't have time to dawdle over every little thing...*

I arrived to find cartons littering the hallways and Dad crouched over a box of nuts and screws that he had saved for reasons unfathomable to me. Mom was going through a file of ancient receipts from my father's long-defunct floral business.

My mother looked tired. "I'm here now, Mom," I said. "Why don't you and Dad take a break?"

"Okay, dear," she answered, settling into her rocker with a weary sigh. "I just don't know where to start."

You can start by throwing everything out! I wanted to respond. Instead I took a peek in the basement. Old phone books were stacked against a wall, pinned in place by rusted yard tools. Fine china was mixed up with cheap dishware. Dozens of balls of yarn, covered with dust and grime, were stuffed in shopping bags and piled on old furniture. My parents could have opened a junkyard. *Lord,* I wailed inwardly, *help me get rid of this stuff!*

It was impossible to tell what was valuable and what wasn't, so I called my old friend Janice, who loves antiquing and shopping in secondhand stores. "I'm on my way," she promised.

Mom and Dad watched as Janice and I plowed through the mess. As I gave this item and that a perfunctory look, I caught Mom watching me, her eyes misty. *What good is a wedding banquet centerpiece from 1949?* I grumbled to myself. I didn't want to get into a discussion about it. Yet I hesitated. Mom and Dad weren't just saying good-bye to a bunch of things, they were letting go of a record of their years together in the community where I was raised. They were leaving behind friends, family, their church—a whole way of life.

This is not the time to get sentimental, I scolded myself.

"Look!" Dad cried. "An old gold piece."

He handed it to Janice. "You're right," she said. "Hang on to this. Are there more?"

Oh no. We'll be here forever.

As the day wore on, I alternated between feeling like a cold, heartless wretch and feeling resentful that, as my parents got older, I seemed to be the one who always had to take charge and play the bad guy. I loved my mom and dad. I didn't want to see them unhappy.

Late in the afternoon, Janice pulled something wrapped in tissue paper from a box and gasped. "It's an old sampler," she said.

I peered over her shoulder. The alphabet, the numbers four to ten and the words *Polly Hall's sampler, age twelve* were stitched into the delicate old muslin. There was a year: 1791.

"She was one of my ancestors," I said, awestruck. "I never knew we had this."

"I knew," Mom said matter-of-factly. "Is it something you want to keep?"

I was about to say that we would be crazy to throw it out when I saw Mom was serious. I stared at her. I knew what she was thinking: You seem to want to throw everything away.

"Listen to what it says here," Janice interrupted, reading from the sampler.

> *Polly Hall is my name*
> *New England is my station*
> *Colchester my dwelling place—"*

"And Christ is my salvation," Mom finished the rhyme, smiling faintly. We all stood in silence for an instant, so quiet

I could almost hear the old house breathe. I wrapped my arms tenderly around Mom's shoulders, then pulled Dad close. I turned my face so they wouldn't see my tears, my mixed-up tears of shame and happiness.

"Mom, I'm sorry," I whispered. "I was only trying to help."

She patted me on the back. "I know, dear. What would we do without you? Your dad and I are just moving so much slower these days."

And I had been moving much too fast. Yes, there was plenty to do in this house, more than my parents could handle alone. But there was time too, time for patience and understanding. You never know the treasures you might find.

"I nearly threw that box out, it was so light," Janice said, folding the sampler carefully.

No, I thought, smiling, *I think we were meant to find it.*

Read on for a sneak peek of the next exciting book in
Miracles of Marble Cove!

Hopes and Dreams
by Susan Page Davis

Margaret Hoskins awoke suddenly, sucking in a breath and sitting bolt upright in bed. The room was dark, with a faint glow from the streetlight at the end of Newport Avenue defining the window, and the numbers on the bedside clock reassuringly normal.

Allan rolled toward her. "What is it?"

"Nothing. A dream. Go back to sleep."

Allan took her at her word and settled into his pillow once more. Margaret lay down but stared at the blue 3:05 on the clock. What on earth was her cousin Buddy doing in her dreams? She hadn't seen Buddy for nearly a year—since the family reunion that had included a rather awkward meeting. She and Buddy had reconnected after a long estrangement, but they hadn't stayed in touch since. And now he had wormed his way into her dreams somehow, along with the surf and Marble Cove. Was this about her latent memories of the time she'd nearly drowned and Buddy had come to her rescue?

She tried to remember other details of the dream, but it fragmented and evaporated. The only other thing that hovered in her mind was the sound of bells. That seemed very odd. Buddy and water didn't have anything to do with bells.

With a sigh, she rolled over toward the wall. No sense letting this trouble her. Allan's soft breathing told her that he'd slipped easily back into sleep, but it didn't come so quickly for her. This would be another long day at the gallery, and she couldn't afford to lose an hour or two. She had no idea what Buddy was up to these days, and fretting over the dream wouldn't help him.

Father, give me rest, she prayed silently. As she relaxed, she added, *And keep Your hand on Buddy.*

She awoke again at 6:30 PM. Allan was dressing, and she threw back the coverlet.

"Sleep well?" he asked.

"Yes. I just had a few wakeful moments after that dream."

"What was it about?" He grabbed his shoes and sat down on the edge of the bed.

"*Hmm,* it's misty now. Buddy, I think. And … and bells. I was swimming. That's about all I can remember."

Allan frowned. "Well, don't let it bother you."

"I won't." Margaret headed for the bathroom. When she came out, Allan had left the bedroom. No doubt he was in the kitchen fixing breakfast. Margaret wriggled into her swimsuit and pulled on her cover-up and sandals. As she passed her daughter's door, she heard Adelaide stirring.

Allan looked up as she entered the kitchen. "You're going swimming?"

"Thought I would. I won't be long."

He nodded. Margaret loved to swim, and early mornings were one of the few times she could get to the beach these days. Usually few people came out at this hour, and she loved the solitude as well as the soothing water.

"Be careful," Allan called as she opened the back door.

She turned and threw him a smile. "I will." He was thinking about Buddy and her dream, Margaret could tell. Worrying just a little bit that she might have trouble in the ocean cove again. She'd had a close call that one time when the undertow seized her. But a man had appeared and hauled her to safety. Only much later had she learned that her rescuer was her cousin Buddy. Now every time his name came up, she thought of how close she had come to drowning.

But she would be safe today. She knew the vagaries of the tides and currents on the beach near Orlean Point lighthouse. With her towel hanging over her shoulder, she hurried down the sidewalk past her friend Diane's house and onto the boardwalk that led down to the sand.

She saw only one figure, far down the shore, walking in the direction of the lighthouse. After dropping her sandals and cover-up on the dry beach above the sheet of wet, packed sand closer to the surf, she approached the waterline. Waves persistently kneaded the shore, then retreated. This morning they seemed gentle, with little foam showing when they broke.

The water was cool, but not bad. With the morning sun now well above the horizon, Margaret didn't mind. It was probably as warm today as it would get this season. Some of the "summer people" thought the Maine coastal waters were too cold for swimming, but she found their temperature bracing. And August was the best month for swimming here.

Wading out until she was waist-deep, she splashed a little water on her arms. A wave licked higher, soaking her to her chest, and she plunged forward, into the welcoming liquid. She swam under the surface for several yards, relishing the water resisting her strokes and kicks. She loved pushing against it, using it to propel herself through a different environment.

She surfaced and shook the hair from her eyes. Taking her bearings from the lighthouse, she swam out from the beach, stroking powerfully against the calm water of the cove. She loved swimming and the fact that it kept her body strong, even though she was past sixty years old. On that bright morning, she felt as free as a harbor seal—content and in control of her life. Swimming was so much better than sleeping. In slumber, she couldn't control her dreams, but here she could control her body and her thoughts.

Margaret liked where she'd come in the past year or two. She'd successfully launched her new business, the Shearwater Gallery, and her painting was better than ever before—selling better too. She had strong supporters in her friends, and her family was also doing well. God had blessed her richly.

She rolled over onto her back for a minute and floated, gazing up into the sky. Herring gulls circled between her and the puffy clouds. The waves nudged her almost imperceptibly shoreward, and she let them carry her. There was nowhere she would rather be right now than in the water off Marble Cove.

Rolling onto her stomach, she fixed her gaze on the lighthouse once more and struck out for shore. The tide was going in, and it wasn't hard to land close to where she'd left her cover-up and towel. While she was swimming, a sprinkling of summer residents had arrived to enjoy the beach. She waded out of the mild surf and across a few yards of damp sand, and a golden retriever/Lab mix ran down the beach toward her, yipping with joy.

"Hello, Rocky!" Margaret looked past the dog and smiled at Rocky's owner—her friend, Diane Spencer, who was strolling toward her carrying her sandals. Though she was fifty-five years old, Diane kept a trim figure and looked youthful in jeans and a gauzy cotton top.

Diane waved. "Good morning!"

"Hi there." Margaret toweled her short gray hair and drew on her striped cover-up.

Diane walked over and waited while Margaret slipped on her sandals and picked up her towel. "Have a good swim?"

"Excellent."

Diane smiled ruefully. "I wish you'd take someone with you, but I guess worrying about you won't do any good."

"I have a great respect for the water," Margaret said. "I don't go in alone unless I'm sure nothing's out of whack. And besides, there are plenty of people here today." She gestured toward the others now strolling the beach and relaxing in the sand. She and Diane set out walking. They passed a couple of moms who sat on a quilt talking and watching their children splash in the waves.

Neither of them spoke of the day she nearly drowned, but Margaret knew Diane was thinking of it.

"So," she said. "It's been a good summer."

"You talk as if it's over," Diane replied.

"Well, you know, it's so short here in Maine, and we're into August now. We have to savor each day."

"I do, and I know you do too." Diane looked back and gave a sharp whistle. Rocky bounded past them and turned to face them, yipping. She smiled. "It's such a relief having my second book finished!"

"I'm so proud of you."

"Well, look at *you*. Last summer you didn't know if the Shearwater would survive the season."

"That's right," Margaret said. "I feel as though it's a well-established business now, and my painting is going pretty well, if I do say so."

"You *should* say so. It's the truth."

They ambled along and climbed the boardwalk leading up to Newport Avenue, where they lived next door to each other.

"You know," Margaret said, "there's only one thing that's kind of nagging at me. Oh, not everything is perfect, of course, but there's one loose end that I don't like to think about."

"You surprise me," Diane said. "Anything I can help with?"

"I don't think so. It's Buddy."

"Your cousin?"

Margaret nodded. Diane knew the story of how Buddy had plagued Margaret since childhood and the difficulty she'd had forgiving him. But then Margaret had learned that Buddy was the mysterious rescuer who had pulled her from the water.

"I haven't kept in touch with him since the family reunion. I should have."

"What made you think of him today?"

Margaret smiled wryly. Diane had the instincts of a psychologist. "I dreamed about him last night."

"Really? Good or bad?"

"Neither. But I was in the water, and Buddy was there."

"Were you scared?"

"I don't know. I was a little shaken when I woke up."

"And you started thinking about how you haven't been in touch with him."

"Yes, I guess that about sums it up. That and the bells."

"Bells?"

Margaret nodded uneasily. "I'm not sure where that came from. It didn't seem to fit with the dream."

Diane was silent for a moment. "Do you want an ongoing relationship with Buddy? Or is this just guilt for being angry with him for so long?"

"I'm not sure. But I feel that we should be closer now. I mean, he saved my life that day, and what happened turned his life around. He stopped drinking, and he really had changed the last time I saw him."

"Why don't you call him?" Diane asked softly. "Just reach out and see if he wants to stay in touch. And if you get bad vibes, you can end the call pretty quickly. That might be a prudent way to test the waters."

"Yes, I suppose you're right. Sort of making an overture from a safe distance."

"Exactly."

"I should do that." As they approached Diane's snug cottage, Margaret looked across the street.

"Hey, there's a vehicle in front of the Simpsons' house. I wonder if someone's renting it."

Diane followed her gaze. The house directly across from Margaret's—nestled between the Bauers' Craftsman bungalow and Mrs. Peabody's lavender Victorian—did indeed have a vehicle parked in its driveway. Diane had never met the owners, as they lived elsewhere, but they sometimes rented the house to summer people.

"That would liven up our street."

"You never know. It could just be Mr. Simpson doing some work on the house."

Diane squinted at the SUV. "Could be. I don't know what he drives."

Margaret stopped with her in front of Diane's gate. Rocky waited patiently beside them, panting gently. "I hope this good weather holds. If there are renters, they're probably here for the beach and the Lobster Festival."

"I didn't go to that last year," Diane said. "Did you?"

"Oh, we always go for the food." Margaret chuckled. "It brings a lot of tourists in. In fact, it may be our biggest weekend of the year businesswise, except for Memorial Day. Kind of a last hurrah of summer. I go for the lobster and the corn on the cob and—well, all of it."

"Sounds like a calorie fest." Diane rubbed her stomach. "You're making me hungry!"

Rocky woofed, and both women laughed.

"Rocky's hungry too," Margaret said.

"I'd better get him inside. I'll see you." Diane headed up her walk, and Rocky pranced beside her. Margaret headed for home, smiling.

★ ★ ★

Margaret and Diane met on Saturday with their friends, Shelley Bauer and Beverly Wheeland, for coffee at the Cove.

"Have you got a new neighbor, Shelley?" Diane asked as they settled in at a corner table. "I saw an SUV there yesterday, and it's still in the yard this morning."

"Yes, I think so," Shelley said. "I saw a woman carrying some luggage in yesterday. I haven't met her yet, and I'm not sure if she's alone. I sort of hoped someone with kids would rent the place this summer."

"We'll have to look for an opportunity to meet her," Diane said.

"So, what about the treasure?" The mystery they'd been investigating obviously occupied more of Shelley's mind than the new tenant did, and she didn't hesitate to swing the conversation around to it. After cracking a cipher in an antique prayer book and discovering yet another old key and a map in the mysterious box Frances Bauer had handed down to Shelley, the friends were even more confused and frustrated than ever.

But they were hopeful too.

"You've got to admit, all the evidence we've uncovered points to there being a real treasure," Diane said, looking around at the others expectantly.

"Yes, there definitely *was* one," Beverly said slowly. "As to whether it's still out there or not, I'm not a hundred percent convinced. After all, Jeremiah Thorpe lived in Marble Cove and pastored Old First over two hundred years ago. I mean, really, it's a wonder we've found any real clues about his treasure."

Margaret smiled at her. "You are our voice of reason, Beverly."

Beverly chuckled. "Do you think it's time to talk things over frankly with Reverend Locke?"

The other women eyed each other, as though each one waited for someone else to speak.

At last Margaret said, "I suppose you're right, Beverly. He's tied in to this somehow, and we need to know how."

"And I want to know who that woman was that he was with so often," Shelley said.

Diane nodded. "I don't think he's keeping it a secret. After all, he was seen with her in town. If he didn't want anyone to know about her, he'd have been more discreet."

"I guess you're right." Shelley sounded disappointed.

Margaret sipped her coffee as she thought about the clues they had unearthed. Everything pointed to a lost treasure connected to Old First, the church where Silas Locke was the minister. She came to a decision and set down her cup.

"All right, here's what I think: We should call Reverend Locke and make an appointment to talk to him about all this."

Diane nodded slowly. "That makes sense. We could all go together."

Beverly's smile held a tinge of relief—she was the only one of the four who considered Old First her home church.

"That sounds like a good idea." Margaret pulled out her phone. "How about it? Shall we call now and make it official?"

"So long as you do it." Diane smiled impishly. "I'm on his bad side."

"Yeah," Shelley said with shudder. "I don't want to be the one to call him either."

"Oh, you two." Margaret shook her head, but she smiled as she chided them. "Beverly, are you all right with that, or would you rather make the call?"

"No, I think I'll defer to the eldest on this one."

"Ha." Margaret didn't mind the gentle jab—Beverly was more outspoken now that she knew them all better, but she was still reserved, and it was gratifying to see her feel comfortable enough to tease a little. Margaret had saved the minister's number in her phone, and she pulled it up on the screen. "Here goes."

After she punched Send, they all waited in silence.

"Hello?"

Margaret smiled and tried to put pleasantness into her voice as well. "Hello, Reverend Locke. This is Margaret Hoskins."

"Hello, Margaret. How may I help you?"

"As you know, some friends and I have been looking into Old First's history and trying to learn about Jeremiah Thorpe. We wondered if we could meet with you and discuss what we've found so far. You might be able to add to the data we've accumulated." Margaret glanced at the other women. Diane nodded approvingly.

"Well ... I'm not sure I can help. What exactly are the four of you hoping to do?"

"I assure you, our intentions are honorable," Margaret chuckled. "Our hope has always been to locate Thorpe's fabled treasure and use it to help restore the church. I'm not sure how that would work out since last month's fire and all, but we haven't given up the quest."

"I see. Well, I suppose I could see you on Tuesday evening."

"Tuesday evening is fine," Margaret said, glancing at the other three. All nodded, with varying degrees of enthusiasm.

"All right then. Can you come to my house? Say, six thirty?"

"Yes, certainly. And thank you very much." She closed her phone. "Well, you heard. We'll go over at six thirty Tuesday."

They sat in silence for a moment. Margaret wondered what they had put in motion. They'd been looking for clues about the colonial minister and his rumored bounty for months, but none of the hints they had found seemed to lead them closer to uncovering it. Were they in for another disappointment, or would they learn something that would lead them to the treasure they had sought so long?

A NOTE FROM THE EDITORS

We hope you enjoyed Miracles of Marble Cove, published by the Books and Inspirational Media Division of Guideposts, a nonprofit organization that touches millions of lives every day through products and services that inspire, encourage, help you grow in your faith, and celebrate God's love.

Thank you for making a difference with your purchase of this book, which helps fund our many outreach programs to military personnel, prisons, hospitals, nursing homes, and educational institutions.

We also create many useful and uplifting online resources. Visit Guideposts.org to read true stories of hope and inspiration, access OurPrayer network, sign up for free newsletters, download free e-books, join our Facebook community, and follow our stimulating blogs.

To learn about other Guideposts publications, including the best-selling devotional *Daily Guideposts*, go to Guideposts .org/Shop, call (800) 932-2145, or write to Guideposts, PO Box 5815, Harlan, Iowa 51593.

Sign up for the Guideposts Fiction Newsletter

and stay up-to-date on the books you love!

You'll get sneak peeks of new releases, recommendations from other Guideposts readers, and special offers just for you . . .
and it's FREE!

Just go to Guideposts.org/Newsletters today to sign up.

Guideposts®

Visit Guideposts.org/Shop
or call (800) 932-2145

Find more inspiring fiction in these best-loved Guideposts series!

Mysteries of Martha's Vineyard

Come to the shores of this quaint and historic island and dig into a cozy mystery. When a recent widow inherits a lighthouse just off the coast of Massachusetts, she finds exciting adventures, new friends, and renewed hope.

Tearoom Mysteries

Mix one stately Victorian home, a charming lakeside town in Maine, and two adventurous cousins with a passion for tea and hospitality. Add a large scoop of intriguing mystery and sprinkle generously with faith, family, and friends, and you have the recipe for Tearoom Mysteries.

Sugarcreek Amish Mysteries

Be intrigued by the suspense and joyful "aha!" moments in these delightful stories. Each book in the series brings together two women of vastly different backgrounds and traditions, who realize there's much more to the "simple life" than meets the eye.

Mysteries of Silver Peak

Escape to the historic mining town of Silver Peak, Colorado, and discover how one woman's love of antiques helps her solve mysteries buried deep in the town's checkered past.

Patchwork Mysteries

Discover that life's little mysteries often have a common thread in a series where every novel contains an intriguing whodunit centered around a quilt located in a beautiful New England town.

To learn more about these books, visit Guideposts.org/Shop